SINS OF THE TITANIC

A James Acton Thriller

By
J. Robert Kennedy

James Acton Thrillers

The Protocol

Brass Monkey

Broken Dove

The Templar's Relic

Flags of Sin

The Arab Fall

The Circle of Eight

The Venice Code

Pompeii's Ghosts

Amazon Burning

The Riddle

Blood Relics

Sins of the Titanic

Special Agent Dylan Kane Thrillers

Rogue Operator

Containment Failure

Cold Warriors

Death to America

Delta Force Unleashed Thrillers

Payback

Infidels

Detective Shakespeare Mysteries

Depraved Difference

Tick Tock

The Redeemer

Zander Varga, Vampire Detective

The Turned

SINS OF THE TITANIC

A James Acton Thriller

J. ROBERT KENNEDY

ISBN-10: 1514639408

ISBN-13: 978-1514639405

First Edition

10 9 8 7 6 5 4 3 2 1

For the victims.

SINS OF THE TITANIC

A James Acton Thriller

"If the American people ever allow private banks to control the issue of their money, first by inflation and then by deflation, the banks and corporations that will grow up around them (around the banks), will deprive the people of their property until their children will wake up homeless on the continent their fathers conquered."

Thomas Jefferson

"These circumstances convince me that the ship seen by the Californian was the Titanic and if so, according to Captain Lord, the two vessels were about five miles apart at the time of the disaster....When she first saw the rockets the Californian could have pushed through the ice to the open water without any serious risk and so have come to the assistance of the Titanic. Had she done so she might have saved many if not all of the lives that were lost."

Lord Mersey in the final report on the sinking of the Titanic
July 30, 1912

AUTHOR'S NOTE

This story deals with one of the greatest maritime disasters in history. Over 1500 souls died that day with heroism and bravery displayed by many. Any reference to actions or deeds by the captain or crew of the RMS Titanic are purely my own invention, and should not be in any way interpreted as an historical account of what any one individual did or did not do on that fateful night. This book is entirely a work of fiction and no disrespect is intended.

This book also deals with a United States Presidential election. I have avoided all references to any characters being Republican or Democrat, and though this book is again "torn from the headlines", any similarity to actual individuals is purely coincidental.

PREFACE

On April 14th, 1912, at 11:40pm, the Royal Mail Ship Titanic hit an iceberg only 37 seconds after it was spotted by the lookouts. A distress call went out almost immediately, however there was only one ship in the area, the RMS Carpathia. The Unsinkable Ship snapped in half less than three hours after the initial impact, the design fundamentally flawed. The watertight bulkheads, meant to prevent water from moving from one section of the ship to the next, were not built high enough. This meant that when one section filled, it spilled over the top of the bulkhead to the next section and then the next, dooming the luxury liner.

This all so the rich could enjoy spectacular lines of sight in their unsinkable ship.

And because of the arrogance displayed in the design of the ship, the largest of its time, the belief it was unsinkable meant lifeboats were an annoyance rather than a safety feature. Too few were installed to evacuate all the passengers, as it ruined the "look" of the ship and took up too much room on the decks where the well-heeled were to stroll after their midday tea.

A decision that would ultimately doom over 1500.

The Carpathia didn't arrive until almost two hours after the Titanic sank below the ocean surface, leaving hundreds behind in the frigid waters of the North Atlantic to die slowly of hypothermia, their cries for help heard by the lucky few to be saved in the too few lifeboats.

After the fact, when interviewing survivors, many reported they thought another ship was in the area, close by, but were assured by authorities they were mistaken, any lights most likely planets or stars, any objects most likely icebergs or debris.

It wasn't discovered until days later that the SS Californian had been sitting unmoving, as little as five miles away, fully capable of rescuing the passengers of the sinking liner. In fact, the lookout of the Californian had spotted the Titanic and its emergency flares, yet their captain dismissed it as some sort of celebration, deciding not to wake their sleeping radio operator.

So it turned out those passengers were right all along.

Still others claimed there was yet another ship, they too dismissed.

But what if those survivors were right all along? After all, they were right about the Californian, and if they were right about that, then why not about this other mysterious ship they claimed seemed to never get closer as they rowed toward it?

And if they were right, and that ship was indeed there, why did it sit by while over 1500 innocent souls perished?

Outside Acton & Palmer Residence, St. Paul, Maryland

"Everybody look at the bodies as if you're shocked but not scared. That means mouths open, eyes wide as if your dentist just squeezed your boob."

Mai Lien Trinh looked wide-eyed at the CIA agent driving the car, unsure of what she meant, her English excellent but her grasp of American humor a work in progress. She looked over at her friend, Tommy Granger, and copied him, his mouth agape, his eyes wide, staring out the window.

And when she looked, the shock didn't need to be faked, her imagination not doing reality justice. A body lay in the middle of the street, a large pool of blood staining the pavement, a second on a nearby lawn, killed by her boss and his wife only minutes before.

Professors James Acton and Laura Palmer.

When she had heard what had happened she couldn't believe how calm they were, it almost as if killing people were something they did every day.

Archeology professors killing people.

She had to remember that these two men had tried to kill the CIA agent now driving them to safety.

Sherrie White.

She seemed young. Very young. Barely older than her, perhaps not even.

How much training does it take to become a spy?

She assumed years.

The car pulled away from the scene of the crime and Mai took a look back, spotting the professors pulling out of the driveway in their own vehicle, Acton's boss and best friend, Dean Gregory Milton and his wife Sandra, in the back seat.

4

She felt Tommy grip her hand, squeezing it tightly. She looked at him and he gave her an unconvincing smile.

It made her feel better somehow.

He's just as terrified as I am.

A police car screeched to a halt, two officers jumping out as they passed, Sherrie pressing on the gas just a little harder.

They stopped at the end of the street, she assumed to allow the professors to catch up.

The turn signal began to click.

Then she caught something out of the corner of her eye and screamed.

A large SUV slammed into the driver side, the entire side of the car caving in, the impact shoving her across the back seat and into Tommy. Her head slammed against his, the impact excruciating, knocking her senseless for a moment as a cacophony of screeching tires and twisting metal attempted to overwhelm the pounding of her head.

Something else replaced everything, a rapid, popping sound, loud, strange, then everything suddenly rushed back into focus.

Gunfire!

Tires screeched behind them and she turned to see the professors' Jeep reversing direction as bullets tore into the windshield. She wanted to scream a warning to them yet she knew it was useless.

They slammed into the parked police cruiser.

The passenger side doors were suddenly opened and someone reached in, grabbing an unconscious Tommy and hauling him out. Mai noticed blood on the window for the first time, he obviously having hit his head hard. She pushed away from the open door in vain, an iron grip on her ankle hauling her onto the pavement. Gunfire continued as they were yanked toward the SUV, the rear door open. Tommy was shoved inside

5

first, Mai next. On instinct she dove for the door on the other side, but someone in the driver seat pointed a gun at her.

"Sit or die."

She sat.

She looked to see a dazed Sherrie pulled from the car and thrown on the pavement, a woman standing over her, aiming a weapon at the young CIA agent.

Two rounds fired into Sherrie's chest.

Mai screamed.

Central Road, Southampton, United Kingdom
April 10, 1912

Henry Dodge held a hand to his heart, trying to control his breathing, his chest heaving as he caught his breath. A woman, parasol in hand, looked at him, whispering to her husband. Dodge bowed slightly at her, causing the woman to hurry on, dragging her husband along, embarrassed at having been caught staring.

He stepped deeper into the alleyway, his feet bumping against a stray crate. He pulled his pocket watch, a Patek, Philippe & Co, given to him by his father on his eighteenth birthday.

11:20 am.

Ten minutes before final boarding.

I just have to survive ten more minutes.

And this was as good a place as any to wait. He had spotted the two men sent to stop him as he finished his breakfast at his hotel. They had looked slightly out of place, bruisers like that not common at the South Western Hotel.

And though they were impeccably dressed, they weren't too subtle, one pointing when he had been spotted, then both clumsily trying to hide behind columns too narrow for their large frames.

Yet he was certain those who had sent them wouldn't send just anybody.

If they had been given time to prepare.

And they hadn't.

For it was only hours ago he had been delivered the documents that showed who was behind the greatest change to monetary policy the world had ever known. America was about to create the Federal Reserve System, with the blessing of the government, the ultimate goal to create a financial system that would stabilize a fractured banking system. It would be allowed to lend and print money and set monetary policy independent of the government so the nation's finances wouldn't be swayed so easily by the whims of public officials.

It was a laudable goal.

On paper.

It effectively privatized the entire monetary system of the United States, handing the US dollar over to a private group of investors, and if the documents sent to him anonymously were genuine, and he had no reason to believe they weren't, the very men behind the creation of what could ultimately control one of the greatest nations in the world did *not* have its best interests at heart.

It was a power grab of unprecedented proportions.

The minutes of a meeting between a group of men, some he had heard of, some he had not, were chilling in their content and intent. These men were powerful. Heads of some of the largest companies in the world, some involved with the Inter-Parliamentary Union, various monarchies and conglomerates that controlled massive wealth as well as political and economic power.

They were the elite, their positions handed down to them through the generations, almost all old money and old titles, their positions absolute.

As was their power.

They called themselves The Assembly. He had never heard of them as an organization, yet if this meeting were any indication, they were an organization that had been around for a long time, with their fingers into everything imaginable. What their motivations were, he had no idea. Money? Power? Both?

With either came the other, neither being mutually exclusive.

But the power *and* the money they would have should their plans succeed could impact the entire world for decades, even centuries to come.

And no one knew.

Except him.

And whoever had changed his life forever by sending him the transcript.

They must have been well informed. His trip today wasn't well known, only he and a handful of business associates were aware of it, though if The Assembly were as powerful as it appeared, then he was certain they'd have access to the passenger manifests.

The envelope had been slipped under the door of his hotel room only minutes before he was to leave for breakfast, his name and the word "URGENT" scrawled on the plain envelope. He had tucked it under his arm then opened it while waiting for his food to arrive.

The handwritten warning inside had him almost tossing the papers aside, it simply too fantastic to be bothered with.

Mr. Dodge,

Be forewarned that they will kill to keep this information from falling into the wrong hands.

A Concerned Citizen

But he had some time so had skimmed the first page, and when he realized the subject matter, had read every word, twice, his breakfast going cold, forgotten as he realized he had to get this information into the hands of his father, a United States Senator, and one of the most vocal of those opposed to the creation of the Federal Reserve System. It was something his father had taken an incredible amount of heat over, subtle threats

9

received suggesting if he didn't change his vote, his reelection would be all but impossible.

It took money to run for the Senate, and though his family had plenty, their pockets weren't deep enough to run a campaign against a serious challenger.

A horn sounded from the mighty ship signaling the final boarding call, causing Dodge to jump. He looked about sheepishly, then inhaled, straightening his bow tie. He stepped tentatively out into the open, hundreds if not thousands of the public milling about, waving at the full decks. The dock was nearly cleared of cargo, several cranes swinging the last minute shipments aboard the massive vessel at Berth 44.

He frowned, wondering if his luggage had been sent ahead as requested otherwise it would be a difficult trip. With two men in the lobby clearly looking for him, he had sent instructions through his waiter to have the luggage brought here and put on board as he ducked out a side entrance.

He shrugged. There was no time to do anything about it should his instructions not have been followed. He patted his inside pocket, the envelope that had changed everything still reassuringly in place.

Stepping into the crowd with purpose, he hurried toward one of the two First Class gangways, fishing his ticket from his other breast pocket. As he neared the staff, their crisp navy blue uniforms looking sharp, as if never worn before today, it became clear White Star Line was sparing no expense to make certain this voyage got off without a hitch.

There was no line up, not at this time, those who had spent the kind of money it took to enjoy the maiden voyage of this marvel of modern engineering in First Class a mostly punctual bunch.

A hand gripped his arm just as he was about to hand over his ticket.

He spun, a lump forming in his throat as his heart nearly stopped, the bruisers from the hotel having found him.

He tried to break the grip with a jerk of his arm to no avail, the man impossibly strong.

He tapped a well of courage he didn't realize he had.

"Unhand me, sir!" He turned toward the White Star Line staff. "Are you just going to stand there, or assist me?"

The two men looked at each other for a moment, shocked, then rushed forward. The grip was immediately loosened and he jerked his arm free, pushing past the two White Star men, stuffing his ticket into one of their hands as he rushed up the gangway. He glanced back to see the two men glaring at him before fading into the crowd, the two staff members joining him as he boarded the ship.

"Are you alright, sir?" asked the man who was inspecting his ticket.

Dodge nodded. "An unfortunate way to end an otherwise enjoyable stay in England."

"Indeed." The man handed him his boarding pass. "I trust your journey will be without incident."

Dodge smiled. "I'm certain it will be."

The man bowed.

"Welcome aboard the RMS Titanic."

Charles Street, Annapolis, Maryland
Present Day
Three months before the shooting

Steve Wainwright looked through the door and sighed at the sight. Box upon box were stacked against the far wall, every square inch of the exposed paneling covered with souvenirs and memorabilia, one entire wall devoted to what appeared to be some sort of research project into the Titanic.

His grandfather's obsession.

His grandfather had died just before the outset of World War II.

Single gunshot wound to the head.

Self-inflicted.

Steve had never met his grandfather, and his own father had barely spoken of him, the pain and shame too great. He knew his father loved the man, yet he was also pretty sure he had never forgiven him for what he had done.

His suicide had left them with a lot of debts, his Navy pension not enough to support the family, and his Grandma Rose had struggled to keep them fed and clothed. World War II had actually helped, the men going off to war, the jobs freed up for women like his grandmother.

It had allowed her to earn a decent living while her two boys went off to fight.

Uncle Mike never returned.

Dead in North Africa.

His dad had made it home, stayed with Grandma Rose to help her out, then when she passed a few years after the war, he had married and started a family in this very home. It had been updated over the years, probably unrecognizable to his grandparents if they were to see it today, but this one room in the basement hadn't been touched in over sixty years.

Where do I begin?

His father had just passed and the family home had been willed to him, his mother having succumbed to cancer not even six months ago. He was convinced his father had died of a broken heart, the two of them inseparable for over sixty years.

It was like losing a piece of your soul.

His father had never been the same, had barely spoken, and it was clear to Steve that the man was just waiting to die.

It hadn't taken long, his father over ninety years old.

He had had a good run.

A run that wasn't worth continuing without his partner.

Steve's chest tightened as he stepped inside the small room tucked away at one end of the basement. It had been locked for as long as he could remember, his father never setting foot inside, a padlock on the door sealing them out, the combination something he and his sister had guessed at for years as children with no success.

Today he had cut it off with bolt cutters, something he had to buy from Home Depot just for this.

Maybe I can return them?

He had asked several of his father's neighbors if they had any and none had, apparently it a tool rarely needed so seldom bought. It seemed in the movies everyone had a set, yet he was pretty sure this was the first time he had ever actually held a pair.

And like in the movies, he almost felt like he was committing a crime by slicing through the metal that had kept everyone out for so long.

He drew in a deep breath through his nose, trying to get a sense of his grandfather.

Instead he was rewarded with stale, musty air.

He stepped over to the wall and unlatched a window, pushing it open, the unused hinges screeching in protest.

"You down there?"

He turned toward his sister's voice. "Yeah." Footsteps echoed through the stairs over his head. "I'm in granddad's room."

"Aww, you said you'd wait!"

"You're late."

His sister Judy stepped into the room, her mouth agape. "I don't know what I was expecting, but…"

She slowly rounded the room leaving her sentence unfinished, a finger running over every surface within reach, leaving a distinct trail in the quarter inch of dust that had managed to accumulate in the closed room.

Probably all the paper slowly disintegrating.

"What's this?" she asked, stopping in front of the wall of Titanic clippings and maps.

He shrugged. "I dunno."

She pointed at one of the boxes labeled 'Dad's things'. "That looks like Dad's handwriting."

Steve stepped over to the wall and nodded, the handwriting not only distinctly different from everything else in the room, but clearly his father's chicken scratches, the man never known for his handwriting skills. Judy pulled the lid off the banker's box revealing an assortment of papers and file folders. One stood out.

"Is that a police file?"

Judy reached inside and pulled out the blue folder, a faded Annapolis PD stamp on it. She opened the file and gasped at the same time Steve did.

"It's a report on Granddad's suicide!" She closed her eyes and handed him the folder. "I can't look."

Steve took the file and dropped into the only chair in the room, the springs protesting under his weight, his grandfather probably the last to sit here. He quickly skimmed the file, mostly routine name and address info, a description of the scene and the position of the body.

He jumped from the chair, looking back at where he had just been sitting.

"What?"

He nodded toward the chair sitting in front of a roll top desk. "That's where he was when he shot himself."

Judy's hand darted to her mouth and she bit her index finger.

And suddenly things he had missed earlier jumped out at him. To the left of the desk the carpet had a dark stain, something he had dismissed as coffee earlier. There were dark brown splotches sprayed across the boxes stacked to the left, several spots on the window he had just pushed open.

Bloodstains!

"No wonder Dad never wanted us in here."

Judy nodded, gripping his arm. "But why wouldn't he clean it up?"

Steve pointed to the floor. "It's been cleaned, just not well. I guess back in those days they left things to the families."

"Probably Grandma was left to clean it up and she couldn't deal with it."

He looked about the tomb, it at once a testament to his family's shame and its remorse. "I remember Mom saying that Dad had locked the room up shortly after the death. Grandma probably couldn't get in here to finish the job."

He returned his attention to the file, flipping to the next page, a piece of paper, handwritten, clipped to the file. He read it aloud for his sister to hear, her eyes once again squeezed shut.

"May God forgive me for what I did."

"His suicide note?" she asked, stealing a quick glance.

He nodded, his eyes narrowing. "Something doesn't sound right. What do you make of it?"

Judy shrugged. "He's asking for forgiveness for committing suicide, obviously."

Steve pointed at the last three words. "Then why is it 'what I did'? Shouldn't it be 'what I've done'?"

Judy leaned in closer, reading the note for herself. "Maybe he wasn't thinking very clearly? He was about to kill himself."

Steve shook his head. "This is written very neatly, signed and dated. It looks like a very deliberate note." He pointed again at the words. "It's as if he regretted something he had done in the past. Can you think of anything?"

Judy looked at him. "You're asking me? You know Dad never spoke about him. I can honestly say I know absolutely nothing about Granddad except that he was in the Navy."

"And the Captain of a ship."

"Right." Judy snapped her fingers. "And didn't he resign, or retire early?"

"After World War One, I think. I remember Mom mentioning it. It was unexpected, apparently."

Judy smiled at him. "I guess we do know a little bit."

"'Little' being the key word here."

He flipped the page and groaned, a crime scene photo showing his grandfather slumped over his desk, the gun on the floor, the note sitting to the side. On the floor sat a poster tube and another banker's box. He moved the folder closer to his face.

April 14, 1912.

He lowered the file and looked about the room, spotting the box sitting on top of a stack near the window, the tube lying beside it. He handed the folder to his sister and retrieved the tube, popping the top off.

"What's that?" asked Judy as he tipped it upside down and shook it, something inside beginning to slide out.

"It was on the floor the night he shot himself." He nodded toward the box. "And so was that. Dad must have moved them."

Something hit his hand and he reached inside with his fingers, fishing it out. Putting the tube aside, he unrolled what turned out to be a large painting. "What the hell is this?" he muttered as he held it up for Judy to see. A naked woman holding an almost translucent scarf stood in front of some sort of stone structure.

"Doesn't look like something Granddad would like."

Steve shook his head. "No. Not at all. And look at the edges. This has been cut out of its frame."

Judy gasped. "Granddad was a thief?"

Steve felt his stomach flip at her words. He couldn't believe it, not for a second, but he was holding the evidence in his hand. Then again, what he was holding could be anything. It could be some worthless painting done by some hack in a street market for a nickel.

It doesn't look cheap.

In fact it looked like a great deal of talent was involved.

He handed Judy the painting and lifted the box from the stack, placing it on the desk. Removing the top, he reached inside to remove the single, thick file folder, a piece of paper clipped to the cover.

"My greatest regret. May God forgive us all."

17

Judy leaned in. "Open it."

He flipped the cover back, a sheaf of papers inside dry to the touch, so much so he feared they might crumble if he were to bend them. Yet the type was still clearly legible. "Looks like a passenger manifest."

Judy leaned in. "Of the Titanic?"

"Yeah..." His voice drifted off as he focused on the handwritten note, his heart pounding with the implications. His grandfather had been Navy, had been captain of a ship during the time the Titanic sailed.

And had killed himself for something he had *done.*

Granddad, what did you do?

He handed the file to Judy who read the handwritten note attached to the first page by a dull paperclip, her voice barely a whisper.

"We could have saved them all."

North Atlantic Ocean
Aboard the RMS Titanic
April 14th, 1912

Henry Dodge folded his napkin neatly, his meal finished. And what a meal. Ten courses, starting with oysters and ending with Waldorf Pudding, it was one of the finest dining experiences he had ever been privileged to partake in. The company was terrific, the well-heeled always welcoming of the son of a United States Senator. He was treated with respect, lest they feel the wrath of the elder Dodge should they want something from the government in the future.

And these people were always wanting something.

John Jacob Astor IV, by far the richest man aboard—and one of the richest in the world—rose, silencing those gathered. "Gentlemen, may I suggest cigars and brandy in the smoking room?"

A round of agreement had the men rising, assisting their wives to their feet, the two sexes to part. He had been paired with a lovely young lady tonight named Madeleine Dumont, travelling unescorted to meet her fiancé in New York, and as he was married, it had been deemed a good match, there none of the pressures of young single people to worry about.

She was ten years his junior, though their conversation had been pleasant, he finding her well-educated and well-versed in world affairs, a refreshing change from his wife who seemed to make it her mission in life to be ignorant of all things non-domestic. It had been a disappointment to say the least. She had an education, a good one, her parents well to do, and during their lengthy courtship she had partaken in conversations covering

19

most topics with what he had assumed was genuine interest, her insights often thought provoking.

Yet after their wedding it was as if a switch had been flipped and all she cared about was climbing the social ladder by managing a good home, being invited to the right parties, and making certain the A-list were always at their own parties. He was certain she was determined to see him follow his father's footsteps, she even fantasizing about it on occasion, with phrases like "when you're a senator" and "when you take over from your father" peppering their conversations.

Unfortunately for her, he had no interest in becoming a politician. He had seen what it had done to his father, and though he was certain his father loved his job, he hated the way he was at the beck and call of those who helped finance his campaign.

He exchanged pleasantries with Mademoiselle Dumont then joined the men as they made for the lounge, standing drink orders delivered into their hands within moments, choices of cigars presented and lit.

Dodge made it a point to note what Astor was drinking and smoking on the first night, hoping to use it as an excuse to open a conversation with the one man who might be able to help him.

The Astor family was apparently opposed to the creation of the Federal Reserve System, and Astor, along with several other prominent men, were travelling back to the United States to try and stop it. If anyone might know who this Assembly was, and how to stop them, he was certain it would be Astor.

Dodge sipped his 1858 Cuvée Léonie, a ridiculously expensive cognac preferred by Astor, the viscous liquid setting his taste buds afire as the delicious fluid rolled over his tongue and down his throat. He took a long drag on his cigar, mixing the two sensations and closing his eyes for a moment.

He spotted Astor, departing one group, heading for another.

He made his move.

Deftly navigating the groups of three and four that had gathered, he approached Astor.

"Sir, I was wondering if I might have a moment of your time."

Astor paused, looking at him.

"I assume about the letter I sent you?"

Wainwright Residence, Collette Court, Odenton, Maryland
Present Day
Two weeks before the shooting

Steve Wainwright looked at the scanned pages on his computer screen, his sister Judy sitting beside him. He shook his head as they slowly read through his grandfather's service record, the files sent to them after he had put in the request months ago. It had taken a call to his congressman a week ago to finally grease the wheels of an impossibly slow bureaucracy.

And now they were reading a rather mundane file, listing their grandfather's personal information, assignments and commendations. He clicked to the next page, finding a list of specific missions.

A spasm shot through his big toe and up to his knee. He winced as he pulled his foot up by the pant leg, crossing it over his knee, massaging away the pain.

"Your arthritis again?"

He nodded. "Getting old."

Judy smiled. "Old? I just had my first great-grandchild. Now *that's* old."

"Hey, I'm older than you."

Judy lay her head on his shoulder for a moment. "And I'll never let you forget it." She lifted her head. "What's that?"

Steve's eyes narrowed at the large blacked out block in the center of the page, one of their grandfather's assignments redacted. "That's odd." He pointed to the dates of the previous and next missions. "Notice anything about those dates?"

Judy shrugged. "Should I? You know I'm not the history buff like you are."

"The Titanic sank April fourteenth. His previous mission ended two weeks before that, and his next mission started three weeks after. Don't you think that's too much of a coincidence?"

Judy squeezed his forearm as she looked at him. "You don't think Granddad had something to do with the sinking, do you?"

Steve felt his stomach churn. "I don't know what to think anymore. But I have to find out."

Judy's grip tightened. "But what if he *did* have something to do with it. Do we really want to know?"

Steve sucked in a quick breath as his heart slammed in his chest, not sure of the answer. If his grandfather did indeed have something to do with the sinking, it could destroy the family's reputation for generations.

Nonsense!

The ship sank because of an iceberg. That was accepted fact, the footage taken of the ship on the bottom of the ocean proving the firsthand accounts from the survivors, so there was no way his grandfather was responsible for sinking the ship.

Yet he was involved somehow, his guilt haunting him until it finally became too much.

"I have to know."

"No matter the consequences?"

Steve frowned, looking at his sister.

"Yes, no matter the consequences."

North Atlantic Ocean

Aboard the RMS Titanic

April 14th, 1912

It was everything Henry Dodge could do to avoid an audible gasp. Astor had sent him the letter? It sort of made sense that he could be the source. He'd definitely have the connections and wanted to see the creation of the Federal Reserve stopped. And if he was the source, then he definitely knew about The Assembly, since they were mentioned in the letter.

He also knew they would kill should it become necessary.

Which meant he had Astor to thank for putting his life at risk.

"You're 'A Concerned Citizen'?" he finally managed to ask.

"Yes, but now isn't the time to speak of such things." He looked about. "You have the letter?"

Dodge nodded.

"On your person?"

"I fear to leave it anywhere else."

"Good man. It is essential you deliver that letter to your father in Washington upon our arrival. He'll know what to do with it."

Dodge felt his chest tighten as someone approached, Benjamin Guggenheim. Astor shook his head almost imperceptibly, the man changing direction slightly, striking up a conversation with a group on another trajectory.

"Why not deliver it yourself?" asked Dodge, his voice low, mimicking Astor's continued enjoyment of his cigar and spirits.

"They would expect me to have it, and I fully expect they will make every attempt to intercept it before I have a chance to deliver it. Hopefully you'll succeed where I'm likely to fail."

"But they know who I am."

Astor paused in mid drink, his eyebrows shooting up. He lowered his glass. "Are you certain?"

Dodge nodded emphatically, catching himself, his earnestness out of place in such sedately civilized company. "Yes, two men came to my hotel but I was able to evade them. They grabbed me just as I was boarding but I managed to get away."

Astor pursed his lips, shaking his head slightly. "I had my man deliver it. They must be watching me closer than I thought." He looked about, the man clearly nervous. "Have you noticed anyone suspicious on board?"

Dodge smiled slightly. "Sir, I'm so on edge, I've convinced myself that nearly everyone here is after me." He bowed slightly toward Astor. "Present company now excluded, of course."

Astor smiled, returning the bow. "Of course." He motioned toward Dodge's pocket with his cigar. "Guard that with your life. As my note stated, they *will* kill for it, however once it is in your father's hands, it will be too late. If I know him as well as I think I do, he will immediately take action, most likely reading it on the Senate floor. Once that is done, their plans will be scuttled, hopefully permanently."

"You know my father?"

"I do have that pleasure."

"Interesting," murmured Dodge. This revelation meant he hadn't been selected at random to deliver the information, but specifically because of who he was, or rather who his father was. It made him all the more determined to succeed. "Surely they couldn't do anything to stop you, could they? You're too, well…" Dodge wasn't certain how to tactfully suggest the man was too powerful and wealthy to be touched.

"Untouchable?" Astor smiled slightly. "Those behind The Assembly are so well insulated from consequences, I would suggest such considerations are of no concern to them. If I were to die, no suspicions would be cast upon any of them."

"But the documents—"

"Would be destroyed, claimed as fake should they not be." Astor looked at Dodge. "Which is why reaching your father is so important. *He* is the type of man who will recognize its importance and reveal it to the world rather than stop to check its veracity, as he will know full well that there will be no way to prove it. He will recognize that the mere contents being made public will be enough to slow down the process being driven through by The Assembly, and perhaps derail it."

"Why not arrest them? Some of their names are in the transcript."

"What have they done wrong in this case? Is it illegal to try and make a profit on the backs of others? If it were, I'd be a poor man right now. There is a difference between being legally wrong and morally wrong, and once the Federal Reserve Act is passed, nothing they do will be legally wrong."

"So my father is the key." Dodge frowned. A pit formed in his stomach. "Will they try to kill him?"

Astor shook his head. "I doubt it, but he's a wise man, he'll take precautions. And once they are stopped…" Astor's voice trailed off as his gaze drifted over Dodge's shoulder. "The men who pursued you, would you recognize them?"

Dodge resisted the urge to look over his shoulder to see what Astor was looking at. "Absolutely."

"There are two men at the far end who seem to be taking a particular interest in us. I will shift positions to allow you to see them." Astor casually turned, his hand extending toward the other end of the room, as if commenting on the architecture. Dodge stepped forward slightly, turning back toward Astor, his heart leaping into his throat as he spotted the two men Astor had been referring to.

"That's them," he hissed.

"Keep calm, young Mr. Dodge. It is curious, however. I wonder how they managed to get on board."

"Could they have snuck on?"

"I doubt that. If I had to hazard a guess, I would think they already had tickets."

"But how? You only delivered the papers to me a few hours before the ship set sail."

"I would suggest that these men had always intended to board."

"But why?"

"To kill me, of course."

Congressman Bill Mahoney's Office
Monroe Street, Rockville
Present Day
Day of the shooting

"Thanks for doing this, Bill, it's appreciated."

Steve Wainwright sat across from Congressman Bill Mahoney's large mahogany desk, the ornate, cherry stained walls and ceiling contrasting sharply with the state of the art computer equipment sitting on the man's desk.

"No problem, Steve. I owe your son for helping me get reelected. I'm happy to make a phone call or two for the Wainwrights." He held up a finger and hit the button to put the call on speaker.

"Congressman, sorry for the delay."

"No problem, Jerry. Do you have what we're looking for?"

"I've got Captain Wainwright's record up on the screen. It's just archival scans, it hasn't been computerized, but you're right, part of it is redacted for some reason."

"I could see that during wartime, but this was pre-World War One."

"I know. Let me check something. They've been digitizing the assignments, maybe we'll get lucky." The sound of fingers tapping on a keyboard came over the speaker, Steve feeling his stomach squirm with anticipation, not sure of what to expect. *"Oh shit."*

"What?" asked Mahoney, leaning closer to the phone.

"I don't know, my computer is shutting down and there's some sort of security alert telling me to stay where I am."

Mahoney and Steve exchanged worried glances. "What did you do?"

"Based on our conversation, I just typed in Wainwrights name and the word Titanic." There was a pause. *"Oh shit! I'm royally screwed, I shouldn't have done this!"*

"Listen, just tell them I'm the one who asked you to do the search. I'll do everything in my power—"

There was a click then a dial tone.

Steve looked at Mahoney. "What the hell just happened?"

Mahoney shook his head, ending the call. "I don't know, but something tells me someone doesn't want us looking into what your grandfather did."

"And it has something to do with the Titanic."

And the very thought of it made him sick with worry.

North Atlantic Ocean
Aboard the RMS Titanic
April 14th, 1912

"Captain, there are reports of icebergs along our course."

Captain Edward Smith looked at Chief Mate Henry Wilde, taking the communication from the radio room. He read them over, his chest tightening slightly. He was under tremendous pressure by corporate head office to set a transatlantic crossing record on this maiden voyage, though he would not do so at the risk of the ship and its passengers.

He handed the paper back, a wave of guilt washing over him, a cold sweat breaking out on his forehead and back. "Continue at current speed."

Wilde stepped slightly closer, lowering his voice so the rest of the bridge couldn't hear their conversation. "Captain, surely head office would understand if we didn't succeed. Icebergs, especially at night, aren't to be trifled with."

Captain Smith glanced at his Chief, desperate to tell him the truth, yet held his tongue. "As you were, Chief."

Wilde snapped to attention as if he were aboard a military vessel then walked away, his troubled expression clearly indicating he wasn't happy with the decision.

He'll report me, for sure.

Smith took in a deep breath, his chest swelling as he tried to force some courage into his butterfly filled stomach.

As he should.

But Sarah and our daughter will be safe.

He turned and headed for his cabin, closing the door behind him and taking a seat in his chair. He picked up a photo of his family, a lump forming in his throat.

He didn't know who they were, but two men had arrived at the White Star Lines offices only minutes before he was due to leave for the ship. They had a handwritten note from his wife and a clipping of his daughter's hair.

And a request that, should it be ignored, would result in him never seeing them alive again.

He had belted the one closest him, but a gun cocking behind him had ended his fight and he had been rewarded with a fist to the midriff. He rubbed his stomach, the muscles still tender.

The "request" had been simple.

Make all haste to a set of coordinates provided him on a piece of paper, it along his route therefore no course deviation necessary. He was then to do something he couldn't understand at the time.

He was to come to a complete stop.

And wait fifteen minutes.

Then resume his voyage, again at best speed.

He would still set the record, an entry would be made in the log that they had stopped because something had been spotted in the water, something that would turn out to be nothing, and no one would be the wiser.

Wiser of *what* was his question.

He had been rewarded with a second blow.

Questions weren't to be tolerated.

Nor failure.

He had to make the rendezvous coordinates on time or his family died.

Rendezvous coordinates.

That must be what they were. There could be no other possible explanation. He could see no reason to stop in the middle of the North Atlantic for fifteen minutes then resume course. It made no sense unless it was a rendezvous.

But rendezvous with whom?

Assembly Covert Communications Facility, Moscow, Russia
Present Day

"There's been activity concerning the Titanic operation."

Ilya Mashkov's eyebrows rose slightly at the revelation. The meeting of The Assembly had been hastily called, an unusual though not rare occurrence. The interests of their organization were varied involving most countries of the world, from private industry to government procurement, from influence peddling to the very administrations themselves.

The Assembly was all powerful.

It *was* the grand conspiracy that the tinfoil hat crowd whined of, yet were still so wrong about. Illuminati, Masons, Triarii, Rosicrucians. They were all real enough, but the power they wielded paled in comparison to The Assembly.

Because it was small.

Twelve individuals sat on the ruling council. Never any more, and only less until a replacement was found. And even then the process could take time. He had been invited in six years ago after his predecessor had died from a bullet to the head.

Who delivered that bullet, he didn't know, though he suspected it was on the orders of the people whose silhouettes were now on screens in front of him. He knew nothing of them. Who they were, where they were, what they looked like, though he could surmise in some cases from the tasks they volunteered to undertake. Since he had been selected by them, he was quite certain they knew who he was, and it was his guess that the oldest member knew who everyone was, one of the benefits of longevity in an organization that appeared to tolerate little in the way of failure.

Dozens had been murdered since he had joined.

He had little problem with that. The common man wasn't their target, it was the uncommon man. Men and women who had gained power of some sort that wouldn't bend to the will of The Assembly when needed, or threatened their desires.

The Assembly could be subtle. Usually the best interests of The Assembly were also in the best interests of those in control. A CEO usually wanted the same thing, a head of state as well.

But occasionally those interests diverged, and that was when pressure needed to be exerted. Sometimes subtle, sometimes not so subtle. And on occasion, violence was necessary, though it rarely came to that. Usually what was required could be attained through political favors or disruption of a corporation's money supply.

Control of banks was key, especially central banks.

Sometimes this influence resulted in strange results. Pipelines not built for environmental reasons, yet Arctic drilling approved. Things that simply made no logical sense. Until you drilled down to the real reason. In The Assembly's case, the Artic didn't have railways, and it was far more profitable to transport oil by rail, if you owned the railway.

But oil was merely one of many economic pies they had their hands in.

The real money was in banking.

And arms.

A slightly unstable world was always more profitable than a stable one. A planet at peace with itself could spell economic disaster, history itself being the lesson there. After World War One, the world was weary of war, and that weariness grew into complacency and the false belief that the "war to end all wars" was actually in fact that. The result? The Great Depression.

World War Two brought the world out of the worst economic decline in modern times and led to an economic boom. The end of the war though didn't mean the end of the need for massive arms spending. Korea, Vietnam and the Cold War fueled spending the world over, which kept economies expanding, technology advancing, quality of life improving.

For those on the winning side.

And The Assembly was always, ultimately, on the winning side.

The end of the Cold War was supposed to bring a "peace dividend" that never really materialized, yet did lead to a weakening of most major armed forces in the world with the exception of China. Bringing back an external threat had been of key importance. Terrorism had helped, allowing for massive investments in security through fueling paranoia on the home front, whether that be airport scanners that could see through clothing, to the militarization of the police forces by letting them purchase army surplus equipment. And Russia's resurgence due to their oil reserves had done wonders, with the military leaders of the Western world realizing that the Cold War wasn't yet over.

All of which meant The Assembly would continue to rake in the money, wielding power over men and women the world over, none with any inkling what was actually happening.

And the beautiful thing, as he had discovered, was that mankind was screwed up enough to actually bring most of what happened upon itself.

The Assembly didn't fly planes into the Twin Towers.

The Assembly didn't create ISIS.

The Assembly was merely there to capitalize on these events, and profit from them, as they slowly guided the entire planet toward some end game he hadn't yet been made privy to, and wasn't sure if he ever would.

They were only twelve people, though their organization was much more, though nobody knew who they worked for. Everything was done through private contractors, some like BlackTide that were now defunct after their failure, others too tightly controlled to ever be known to the public.

If The Assembly wanted something done, their hands were never soiled, there never a possibility of anything being traced back to the organization.

Yet now it appeared something was wrong.

Titanic?

"Forgive me, since I'm new, I'm not familiar with our involvement with the Titanic."

"What our involvement was is of no importance however a file will be provided. What *is* important is the fact someone is beginning to ask questions about a naval officer involved."

"Who?" asked one of the others.

"Captain Johnathan Wainwright. He committed suicide in 1940, but it appears someone is asking questions and may have found a link to the Titanic operation."

Mashkov felt his chest tighten slightly. He hated not knowing what was going on, and it was as if the others took delight in making it clear that he was the only one who was out of the loop.

Or were they just as much in the dark as he was?

Only two people seemed to be talking, the others all silent.

Better to remain silent and be thought a fool than to speak out and remove all doubt.

It was one of his favorite Abraham Lincoln quotes that too many politicians today seemed to not heed.

Tipping islands, anyone?

And he'd be a fool himself to ignore the sage advice.

He listened.

"I thought with his suicide we'd be done with the affair. There are no longer any survivors from that era. What makes you think there's a problem?"

"A records clerk did a search on Wainwright's name and the keyword 'Titanic'. It triggered a security alert that we had inserted into the system years ago, and our resources were notified immediately."

"What do you propose we do?"

"There can be only one response. If it were to get out what really happened that night, there could be substantial repercussions that could lead to our discovery, though I feel the risks to that are minimal. Regardless, it could result in a witch-hunt that may disrupt our interests significantly over the short term."

"You are proposing the problem be cleaned up."

"Yes."

"Is that absolutely necessary? Don't we risk drawing even more attention to ourselves?"

"The sinking of the Titanic is one of the most famous incidents in modern history and holds a certain fascination with the public, especially after that damned James Cameron movie. Should it come out that those people could have been saved, everyone will be seeking the truth, from governments to press to conspiracy nuts. Our security procedures weren't as tight back then out of necessity. All it would take would be some stray reference to us that might have serious repercussions."

"I agree," said the only other person who had been speaking. "Does everyone agree?"

Mashkov leaned forward and pressed a green button beside his terminal. Once the last button had been pressed, a tally flashed on the screen.

Twelve to none.

"It is agreed then. All who have been exposed to the information will be eliminated."

North Atlantic Ocean
Aboard the RMS Titanic
April 14, 1912

Henry Dodge patted his breast pocket, the envelope still secure on his person. Yet at this moment, he felt anything but. The sight of the two men, bold as brass, within sight of him, making no attempt to hide themselves, had his heart racing since Astor's spotting of them.

And his heart had only just recovered from his initial scare before boarding.

This trip, which he had been looking forward to for months, was turning into the most terrifying, stressful event of his life. He was by no means a courageous man. He had never joined the military, had never charged into a fight, verbal or otherwise. If he had to describe himself, he would lean toward the almost timid side.

He definitely took after his mother.

Which might be why his wife seemed to think she could control him.

He looked in the mirror, adjusting his tie.

If I survive this, there's going to be some changes at home.

He took a long breath, squaring his shoulders and inflating his chest.

Perhaps a little more intimidating than normal?

He narrowed his eyes slightly, wiping any trace of good humor from his face.

Definitely more intimidating.

He pictured the two bruisers, their suits barely containing their bulging muscles.

Now that's intimidating.

He would be no match for them in a fight. Of that there was no doubt. And they were most likely armed, which would put a quick end to any contest should it occur.

If only it were wrestling.

His father had insisted on trying to make a man of him when he was younger, forcing him to join the Greco-Roman wrestling team. He had been quite good at it, actually. He never won any tournaments, though always placed decently, never humiliating himself.

Yet he had hated it.

Grappling with sweaty boys was not his idea of a good time and the locker room had always been a horror show of bodies developing far faster than his.

Baldy.

He frowned, looking down the mirror slightly.

If they could see me now.

He chuckled, shaking his head, noting it the first time he had genuinely laughed since receiving the envelope under his door.

So sad considering the amount spent on this voyage.

One final check in the mirror and he opened his cabin door, stepping into the hallway, nodding to an elderly couple heading to the deck, arm-in-arm.

"How do you do," said the gentleman, Dodge returning the greeting. He let them pass and was about to follow when he saw the bruisers at the end of the hallway.

His stomach flipped as they spotted him.

He turned the other way, rushing as gentlemanlike as he could to the far end of the corridor, making his way to the deck in a more roundabout fashion. He hadn't intended to go outside, it too chilly for his liking, yet if there was one place he could be certain there would be plenty of people at this time of night it would be there.

He hoped the eyes of the passengers would protect him.

The air was bracing, the North Atlantic a cruel mistress to those not prepared for her harshness, and his attire certainly left him unprepared.

He shivered.

The pounding of footsteps behind him had him rushing down the deck, away from the door he had just stepped through. Crossing the width of the ship to the starboard side, he tried to put some distance between himself and the men but it was no use, he knew.

Suddenly somebody stepped out in front of him from the shadows, startling him.

It was Astor.

He stopped.

"They're after me."

He nodded, looking down the deck. "They searched my room during dinner."

Dodge frowned. "Did they find anything?"

Astor shook his head. "No, I put the papers in the ship's safe. I knew they'd try my cabin the first chance they'd get should anyone be aboard."

"A prescient move."

Astor smiled. "Indeed." He frowned. "Here they come."

"Go, nothing must happen to you."

Astor shook his head, popping his cane up, grabbing it tightly in the middle. "I've never shied away from a fight, and I'm not going to start tonight."

Dodge suddenly felt inferior to this man in yet another way. His wealth, power and accomplishments were probably unmatched on the ship, yet his courage appeared to be as well.

Dodge turned toward the men, looking about for a weapon, finding none.

The two men stopped in front of them.

"Gentlemen, our employers would like their property returned," said the first, smaller than the second, though to suggest he was small would be a mistake.

"I'm sure we have no idea what you're referring to," replied Astor, thankfully, Dodge's tongue stuck to the top of his suddenly dry mouth.

Somebody shouted far above them, the words inaudible.

The man smiled, revealing a cracked front tooth, what remained black as coal. "Mr. Astor, sir, please don't waste our time. You know exactly what we are referring to." He held out a hand. "If you would kindly hand it over, all will be forgotten."

More shouts from above, again inaudible, their tone though clear.

Something was wrong.

But no one seemed to notice, the casual strolls continuing, even their own little confrontation going unnoticed.

Astor jabbed the air with his cane. "Do you honestly believe that if I did have whatever it is you are looking for, I would be stupid enough to carry it on my person? Do you honestly believe either of us would be stupid enough?"

The envelope in Dodge's pocket suddenly felt ten pounds heavier.

The sound of the engines changed and he could feel the boat begin to turn to the left slightly, the shouts above continuing.

Yet no one, including Astor and the bruisers, seemed to notice.

Something is definitely wrong.

What that could be, he had no clue. He peered down the deck but could see nothing, the lights too bright to see if anything was in their path.

The larger man opened his lapel, revealing a shoulder holster. "We must insist, gentlemen. Either you provide us with the papers you stole, or take us to them."

The ship vibrated then shook, Dodge reaching out for something to catch his balance as a strange sound rapidly approached.

And that was when he saw it.

A massive iceberg, passing by the starboard side, towering over their heads, impossibly close. The noise grew as it neared them, chunks of ice scattering across the deck much to the shock and surprise of those casually strolling only a moment before.

Dodge looked at Astor, fear on his face, but felt almost reassured at the calm on the older man's face. Suddenly Astor's cane whipped out, smacking the larger man on the side of the head, the man collapsing in pain, grabbing at the point of impact as Astor raised his weapon for a second blow.

The other man was shocked at first, it unclear whether or not it was from the iceberg or Astor's attack, but a growl erupted and Dodge reacted, surprising even himself. He rushed forward, leaning over, shoving his shoulder into the man's midriff, lifting him off the ground as he wrapped his arms around his opponent. Surging toward the railing as the iceberg passed their position, he roared as the man began to fight back.

They hit the railing bringing Dodge to an immediate halt. He released his grip on the man's back, his foe's momentum carrying him backward and over the side. He didn't hear or see the splash as the man hit the water, his eyes drawn to the shocking sight of the iceberg continuing down the side of the ship.

Out of the corner of his eye he saw Astor's cane swing again.

The man was down, blood flowing from his head. Astor bent over and pulled the man's gun from its holster. He looked at Dodge. "Help me."

Dodge stepped over and helped Astor lift the man to his feet. "Is he dead?"

"Not yet."

Dodge looked around to find no one paying attention to them, all eyes on the iceberg and the ice scattered on the deck. "Then we have to hurry," said Dodge, his decision made. These men meant to kill them, and once the excitement of the close encounter with the iceberg was forgotten, their opponent would have the opportunity to try again.

He grabbed the man's belt and hauled him toward the railing, shoving him over the side, Astor's surprised expression leaving him slightly uncertain as to whether or not it had been a wise move.

"I do believe I have underestimated you, Mr. Dodge."

Dodge said nothing for a moment, instead shaking uncontrollably as both the cold and the adrenaline fueling his momentary bravado took hold. "I-I think I su-surprised myself."

Astor looked about then took Dodge by the arm. "Let's get inside. We'll report them as having fallen overboard when the iceberg hit. No one will doubt us."

Dodge nodded, allowing himself to be led inside by the older man, still stunned at what he had just done.

You killed two men!

He rubbed his hands together as the warmth began to return to his body. His hands continued to shake and he was at a loss as to how to calm his heart, now hammering in his chest.

Two crewmembers rushed by, concern written on their faces.

It wasn't until they were almost out of sight he noticed they were wearing life vests.

"I think something's wrong."

Yet Astor seemed to already know.

"I have to get to my wife; she will be upset, I'm sure."

"But shouldn't we be telling the Captain about what just happened?"

Astor looked at Dodge.

"I fear none of that will matter in a few hours."

Collette Court, Odenton, Maryland
Present Day

"I dunno, looks the same to me."

Steve Wainwright sat at his desk, the painting discovered rolled up in his grandfather's basement clipped to an easel poached from his wife who stood next to him. On his computer screen was a Wikipedia article about the most valuable item lost on the Titanic, a painting that looked, to his untrained eye, identical to the one standing before them.

"Me too," agreed his sister Judy. "It's either the same painting or a very good forgery." She looked at his wife, Sally. "You're the artist in the family, what do you think?"

"I'd hardly call myself an artist." Sally shrugged. "I don't know. To me it looks identical, but I wouldn't know where to begin to figure out if it's real or not."

Steve looked from the screen to the painting, sighing. "Then where should we begin?"

Judy scratched the back of her hand. "I think we need an art expert."

Steve was *not* an art buff. "Okay, where the hell do we find one of those?"

"Art gallery?" suggested Sally.

"No way!" Steve shook his head emphatically. "I wouldn't trust them to not claim it was a fake and steal it." He tapped his chin. "No, we need somebody impartial, not motivated by money."

Sally put a hand on his shoulder. "An academic. Like from the university."

Steve snapped his fingers. "I'll give Greg a call! He's the dean of St. Paul's and they're not that far from here."

"Who's this Greg?" asked Judy.

"Young guy, forty something, met him at a charity event, fundraising for wheelchairs. He's in one. Gunshot wound to the spine." He began to Google the university. "Sharp cookie. He'll know exactly who we need to show this thing to."

"How was he shot?" asked Judy as Steve looked up the number, grabbing the cordless phone off his desk.

"Not sure," replied Sally. "It was in New York City, I think. Just wrong place at the wrong time, I guess."

Judy shivered. "New York City. I'll never go there, too violent."

"It's not like it used to be," said Sally as Steve dialed. "You used to not be able to walk around in Times Square but now it's family friendly."

Judy turned her nose up. "Can't imagine taking my grandkids there."

"M&M's has a huge store there."

Judy's face brightened. "Really?"

Steve held up a hand, killing the conversation. "Hi, can I speak to Dean Milton, please?"

"Who may I ask is calling?"

"Steve Wainwright. We met at the Wheelchairs for Veterans fundraiser last year."

"One moment, please."

Muzak of some type began to play and he turned in his chair. "I'm on hold."

Suddenly a click had him sitting upright.

"Steve, Greg here, to what do I owe the pleasure?"

"Hi Greg, I hate to bother you with this, and if you're not the right person, just let me know, but, well, we were going through my grandfather's

46

basement and came across a painting that, well…" His voice trailed off as he looked at the painting, the woman looking off to the side, as if unconcerned she were nude in what might be a private garden.

"Well?"

"This is going to sound crazy."

"You'd be surprised at what I've heard over the years."

"I doubt you've heard anything as crazy as this."

"Just tell him!" urged Judy.

"Okay, Greg, here's the thing. We think the painting might have been taken from the Titanic."

There was a pause on the other end of the line and Steve began to wonder if their connection had been lost.

"Do you mean recovered as part of one of the exped—"

"No," interrupted Steve. "Taken the night of the sinking."

"I see." There was another pause. "Can you bring the painting in?"

"Absolutely. When?"

"How soon can you get here?"

"We can be there in an hour."

"Good. I'll clear my schedule and have our expert meet you."

"Oh, you're not the expert?"

Milton laughed. "Ah, no. I've got someone on staff here who's perfect for this type of thing. And I can assure you, he's seen a lot of strange things in his time, so he won't be quick to dismiss your story."

"Sounds like the right man for the job. Who?"

"You met him and his fiancée, now wife, at the fundraiser last year."

"Oh, the archeology professor." Steve searched his memory. "Sorry, I can't remember his name."

"Professor James Acton."

North Atlantic Ocean

Aboard the RMS Titanic

April 15th, 1912

Captain Smith listened to the reports coming in from across the ship, his insides churning with the horror of what was to come, his outward appearance stoic, confident. Flooding had already begun, the water rapidly rising, and the naval architect Thomas Andrews, on board for the maiden voyage, had already informed him of the fatal flaw.

The watertight bulkheads weren't high enough.

The water would fill section after section, pouring over the bulkhead walls until the ship would finally sink.

It was inevitable.

"The nearest ship is almost three hours away. The Carpathia."

"That's not enough time!" cried First Officer Will Murdoch.

"Calm yourself, Mr. Murdoch. We must not panic the junior officers or the passengers."

Murdoch squared his shoulders. "Yes, Captain, of course. I apologize."

Smith smiled gently. "You're a good man, Will. Remember your training and you'll get through this. We all will."

Murdoch lowered his voice. "But, Captain. The lifeboats…"

Smith nodded, knowing exactly what Murdoch was referring to.

The lifeboats were launching, yet there weren't enough.

The Unsinkable Ship.

Absurd.

He looked at the chart showing their exact location and frowned.

They were less than an hour from the coordinates where he was supposed to have stopped.

His stomach flipped.

Would the men who held his family show mercy should he die here tonight?

His finger tapped the location of the planned stop.

It has to be a rendezvous.

Which meant there was a ship out there that could save them all if it were big enough.

But would they ignore the distress call?

They had so far, the Carpathia the only one to respond.

What kind of people would stand by while an entire passenger liner sank?

Unknown Assembly Facility

Present Day

Jerry Sparks sat, quaking in a chair, his hands cuffed behind his back, a hood over his head. Beyond the sound of his own rapid breathing against the cloth, he heard nothing.

Except footsteps.

Slow, deliberate footsteps, pacing around and around him.

No voices, no other sounds like traffic or the hustle and bustle of a city.

Not even the sounds of an HVAC system keeping wherever he was cool.

It was more terrifying than anything he could imagine.

He had been escorted out of his office within minutes of the security alert appearing on his computer, the Military Police taking him to their offices and holding him there, the Sergeant apologetic.

"Just following orders."

They had chitchatted for almost half an hour before two men in suits and dark glasses appeared, IDs flashed, cuffs slapped on his wrists. He had been placed in the back of an SUV, the hood pulled over his head, then driven in silence for about fifteen minutes.

He had heard nothing but the sound of the engine.

He had been led to wherever he was now, only a couple of minutes' walk from the vehicle, and still nothing had been said.

Just a hand shoving him into a chair then silence.

Until the footsteps.

"Do you know why you are here?"

He nearly jumped from the sound, a woman's voice, slightly deep, confident—German perhaps—echoed, the room he was in apparently large.

"N-no," he replied, his stomach flipping, his heart racing. "Because of the records search?"

"Very good. Why did you execute that search?"

The footsteps continued to circle him, the questions coming at him from all directions, his head spinning to follow. "I-I was doing someone a favor."

"Who?"

Tell him! If he knows you were doing it for a Congressman, then maybe everything will be okay.

"Congressman Mahoney."

The footsteps stopped for a moment, then resumed.

That must have surprised her.

"And why was he asking you to conduct this search?"

He shrugged. "I'm not sure. I got the impression it was a favor for a friend. Maybe a constituent?"

"And the name of this friend or constituent?"

"I have no idea, but I think they might have been related to Captain Wainwright."

"Are you sure?"

He shrugged, the hood rubbing on his nose. "No, just a hunch."

She was behind him now, the sound of her shoe scraping as she turned, distinct. "Thank you, you've been very helpful."

Two steps sounded on the floor then stopped directly behind him.

There was a click.

A loud bang.

A moment of searing pain.

51

Then nothing.

North Atlantic Ocean
United States Naval Vessel—Identity Classified
April 15, 1912

"Captain, I'm receiving a CQD signal from the RMS Titanic. They're sinking."

Captain Johnathan Wainwright spun toward his communications officer. "Repeat that."

"CQD signal from the RMS Titanic, Captain. They report they are taking on water and are sinking fast."

Unbelievable!

"Location?"

"Fifteen nautical miles due east."

Wainwright frowned. His orders were clear. He was to make best speed to his coordinates then hold position until ordered to get underway again. He had to admit they were the strangest orders he had ever received in his time as captain, and in all the years he had been in the navy, he couldn't recall a ship simply sailing into the middle of the North Atlantic and stopping for no reason.

Then ordered to Darken Ship.

They were a massive hunk of floating metal in the middle of commercial shipping lanes.

It simply didn't make sense.

But as had been made abundantly clear to him by Admiral Coolidge, he wasn't in charge.

Commander Whitman was.

Whoever the hell he is.

Whitman had boarded in Norfolk with five other men, disappearing to segregated quarters, their equipment isolated in the hold until several hours ago when it had been ordered moved to the deck.

He still didn't know who they were or what department of the government they worked for. Their uniforms had no insignia, though they had the bearing of military when they arrived. He had spoken to Whitman for all of two minutes when he had been delivered his sealed orders.

And that was it.

But his orders be damned, there was a civilian ship sinking, thousands of lives were at stake, and he would not be left sitting here in the dark, waiting for only God knew what.

"Send a message to the RMS Titanic that we are responding, ETA one hour."

"Yes, Captain!"

"Belay that order."

Wainwright spun toward the voice as his comm officer froze.

It was Whitman.

"She's sinking, Commander. It is our duty to provide aide."

"Negative. This mission is Top Secret. Our being here can never be known." He turned to the comm officer. "Who beyond this room knows of the CQD transmission?"

"Only the radioman."

Whitman turned to Wainwright. "I remind you, Captain, that every one of your crew are sworn to secrecy. Should anyone reveal what is about to happen, they will be subject to court-martial, and possibly the death penalty."

The entire bridge crew looked at Wainwright, some of these men barely in their twenties.

The fear on their faces enraged him.

Yet Whitman was correct. The orders from the Admiral were clear. Whitman was in charge. The mission was highly classified. And no matter what was seen or heard, none of it was to ever be repeated.

In fact, the entire crew had been ordered below decks upon their arrival, only essential personnel topside during this phase of the operation.

Wainwright breathed through his nose, his lips pressed tightly together. "What are your orders, *Commander*?"

"Maintain radio silence and Darken Ship conditions. Make best speed for their coordinates, stopping two nautical miles from their position."

Wainwright's eyes narrowed. "Why two miles? If we're to render assistance, we should be much closer."

Whitman looked at the Captain. "We will not be rendering assistance of any sort."

Wainwright's chest tightened, his blood beginning to boil. "Then why for the love of God are we going there?"

"Because, Captain, our mission is aboard that vessel, and I have every intention of completing it, whether the Titanic is sinking or not."

Saint Paul's University, St. Paul, Maryland
Present Day

"Thanks for seeing us on such short notice, Professor."

Professor James Acton extended his hand, greeting Steve Wainwright, his wife and his sister. Greg Milton, Acton's best friend and boss, sat in his wheelchair nearby, his back still giving him troubles, but troubles he would gladly deal with considering the doctors had told him he would most likely never feel a thing below his waist again.

They had been proven wrong, and though he could now walk, he fatigued easily, and as the hours passed, he would find himself in need of his chair, his back threatening to give out.

Acton always felt a twinge of guilt every time he saw his friend in his chair. Though Milton had never blamed him, and called him a fool for doing so, he had never been able to forgive himself for getting his friend involved in his troubles. He had been pursued by America's elite Delta Force operating under false intel indicating he was the leader of a domestic terrorist cell, their orders to eliminate him and his followers.

Too many had died before the soldiers had discovered the truth and refused to carry out their illegal orders.

By then his friend had been shot and left for dead.

Ever since those events, the men of Bravo Team, the Delta unit that had taken so much from him, had made it their mission to help him whenever he or a loved one got into trouble, and that seemed to happen more often than it should, though he had no regrets. Once he had moved past those events, he had realized how great these men were and now even considered them friends, though not necessarily good friends, the nature of their job so secretive, it wasn't like they got together on vacation or went to each other's homes for barbecues.

Though he had a feeling if he were to show up, he'd be welcomed with open arms.

He had met the love of his life, Professor Laura Palmer, during those initial events. She had risked her life to help save a man she had only read about in magazines and their love had been forged under fire, a type of love that quite often flamed out fast, but not for them. Perhaps because they found themselves in adrenaline-fueled firefights so often, the spark was kept alive.

Acton looked at his watch and frowned. "My wife is supposed to—"

"Hello, sorry I'm late!"

Acton grinned as Laura entered the room, tossing her satchel onto a table near the door. "This is my much better half, Professor Laura Palmer. She's an archeologist and anthropologist at the Smithsonian in DC," explained Acton as Laura shook hands. "I've asked her to join us as she was on one of the teams that examined some of the artifacts brought up from the Titanic."

Laura gave Milton a cheek kiss and looked about, Acton recognizing the excitement in her face. "So, where is it?"

Steve Wainwright held up a tube, about five feet long. Acton almost cringed as he thought of the damage that could have been done to what might actually be a priceless work of art.

"May I?" he asked.

Wainwright nodded, handing it over. Acton pulled the top off as Laura snapped on gloves. He handed her the tube then did the same. She carefully extracted the canvas and began to unroll it on the lab table without forcing it flat, the material demanding to return to the shape it had come to know over decades, perhaps a century.

It would take time to flatten it safely, though it could be done.

He frowned, pointing at several pronounced creases before even looking at the painting itself. "It looks like it was folded up at some point, into a square."

"Tsk-tsk," clicked Laura, shaking her head. "Who would do such a thing?"

"Someone who didn't know any better?" suggested Milton as he rolled to the table. "So, is it the painting?"

Acton held the top open, Laura the bottom as one of his grad students, Mai Lien Trinh, snapped photos. "Cursory examination suggests it is La Circassienne au Bain by Merry-Joseph Blondel. We'll need to do a lot more testing to confirm it, however." He gently let the canvas roll back up, Laura doing the same. He turned to Steve Wainwright. "You found this in your grandfather's basement?"

Steve nodded.

Acton took a seat, motioning for the others to do the same, he always feeling a little odd looking down at Milton. He nodded toward the painting. "Let's assume that it's real. If it is, it should be on the bottom of the Atlantic. That painting was *not* one of the artifacts recovered in recent years, and even if it were, for you to have it would be impossible. On the black market it would go for millions, and from what I understand, your grandfather and father were not exactly in the stolen arts business."

Steve chuckled. "Nooo, definitely not." He motioned toward the painting with his chin. "What can you tell us about it?"

"It was painted in 1814 by Merry-Joseph Blondel," explained Laura. "It's a life size oil painting, a portrait of a Circassian woman at a bathhouse. Initially it wasn't too popular, considered rather bland, but prints of the painting proved popular with the public and Blondel himself began to gain stature so the painting's value began to increase. It eventually ended up in

58

the hands of…" She pulled out her cellphone, tapping a few keys. "Sorry, the name escapes me…ah, here it is, Mauritz Hakan Bjornstrom-Steffansson. He was a passenger on the Titanic, heading to the United States on a chemical engineering scholarship."

"And he owned a painting like that?" asked Judy, her narrowed eyes suggesting disbelief.

"His father was quite wealthy, wood pulp apparently."

"Oh."

Steve leaned forward. "So this Steffansson character, did he die with the others?"

Laura shook her head. "No, he was one of the survivors."

"Must be nice to have money, allows you to claim you're a child or don't have a penis when they call women and children first."

"Steve!" Sally slapped her husband's shoulder.

"Sorry," mumbled Steve, Acton suppressing a smile.

I wonder if we'll be like that at their age.

He glanced at his wife, thanking God she was still alive, her recent gunshot wound to the stomach now healed, but her body still not fully recovered.

She looks tired.

She was getting better, her stamina slowly building, though she hadn't been back to work yet, this her first academic outing since the shooting and the subsequent events in Paris that had almost seen them killed along with everyone else at the American Embassy.

We're home. Nothing will happen to us here.

He looked at the painting.

Yeah, right.

"Mr. Steffansson filed what was the largest insurance claim of the voyage, one hundred thousand dollars," continued a smiling Laura, she not bothering to suppress her delight in the elderly couple's interplay.

"Doesn't sound like much," said Judy, clearly unimpressed.

"That would be over two million dollars today," said Milton.

"Oh."

"And because it was thought lost on the Titanic, and for it to have actually survived, however that happened, it is probably worth much more now since pretty much anything from the Titanic goes for ridiculous prices." Acton nodded toward the painting. "*If* it's real, I'm sure it would go at auction for millions."

Sally exchanged an excited glance with her husband. "So what you're saying is we're rich?" he asked.

Acton shook his head. "No. Since it clearly didn't belong to your grandfather, it would most likely be considered stolen, so would probably be returned to the family."

"Or the insurance company who paid out the claim," said Laura.

Acton nodded. "Never thought of that. Either way, I doubt you'd be allowed to keep it." He leaned forward slightly. "What I want to know is how could your grandfather have possibly got his hands on this? This painting until today was thought to be on the bottom of the Atlantic."

Steve shook his head. "I have no idea. He was a US Navy captain at the time, I know that, but I always thought the only ship in the area was civilian and it arrived too late."

Acton pursed his lips, his eyebrows rising slightly. "Well, that's not actually entirely accurate."

Steve narrowed his eyes, joining the puzzled expressions in the room. "What do you mean?"

"There was actually at least one other ship, close enough to save everyone on board."

North Atlantic Ocean

United States Naval Vessel—Identity Classified

April 15, 1912

It was heartbreaking.

The panicked screams, the cries for help, the desperation of those perishing before Captain Johnathan Wainwright's eyes was overwhelming. He considered himself a man, tough as nails, and had never shed a tear in his life, not even when his son had died from smallpox.

Yet today it was everything he could do to keep from weeping openly.

Instead he let it turn to rage.

A rage he had no outlet for.

The night sky was lit up, flares launched at irregular intervals, the generators located in the stern still providing power to most of the doomed ship, her lights for the most part still on as she seemed to be sinking from the bow.

Which meant he and the bridge crew had a clear view of the horrors.

Several lifeboats were in the water, but too few. He could see they were having trouble deploying many of them, and some successfully launched were inexplicably half-full, if that.

What is going on over there?

There were few people in the water at this point, most wisely staying on the deck for now. Those in the water wouldn't last long, the cold of the Atlantic would be claiming their souls far too soon.

And he was powerless to save them.

It wasn't right.

He adjusted his view, catching sight of the small boat being rowed by Commander Whitman's team as it sliced calmly through the water, their mission a mystery.

A flare screeched into the sky, an errant shot sent at an angle, directly toward them. It burst low above the water, the intense light unsteady as it burned, long shadows cast across the deck for a full minute before it hit the water, bathing them in darkness again.

Shouts rolled over the waves and he peered through the binoculars, a pit forming in his stomach.

They had been spotted.

Saint Paul's University, St. Paul, Maryland
Present Day

"Huh?"

Acton delighted in stunning people with a little bit of history. It was one of the many reasons he loved his chosen profession. History was fascinating. The problem was it was too often presented in forms so boring to children, that by the time they became adults, they usually hated it.

Which was why he tried to keep his lectures as engaging as possible, his classes very popular, especially since he had gained a little notoriety over the years.

And they don't know the half of it!

"The Carpathia was the ship that responded to the CQD signal from the Titanic, but it was too far away to save those who couldn't get into the lifeboats."

"CQD?" asked Judy. "Is that like an SOS?"

"Yes," replied Laura. "SOS was relatively new at the time so a CQD signal was sent, then they began to alternate between the two. Both are considered a mayday call."

Acton raised a finger. "Fun fact. Where did the term 'mayday' come from?"

Milton stifled a grin, accustomed to Acton's tangents.

Acton ignored him.

Judy shrugged. "Some commie thing?"

It was Acton's turn to stifle it. "No, though some might suggest close. It's actually a play on the French *m'aidez* which means 'help me'." He waved his hand, erasing the tangent. "Sorry, back to what I was saying. The Carpathia was the closest ship to *respond*, but it wasn't the closest ship."

"What?"

Steve's outburst sent a shiver up Acton's spine, the pleasure endorphins kicking in as his delight in educating grew. "The SS Californian was actually within sight of the Titanic as she sank. Her crew could see the distress flares, and even noted that the deck lights seemed to be odd, probably because they were tilted on the horizon due to her sinking at the bow."

Judy seemed to have checked her skepticism, instead leaning forward, enthralled. "Why didn't they help?"

"Their Captain apparently thought it was just a fireworks display, and rather than wake his radio operator, he told the crew to just monitor the situation visually. They were stopped for the night because of heavy ice so the lookouts watched it sink and eventually disappear on the horizon. It wasn't until the next morning that they turned on their radio and discovered what had happened."

"That's insane!" cried Steve. "How could that possibly happen?"

"Rules were different back then. Actually, the sinking of the Titanic probably *saved* lives in the long run. Because it was so high profile, new rules were brought in that required enough lifeboats for every passenger, standardized distress signals, standardized response to any suspected distress and a lot more, including design changes. Unfortunately, all of these things were too late to save the Titanic."

Judy's mouth had been open in shock for several minutes, widening it seemed with each word out of Acton. "When this ship—the Californian?—discovered what had happened, did they at least help?"

"Sort of. They actually steamed away then came back in a roundabout fashion. Their captain claimed heavy ice in the area, however many people think he could have safely sailed to the Titanic directly. By the time they arrived, the Carpathia had already taken aboard the survivors. The Californian stayed behind to look for more survivors in the water, but there were none."

"So if the Captain had woken his radio operator, they might have saved some of those people." Steve shook his head. "Unbelievable."

"It is, isn't it. But that's not the only thing."

"What do you mean?"

"Like I said, there were reports of *at least* one other ship in the vicinity."

"You mean…"

"Some people claim there was yet another ship."

North Atlantic Ocean
United States Naval Vessel—Identity Classified
April 15, 1912

Brett Jones pulled on the oars, glancing over his shoulder at the stricken ship. When he had been tasked for this mission he had been eager for a glimpse of the already famous Titanic. To be aboard her for her maiden voyage would be historical, though it would be something he'd never be able to share with his grandchildren.

Otherwise he'd have to kill them.

Especially now.

He had been sent on some ruthless assignments by his anonymous taskmasters over the years, though he had to admit this was pretty coldhearted. The ship that had brought them here was less than two miles away and could easily save hundreds of these poor, condemned souls, but Commander Whitman had forbidden it.

He's a bastard if there ever was one.

Jones had only met the man once before on a mission that had resulted in half a dozen dead, some politician's family in England who had apparently wronged someone.

Who, he didn't question.

He had spent a couple of years in the military but had been dishonorably discharged, his inability to obey his superiors constantly getting him in trouble despite his superior combat skills.

He wasn't Army material.

But he was somebody's.

He had been approached within weeks of his ignominious departure by a man in a suit and a hat, the brim pulled low. He had laughed at him, the man almost a caricature of what the entertainment industry thought spies should look like.

He had given him an envelope with two hundred dollars and a piece of paper with an address and time.

"Be there if you want more."

Two hundred dollars was more money than he had seen at one time in his entire life.

He had tied one on, buying the entire bar drinks all night, making out with some of the sleaziest girls one could imagine, girls who wouldn't give him the time of day the night before.

It had been an amazing night.

One he could barely remember.

Yet it had given him a taste of the good life.

And he wanted more.

He had gone to the meeting, been interviewed, mostly questions about loyalty to his country—he had none after his discharge—his family—he had none—and his friends—few, none close.

He was a loner and alone.

Apparently perfect, from what he had learned since.

It had been several weeks before his first assignment. A simple courier job. Pick up an envelope, deliver it. More courier jobs followed, then after several months, things got interesting.

Weapons were provided, partners, and some action was involved.

It wasn't until his second year that he had to kill someone.

By then he was too addicted to the money to even question carrying out the job.

He had done it.

And vomited the first moment he was out of sight of his partner.

It became easier.

Too easy.

Now he was almost always assigned the kill-jobs, as some of the others called them. He almost never worked with the same person twice, which was why he had been surprised to see "Commander Whitman" again. The last time they had met he was an Army Major named Fitzgerald. The fact they had met before wasn't acknowledged, instead a knowing look exchanged then nothing.

And that was the way it was in this business. Working for someone, who he didn't know, killing people for huge sums of money. It was eating away at his soul, he now numb to it all. His life consisted of long bouts of alcohol, opium and women with questionable backgrounds interrupted periodically for brief stints of work.

He was living the dream.

And it was killing him.

Physically and mentally.

Until he met Margo.

She had changed everything.

A sweet girl, cute as can be, demure but not too compliant.

She was a waitress at a bar he frequented. Never put up with much from the patrons, *never* dated them.

Until him.

But that wasn't because of the bar. He had met her waiting for the bus, her struggling with a load of groceries. She had agreed to a familiar face helping her, then invited him in for a lemonade, her mother chaperoning.

He had made it a point to try and be at the same bus stop at the same time, often waiting for over an hour for her to show up and pretend it was just a coincidence.

And the lemonades had continued.

As had her mother.

And now they were officially courting.

She knew nothing of his life, and he wanted to keep it that way, but if they were to make a go of this relationship, things would have to change.

Which was why he had begun hiding away a large portion of his paydays. He was going to leave the business, marry Margo, and start a family.

If they'd let him.

The screams and cries for help were all around them now, lifeboats making their way toward their ship, apparently revealed by a flare. The boat bumped into something and a frozen hand broke the surface beside him, an unfortunate soul who had apparently jumped overboard early in a fit of panic.

He ignored it.

By the look of things, there would be many more such deaths before the night was through.

The boat bumped against the side of the massive vessel and he raised his oar, looking up at the hulking mass towering above them.

And the closed cargo hatch directly overhead.

"I thought it was supposed to be open?"

Commander Whitman looked at him. "The original plan had them opening it for us at the rendezvous." He motioned with his hand at the ship above. "With all this going on, who the hell knows if they're even alive?" He pointed to several lines leading to the water, apparently left behind by lowered lifeboats. "Let's start climbing gentlemen." He pointed at one of the men. "You stay with the boat. Under no circumstances does anyone come on board, understood?"

"Yes, sir!"

Whitman led the way, the man's skills at rope climbing exceptional, the rest of the team following. Whitman disappeared over the railing above and Jones continued after him, the panicked passengers getting louder with each pull on the rope.

He reached the brightly lit deck and peered over to find hundreds of pairs of feet rushing to and fro. A hand reached over and grabbed him, hauling him to the deck. It was Whitman. He looked about and no one seemed to be paying them any mind, their clothes worthy of any second class passenger.

The rest of the team quietly joined them then Whitman led the way toward the First Class purser's office, his briefing indicating it was located near what was called the Grand Staircase on the starboard side of the ship. Crew were struggling to load passengers into lifeboats on the boat deck, their shouts growing more desperate as time ran out. Cries of women and children filled the air, the panicked, angry shouts of men competing with the wails.

And some simply stood in stunned silence, the expressions on their faces an odd sort of shocked resignation, as if they realized their fate was already set, these poor souls already dead.

It made him wonder what he would do if he knew he were going to die.

I wouldn't be just standing around!

He'd grab a bottle and a woman and have a grand old time.

At least the old version of him would.

But now with Margo in the picture, what would he do?

If they were together, like some of the couples he saw clinging to each other as they passed, he'd do everything in his power to save her. To get her on one of the lifeboats, then do his damnedest to survive.

But should he die, he'd take tremendous satisfaction in knowing she had lived.

71

He had no illusions though that they'd be reunited in the afterlife.

He was going to Hell.

A man didn't kill as much as he did without his soul being condemned.

The purser's office had been abandoned, its door ajar, the ship at a concerning angle now, stray objects rolling slowly across the deck as the bow sank deeper into what would become the icy grave of so many.

Commander Whitman immediately made for the safe, it locked, one of the men pulling out some gear, his job to crack it.

But Jones had a different job.

One that would certainly cement his place in fiery brimstone.

Saint Paul's University, St. Paul, Maryland
Present Day

"Another ship?" Steve Wainwright shook his head. "How come nobody knows about this?"

Acton shrugged. "It wasn't in the movie, I guess." He winked at Laura. "Now remember, the Californian is proven, historical fact. There was an inquiry and everything. Nobody disputes that it was in the area, though some dispute how far away it actually was."

"And this other ship?"

"That hasn't been proven. There were reports of another ship nearby that definitely wasn't the Californian or the Carpathia. People reported seeing it nearby, close enough that some lifeboats tried rowing toward it, but they reported that they seemed to never get closer. This has never been proven, but the witnesses when interviewed were adamant there was another ship."

"Who could it have been?" asked Judy. "Wouldn't they know what ships were in the area at the time?"

Acton nodded. "Yes, they would. All civilian ships reported their intended courses and radioed updates if things changed. The wireless operators were in constant contact with each other relaying updates including weather and sea conditions. The problem with the witness testimony is that there was no other ship in the area, so their statements were dismissed."

Steve was pinching his chin, staring at the floor. "You said *civilian* ships reported their courses. What about military?"

Acton's breath caught for a moment. "You said your grandfather was a Navy captain?"

Steve nodded, his face clouding over. "Yes."

Acton looked at Laura then Milton. "Then I think we might have just found our mystery ship."

North Atlantic Ocean

RMS Titanic

April 15th, 1912

Brett Jones spotted his target helping a young woman into one of the lifeboats, impeccably dressed as expected in a blue serge suit with a crisp blue handkerchief sporting the initials A.V. His polished brown boots matched his flannel shirt. He held the woman's hand, her tear stained cheeks and trembling lip suggesting this was his wife.

"Might I join my wife? She's in a delicate condition."

Delicate.

He knew from his briefing that she was pregnant, the reason for their return. She wanted the child to be born in America, and if it weren't for that reason, they would never have boarded the ill-fated Titanic.

"I'm sorry sir, no man is allowed on this boat or any of the boats until the women and children are off."

Astor nodded. If he were upset, he was hiding it like any good gentleman would. "Well, tell me what is the number of this boat so I may find her afterward."

"Number four, sir."

Astor gave his wife's hand one last squeeze then stepped back as the crew began to lower the boat to the freezing ocean below. He calmly lit a cigarette then stepped forward, tossing his gloves down to his wife, before stepping back and out of the way of the busy crew. When his wife was out of sight, a much younger man joined him, then after a few words, walked away in a hurry.

He approached Astor from the side, jamming his finger in the man's back. "Mr. Astor, come with me." Astor froze for a moment, then nodded, stepping away from the wall. "Let's go to your room, shall we?"

Astor again said nothing and they walked in silence as the chaos continued around them. Astor's suite, C-62, was impressively massive, one of the finest available and unthinkably expensive, Jones was certain.

A touch of envy took hold.

"Do you have the papers you stole?"

Astor took a drag of his cigarette. "Surely you don't expect me to cooperate."

Jones smiled. "Of course I don't, but I have to ask."

Astor stubbed his cigarette out in an ashtray probably worth more than the average annual wage of one of the men who toiled to build the doomed vessel. "I can assure you, my good sir, that I do not have any papers on me."

"The chief purser's safe then."

Astor smiled. "If you already know, then why ask?"

"Again, I have to."

Astor motioned to the wall safe. "Would you like me to open it?"

"Please."

Astor complied then stood back. Inside were several stacks of notes in various currencies, along with a few items of jewelry. Jones stuffed the cash in his pocket, clasping a fist around the jewelry.

"Real?"

Astor raised his eyebrows slightly, as if the question were ridiculous.

Of course it is.

He shoved the jewels in his pocket.

"Is that why you're here, to rob me?"

Jones smiled. "No. I'm here to deliver a message."

76

Astor pursed his lips.

Jones raised his weapon.

"And what exactly is this message?"

"My employers wanted you to know that you should never have betrayed them."

A foot scraped behind him and he spun toward the noise to find the young man from earlier rushing at him. Jones sidestepped the charge, shoving the man off balance with his free hand, sending him tumbling into a table, it shattering from the impact. Astor moved to help the man when Jones wagged his gun back and forth.

"Un-uh. Get back."

Astor frowned but complied as the young man struggled to his feet, his face flush, a small gash on his upper cheek sending a trickle of blood down his face.

"And you are?"

"Henry Dodge."

"Ahh, Mr. Dodge. I see my colleagues failed to deal with you. Unfortunate." The man paled, clearly aware of what he was referring to. Jones shrugged. "No matter, you'll be dealt with now."

"Why?"

Jones' eyes narrowed as he turned toward Astor. "I beg your pardon?"

"Why? What's the point? We're all going to die here tonight."

"Perhaps. Perhaps not. My job is to make certain you do."

"I just put my pregnant wife on a lifeboat. They are *not* allowing men aboard. There aren't enough lifeboats for all of us. We *are* going to die." He nodded toward Jones. "Including you."

Jones smiled. "No, I won't be dying today, Colonel."

Astor and Dodge exchanged glances. "How do you plan to escape?"

Jones' smile broadened. "The same way I came aboard."

Both men looked puzzled, then the young man's jaw dropped. "You came on a ship!"

"Give the man a cigar!" He pointed at Dodge with his gun. "Colonel, I'd tell you to hire this man right now, before he gets away, but alas, it's too late."

Astor put a hand on the young man's shoulder. "I would be honored to have this gentlemen in my employ." He nodded toward the pocket Jones had stuffed the money into. "You have enough cash and jewels there to change your life forever. To make a good life for you and your family. Why not take it?"

"I am taking it."

Astor smiled. "I'm not referring to the money, I'm referring to the opportunity. Take the opportunity to change your life." He paused, glancing at Jones' left hand. "I see you're not married."

Jones looked at Astor. "Standard operating procedure would be to remove all identifiable jewelry, so I wouldn't jump to any conclusions."

Astor smiled. "You have tanned hands, mister, with no tan line on your ring finger."

Jones glanced at his hand and chuckled. "You're a sharp man, Colonel."

"Thank you, sir. And I'm sharp enough to know you have someone important to you in your life."

Jones frowned, unsure of how the man could possibly know that.

He's playing for time.

"You wonder how I know that."

Jones said nothing.

"You work for The Assembly."

Jones' eyebrows popped almost imperceptibly.

"You seem surprised."

Almost imperceptibly.

Again he said nothing.

"Then let me enlighten you, sir. The Assembly is an ancient organization, no one really knows how old as it is very secretive, but let us say at least many centuries. The members are few, only a dozen, and change only through death or murder. They are usually succeeded by family members, or when that isn't possible, by a unanimously agreed upon new member, welcomed into the fold of unthinkable wealth and power. These men control the lives of millions, millions who have no clue they are being controlled. And those millions, good sir, include you."

Jones still said nothing, his mind soaking up all the forbidden knowledge. He knew there was big money behind whoever had been hiring him, and their targets were always political or financial, so they were powerful.

But he had, for some reason, always assumed he was working for the United States government, some sort of top secret spy, working for some even more secretive agency.

It had never occurred to him that he was working for a private group, centuries old, that was manipulating world events for their own benefit.

Though if he were truly honest with himself, he had known he wasn't really working for the government. His government wouldn't kill its own citizens for financial gain.

No, he had always known he was working for bad people.

Incredibly powerful, bad people.

He inhaled deeply, yet still said nothing.

"I can tell from your demeanor, sir, that you knew how dangerous your employers were, though you didn't know who they were." Astor pointed to the safe. "Yet, despite knowing how dangerous these people are, you took the money and jewels. A man like you would only do that for one reason."

Jones felt his chest tighten.

"You are looking to escape this life."

The man was good. Too good. He seemed to be able to read him like a book, and it was making him uncomfortable.

Shoot him already!

Water washed over his feet, the icy Atlantic reminding him of the time constraint they were all under. He glanced at a clock on the mantle.

Time to go.

He aimed his weapon at young Mr. Dodge. "Your copy of the papers."

Dodge looked at Astor, who nodded slightly. He reached into his pocket and produced an envelope, handing it over to Jones. Jones glanced inside then placed it in his breast pocket.

"You have what you came for, now why not leave us to die in peace?"

Jones looked at Astor, a bemused smile spreading across his face. "You are indeed remarkable." He looked at a picture of Astor and a young woman on the mantle, beside the clock. He motioned toward it with his chin. "Your wife?"

"Yes."

"Beautiful woman."

Astor said nothing.

And she was a beautiful woman. Jones recalled hearing about the scandal when Astor had married her, barely eighteen, he almost fifty and only two years since his divorce. It had been the talk of the gossip columns for months leading the newlyweds to flee the country on an extended honeymoon in Europe and Egypt, accompanied by one of their few supporters, Margaret Brown.

She reminded him of Margo.

And he made a decision.

"Colonel, you are a man of honor."

Astor bowed slightly.

"And you swear you are not going to attempt to save yourself by taking the berth of someone else."

"I swear."

Jones turned to Dodge. "And you, sir?"

"I swear."

Jones returned his weapon to its holster, patting the envelope. "Then as far as my employers are concerned, I killed you after I retrieved the papers." He turned toward the door then paused. "And gentlemen, should you think rescue is on its way, and you may yet be saved by an arriving ship, I am truly sorry to tell you that it is not. The Carpathia will arrive far too late to save you." He bowed slightly. "Good evening, gentlemen, and may God have mercy on your souls."

Jones quickly left the room, striding with purpose, his feet working against the icy cold water that now reached his ankles. His mind was racing with what he had done. Or hadn't done. It was the first time he had betrayed his employers, the first time he hadn't fulfilled his mission.

And if these two men didn't die tonight, he'd be dead for certain.

His feet were blocks of ice by the time he returned to the First Class Purser's office. He rapped on the door three times. It opened slightly, the sliver revealing the eye of one of his team, the door jerking open to allow him inside.

"Status?" asked Commander Whitman as he rifled through the contents of the safe, looking for Astor's papers.

"The mission was successful," he replied, holding up the envelope. "I encountered Mr. Henry Dodge and he kindly provided me with his copy."

Whitman nodded, continuing his search then stopped, yanking an envelope out of the pile. Jones looked about the room, the three safes opened, their contents spilled on the floor, mostly letters and wads of cash. In one corner sat a stack of paintings, probably priceless—or at least fabulously out of his budget. One stood aside, as if it were more valuable than the rest, of a naked woman with a cloth wrapped around her back, standing in front of what might have been a stone archway.

She reminded him of Margo.

Whitman shook the envelope triumphantly. "This is it. Let's go."

Jones caught sight of a cloth bag sitting on the floor, its contents spilled open, gems of spectacular color twinkling at him. Whitman left the room, the others following, and Jones made a split second decision as the door swung shut from the tilt of the ship.

He picked up the bag, shoving the spilled gems inside, then the bag into his pocket. He stepped to the door, looking back at the painting.

It is *Margo!*

He pulled his knife, his heart pounding with the foolishness of what he was about to do.

Saint Paul's University, St. Paul, Maryland
Present Day

"The entire idea is preposterous," said Milton. "A US Navy ship that just stood by and did nothing while the Titanic sank?" He shook his head. "I can't believe it."

Acton pressed his lips together, his head bobbing in agreement. "I can't believe it either. There's no way a navy ship would stand by and watch as over one thousand people died."

"The Californian did," said Judy.

Laura shook her head. "That was a civilian ship holding position in iceberg filled water with arguably an idiot for a captain. I doubt the same could be said for a military ship." She sighed. "It just doesn't make sense."

"*If* the ship were there, then they must have been under orders that prevented them from helping," said Milton. "That's the only thing that makes sense."

"But orders that would include letting so many innocent people die?" Steve shook his head. "I refuse to believe my grandfather was such a man." He wiped a tear away before it escaped.

"But we know it's true," whispered Judy, putting a hand on her brother's shoulder.

"What do you mean?" asked Acton.

"Show him."

Steve frowned, giving his sister a look that at once conveyed anger and resignation. He removed a file from a satchel he had been gripping in his lap all along. "We found this with the painting," he said, handing it to Acton.

Acton opened the folder and found photocopies of several documents. "What am I looking at?"

"The first page is his suicide note."

"May God forgive me for what I did," read Acton for the benefit of the others. He flipped the page.

"And that was found with a manifest of the passengers that died."

"We could have saved them all."

Acton leaned back in his chair, his eyes wide as he exchanged looks with Laura and Milton. He closed the file. "It seems to me that this confirms he was there. It doesn't explain why, though."

"Or why they didn't help," said Milton. "There was no way they could know the Titanic was going to sink. If they—"

"Unless *they* did it!" cried Sally, who had been quiet for most of the meeting. "Could he have, Steve, could he?" She dropped her head into her hands. "What kind of a monster would do such a thing!"

Acton leaned forward, lowering his voice. "No, there's no way the Titanic was sunk in any other way than what history recorded. The expeditions to the wreck have proven it was torn open by an iceberg. A torpedo or other type of weapon would have left a distinctly different hole in the hull. There's no way Captain Wainwright was responsible for the sinking."

"You're sure?"

"Absolutely."

Sally sat up, wiping a few tears away with her fingertips. "I'm sorry. This is all just so overwhelming. I just keep picturing that movie and how those poor people died. So terrified. So helpless." She shivered. "So cold."

"Don't believe everything Hollywood tells you," said Steve, putting an arm over his wife's shoulders.

"Actually, that movie was fairly accurate when it came to the sinking," said Acton. "These people died horrible deaths, there's no question about that." He nodded toward the painting. "Here's the thing. If your grandfather was in the area with his ship, and he had this painting in his basement, I can think of only two reasonable ways for that to have happened." He held up his index finger. "One, he did pick up at least one survivor, who had the painting with him. That explanation would only make sense if that survivor then died, since all known survivors were rescued by the Carpathia, though I guess there's a chance they could have survived and been sworn to secrecy."

"Tough secret to keep," said Milton. "The manifest of those taken aboard the Carpathia was thoroughly checked. There's no way someone could pop up later and say they were on board and missed."

"Which is why I don't believe that's what happened," said Acton. "What are the chances of one survivor being found, alone, with an eight-foot by four-foot painting? The mystery ship was too far away to swim to, so I just can't see it happening."

"And the second possibility?" asked Steve.

"That someone from your grandfather's ship went aboard and stole it."

North Atlantic Ocean

United States Naval Vessel—Identity Classified

April 15, 1912

Captain Johnathan Wainwright watched as the team was hauled aboard. He had been forced to steam away a short distance, the survivors having spotted their silhouette on the horizon.

It had been heartbreaking.

It went against everything he had been taught to believe in as a mariner, it went against the accepted code of conduct that governed his kind for centuries, and it was completely un-American.

With the last man retrieved and Commander Whitman entering the bridge with a satisfied expression on his face, he gave the order he had been dying to give. "Prepare to take on survivors."

"Belay that order!"

Wainwright spun toward Whitman. "You've completed your mission?"

"Yes."

'Successfully?"

"Yes."

"Then there's no longer a reason to let these people die." He was about to reissue his order when Whitman stepped closer, his weapon drawn, held tight to his side so it wasn't obvious to the rest of the crew.

"In order for the mission to succeed, no one must know we were ever here."

Wainwright glanced at the weapon then glared at Whitman. "But it is completely believable that we'd be in the area. We can render assistance and no one will know why we were here. No one will know your men are on board."

"Captain, the biggest ocean liner in the world is sinking out there. This will be the biggest story on both sides of the Atlantic for weeks if not months. Questions *will* be asked as to why this ship was in the vicinity, then why it failed to respond to the distress call, and then why it sat several miles away, dark, doing nothing, for almost an hour." Whitman shook his head. "No, Captain, too many questions will be asked." He leaned in closer. "And remember, Captain, since you were never supposed to be here, these people would have died anyway." He stepped back, raising his voice slightly. "We have our orders, Captain. Make best speed for Norfolk."

He turned to face forward, his weapon now holstered, hands clasped behind his back. Wainwright reluctantly issued the orders, several of his men looking at him questioningly, no one comfortable with the situation, but after a moment's allowed hesitation, the ship was under way.

And the screams of the desperate and dying faded with the sound of the engines as they put distance between them and their unforgiveable sin.

Saint Paul's University, St. Paul, Maryland
Present Day

"That doesn't make any sense," said Steve. "If they went aboard the ship, then wouldn't that mean that was the mission all along?"

Acton threw up his hands. "I know, it sounds ridiculous, but doesn't it fit the facts? Your grandfather was a US Navy Captain. His suicide note and the note found with the list of the victims suggests he feels he could have saved them. If he had any hope of saving them, then he had to be in the area. If he was in the area for anything but a secret mission, he would have ordered his crew to save the passengers, but he didn't. There were witness accounts suggesting another mystery ship, and that it seemed to keep its distance from those rowing toward it. A painting thought to be on the bottom of the ocean is found in your grandfather's basement, with no plausible way for it to have come into his possession outside of that night in 1912." Acton shook his head. "The only thing I can think of is that his ship had to be there to *meet* the Titanic, because there's no way a US Navy ship, on a covert mission, would stop to steal a painting from a sinking ship, while watching over a thousand people die. They *had* to be rendezvousing with that ship."

"That might explain why the captain of the Titanic was steaming at full speed even though there had been icebergs reported in the area," said Milton, his foot tapping in excitement.

Acton smiled slightly at the sight of what once couldn't move.

"Are we really saying what I think we're saying?" asked Steve.

"I think so," said Acton. "I think the United States Navy sent a ship on a highly classified mission to rendezvous with the Titanic in order to retrieve something or someone on board. During that mission, the Titanic struck an iceberg, the Navy ship steamed to the location, sent a team aboard to execute their mission, then left. While on board, one or more of the team stole this painting, and perhaps other items."

Steve shook his head. "I can't believe my grandfather was a thief."

"Neither can I," said Acton, "and Captains wouldn't accompany a team like that, so if I had to guess someone took it upon themselves to steal it. The real question now is what were they after?"

Steve shrugged. "I don't know, but whoever was behind it I think knows I'm looking into it."

Acton's eyes narrowed, the hair on the back of his neck standing up as the other shoe was about to drop. "What do you mean?"

"When I was with Congressman Mahoney, the clerk who was searching the database for my grandfather's records said there was some sort of security alert on his computer and then the line went dead."

Acton looked at Laura, concern on her face. "A search of your grandfather's records a century later triggered a security alert?" Acton leaned back in his chair, slowly nodding.

"What?" asked Laura, looking at him.

"I think this proves that our theory is correct."

Milton shifted in his chair. "And somebody wants to keep it a secret."

Laura frowned. "I wonder how far they're willing to go."

North Atlantic Ocean

United States Naval Vessel—Identity Classified

April 15, 1912

Captain Johnathan Wainwright sat in his cabin, debating what to write in his log, and at the moment could think of nothing. The wireless operator had been busy monitoring the signals being bounced around and the news was horrific.

Over one thousand dead at last estimate.

And we could have saved them all.

The Carpathia had arrived as quickly as it could, yet hours after the ship sank below the surface. Hundreds had frozen in the water, the lifeboats too few.

His fist clenched into a ball and he slammed the top of his small desk.

I have to know why.

He leapt to his feet, exiting his cabin, the guard snapping to attention. Storming through the cramped corridors, he quickly made his way to the area repurposed to hold the team he had been ordered to transport.

He was about to knock when he cursed and threw the door open.

He surveyed the shocked faces, Commander Whitman not among them.

"Where's your commander?"

"Up top, Captain," replied one of the men as they all struggled to their feet. It made him think they were all military men, which made what had happened even more appalling in his mind. That military men could follow orders that would leave so many dead was unthinkable.

What did you do?

His chest tightened as he realized he had become one of them. Complicit in the deaths of over one thousand innocent souls, all for the sake of following orders.

He spotted something rolled up in haste under a blanket. He reached over and grabbed it, one of the men reaching to stop him. Wainwright glared and the man backed off. Unrolling it, he immediately went red at the sight of what was most likely a priceless painting, hastily cut from its frame, the edges jagged and torn.

"What the hell is this?"

Nobody said anything.

His eyes bore into the man who had tried to stop him.

"Answer me, that's an order."

The man looked at him for a moment as if he were debating whether or not this was an order he cared to follow. Finally, he shrugged. "A souvenir."

Wainwright rolled up the painting, sucking in rapid, angry breaths through his nose before launching into a tirade. "I may have to put up with a lot of things, but theft isn't one of them. *You* may not care that we could have saved those civilians, but I can assure you the men on this ship do!" His lip curled into a sneer then he jabbed the thief with the painting. "Tell your commander I want to see him immediately."

The man nodded but didn't move.

Wainwright stepped out of the room and stormed back to his cabin, tossing the painting on the desk before dropping into his chair.

He yanked at his hair as he tried to calm himself, his rage threatening to consume him as he stared at the painting.

Was that all this was? An opportunity to steal?

He couldn't believe that. He *refused* to believe that. There was no way the United States Navy could be involved in a robbery. At least not a robbery

91

like this. He could see them stealing something from a foreign government, absolutely, but a painting?

Never.

Not *his* navy.

But it was *his* navy that had ordered him to cede command to Commander Whitman, and it was he that had ordered them to stand by and watch as over one thousand died.

There was a knock on his door.

"Enter."

Commander Whitman stepped inside. "I understand you were looking for me, Captain."

Wainwright nodded. "Close the hatch."

Whitman complied then noticed the painting on the desk. "That shouldn't have happened."

Wainwright glanced at the painting, his blood still boiling. "Explain."

"One of my men took it upon himself to take a souvenir. I had ordered it destroyed."

Wainwright's hand instinctively moved toward the painting as if to protect it. "This is a piece of history, Commander. Civilized men do *not* destroy art." His eyes narrowed. "*Mr.* Whitman. Are you even navy?"

Whitman smiled slightly. "I'm sorry, Captain, but that's classified."

Wainwright felt a hint of relief. "I didn't think so. No navy man would allow people to die at sea. It's just not done. The next time it could be you floating in the water, hoping someone comes along to save you. If it were an option, no one would do it. There's a code, Commander, and you have no concept of that." Wainwright rose. "I expect you and your men off my ship as soon as we are docked."

"Yes, Captain."

Whitman opened the hatch then turned back toward Wainwright, nodding at the painting. "I suggest you destroy that immediately, Captain."

"As I said, it's a piece of history."

"It's supposed to be on the bottom of the ocean."

"Fortunately it was saved."

Whitman shook his head, jabbing a finger at the painting. "That, Captain, is evidence we were there. It must be destroyed."

Wainwright sucked in a deep breath, his chest expanding as he glared at the man. "I will *not* destroy it."

"Then, Captain, you'll have to take it to your grave, as no one can ever be allowed to see it."

Congressman Bill Mahoney's Office
Monroe Street, Rockville
Present Day

Congressman Bill Mahoney rested the back of his head against the elevator wall and closed his eyes, the vibrations of the car almost soothing. It had been a long, tough day and it would take a lot more than the thirty-second ride to help him unwind.

Three fingers tonight.

The elevator chimed and the doors opened a moment later, the smell of the underground parking lot filling his nostrils. He sighed, pushing himself off the back of the elevator and stepping onto the concrete, his footsteps echoing as he made his way to his car.

A door opened to his right, then another.

He was too tired to care.

An engine roared to life as he reached for his fob, pressing the button.

His Ford Taurus' lights winked at him from down the nearly empty row of parking spaces.

"Congressman Mahoney?"

He turned toward the woman's voice behind him, his eyes barely open. "Yes?"

A gun was drawn, pointed directly at his chest. "Come with us, please."

A surge of adrenaline pulsed through his veins as he was jolted awake. "Wh-what's all this?"

Two men flanked him, grabbing him by the arms as the vehicle that had just started pulled out of its parking spot, a black SUV with heavily tinted windows and government plates coming up beside them.

"Who are you people?" he demanded, beginning to struggle against the silent men as he was half pushed half carried toward the rear door. Someone inside pushed it open and reached out, yanking him inside, one of the men following him in, the door slamming shut as the woman climbed into the passenger seat. The driver suddenly accelerated, the tires chirping on the concrete, the surge pressing him into his seat.

"What the hell is going on?"

He tried to make his voice as confident as possible, yet even he could hear the tremor in his voice.

"No talking," said the woman as she turned toward him holding a hood. "Put this on." Mahoney hesitated. "Now."

He took the hood and pulled it over his head, the feeling instantly claustrophobic. He could feel the moisture from his rapid breaths blow back against his face, a line of sweat immediately forming on his upper lip, the temperature increasing noticeably as the vehicle came to a stop, the front window lowering, the familiar beep from the security pad indicating they had a pass for the garage.

Government plates?

The SUV tilted up as they exited and they were soon on the city streets. He tried to keep track of where they were, the perceived speed, the stops and turns giving him a pretty good idea where they were for the first few minutes, but soon they had made a turn into an area of town he had no familiarity with, leaving him hopelessly lost.

They eventually slowed, the vehicle tipping forward as they entered what he assumed was another parking garage. The vehicle made at least half a dozen hard left turns as they descended several levels before finally coming to a stop, all four doors in the vehicle opening almost at once.

Someone grabbed his arm, pulling him semi-gently toward the door. He slid across the seat and stepped down to the ground before being led a short distance then placed in a chair, his hands yanked behind his back and cuffed.

"Why were you asking questions about Captain Wainwright?"

He almost jumped at the sound of the woman's voice, her accent distinctive, European. *German?* He had the sense by the way she deliberately pronounced each word that she had struggled for years to rid herself of what she felt was a childhood curse.

He personally loved the sound of European women.

But not today.

"I'm sorry, but I don't know what you're talking about."

That was stupid. They obviously know!

"Congressman, you'll save us all a lot of time if you simply cooperate. I will ask you one final time. Why were you asking questions about Captain Wainwright?"

He wasn't sure where the bravado was coming from, but he couldn't believe the words coming out of his mouth. "Why do you want to know? He's been dead for over fifty years."

"What is of our concern is none of yours."

"Our? Who are you people?"

"Again, none of your concern. I will ask you one last time, politely. Then my associates will assist me. Why were you—"

"None of your goddamned business. I'm a United States Congressman, and I demand to be released. If you think—"

Something hit him with incredible force in the face, his nose immediately breaking, the taste of blood filling his mouth as he gasped, the surprise making the pain all the more worse. His eyes watered and his ears rang, the pain overwhelming his senses.

He heard the thud before he felt it, something hitting him across his entire stomach, the hood over his head preventing any warning. The blow forced all the air out of him and he sucked in a painful breath almost immediately as he doubled over, his cuffed hands tugging against the chair back.

Someone grabbed the back of his suit jacket and yanked him upright just before another blow slammed into his stomach, the pain intense, crippling, the blow slightly off target, contact with a rib definitely made.

He was sure he heard it crack.

"P-please, no more!" The words were gasped out, his breaths rapid and shallow, the pain too great to do any more. He had read about torture in the past and had dismissed those who had broken as weak-willed cowards.

But he had never experienced pain before, not like this. Yet it wasn't just the pain, it was the fear of not knowing when the next blow would come, what part of his body would be hit next.

The grip on his jacket broke and he sagged over as far as his cuffed hands would allow him, sobs racking his body, the shame of breaking so fast feeding on itself, the realization he wasn't the man he thought he was almost overwhelmingly emasculating.

He felt pathetic.

"I will ask you *one* last time, Congressman. Why were you asking questions about Captain Wainwright?"

He squeezed his eyes shut as blood poured from his nose, collecting at the tip then dripping onto the inside of the hood. His heart slammed in his chest as a pit formed in his stomach as he realized he was about to do the unthinkable. He was about to open his mouth when an image of his wife and children flashed before his eyes. What would they think of him if he threw Steve Wainwright under the bus? What kind of example would he be setting for his son?

No, Steve Wainwright wasn't going to be thrown under the bus by him.

"I received a letter in the mail—anonymous—that said I should look into Captain Wainwright's involvement with the Titanic. I-I thought it was just some sort of conspiracy nut, but I had a friend who would be able to look into it quickly enough so I gave him a call."

"Who was that?"

His lip trembled. They had found him, and if they had found him, then they had definitely found Sparks.

It was a test.

"Jerry Sparks. I asked him to search the records and a security alert appeared on his screen then we were cut off."

"And where is this letter now?"

His mind raced, the problem with an impromptu lie the fact you never had the chance to rehearse the challenges. "I, uh, shredded it. I thought that it was best to not be involved once Jerry said there was some sort of security warning."

The woman's footsteps neared then stopped directly in front of him.

"I think you're lying to me, Congressman."

He flinched, her voice so close she must have been leaning over and speaking into his ear. "I-I'm not."

"We know it was a constituent of yours that asked you to conduct the search."

Oh God!

"We know they are related to Captain Wainwright."

How could they know?

"You have one last chance to name this person. Should you lie to me again, not only will you die, but your family will as well. And so will everyone named Wainwright that lives in your constituency."

"Y-you're insane!"

"No, Congressman, I'm extremely motivated." A hand gripped his shoulder. "You have five seconds before my colleagues continue their work."

He felt her push off his shoulder, the footsteps receding several paces, the sound of something dragging on the ground nearby suggesting to him a two-by-four, or something similar, being readied again. He couldn't hear her countdown, and wasn't even certain she was giving one, but his own thundered in his head, and as he reached the end, every muscle in his body went slack, a hot stream of urine soaking his pants.

"Steve Wainwright."

Harlem, New York City
April 26, 1912

Brett Jones took Margo's hand, squeezing it in thanks as she turned to get a glass of milk from the counter. Jones winked at her, she smiling, then he tucked into his breakfast of bacon, eggs and toast, life good in the Jones' household since his return from the Titanic job. He had quickly begun to break down the large bills in various parts of the city, the gems sold off one at a time on Maiden Lane to jewelers who asked no questions as long as the stones weren't set. Their nest egg was rapidly growing.

But he went through life every day looking over his shoulder.

And it was slowly driving him crazy.

If he had at least heard something from his employer, The Assembly, as Astor had called them, he'd feel better. Yet there had been nothing. Not a single word. No new jobs, nothing.

"Whitman" must have told them about the painting.

If he was blacklisted, then so be it. He wanted out anyway. And if they wanted him dead, he was certain he would be by now.

We have to disappear.

There was no choice. The big question was whether or not Margo would agree to leave with him. He just couldn't see it happening. She had a large family, all in the area, and she was very close with them. To ask her to leave all that, to never see them again, was something he just couldn't do.

And if The Assembly might one day come after him, they might come after her too.

And he couldn't let that happen.

He loved her too much.

Which meant he had to leave her, let her get on with her life with someone else, someone who wasn't a target.

There was a knock at the door.

"I'll get it," said Margo, but Jones raised a hand to stop her.

"You sit and eat, hon, before it gets cold."

"But yours will get just as cold."

Jones grinned, motioning at his plate. "Your food's too good, hon, I'm done."

Margo looked at the nearly empty plate and shook her head. "Did you even chew?"

"Like a duck, babe, like a duck." He wiped his mouth with his napkin, tossing it on the table as the knock repeated. "Yeah, yeah, I'm coming." He opened the door and nearly shit his pants.

"Commander Whitman."

"Come with me."

"I'm in the middle of breakfast with my girl."

"Now."

He frowned but realized there was no choice, two other men down the hallway, clearly backup. "Fine." He stepped back inside and grabbed his jacket and hat. "Hon, I'm stepping out for a few minutes. Business."

"Okay, dear." He could hear the chair scrape as she rose, her footsteps approaching. He quickly stepped into the hall, closing the door, not wanting her to see these men, nor they her.

He followed Whitman in silence, down the several flights of stairs and into a car waiting on the street. The two men stayed outside.

"I've been sent to deliver a message."

Jones could feel his stomach fill with butterflies.

Did it include bullets?

He said nothing.

101

"They know what you did."

"What? The painting? I said I was sorry. That Captain took it before I could burn it."

Whitman smiled slightly. "This has nothing to do with the painting, or the cash and jewels you've been spreading around town."

Jones felt a lump form in his throat.

They know.

"A body was recovered and identified yesterday."

Jones said nothing.

"Retired Lieutenant Colonel John Jacob Astor the Fourth."

Sweat began to bead on his forehead.

"Imagine our employer's surprise when it was found he drowned with no gunshot wounds on his body."

A trickle of icy cold sweat raced down his back, his shirt slowly dampening.

He eyed the door.

"Care to explain?"

His mouth was dry and he had to peel his tongue off the roof. "I must have shot the wrong man."

Whitman smiled. "I'd believe that if you hadn't brought me the envelope with the papers we were looking for."

Shit!

"Here's what I think happened. I think you had an attack of consciousness, brought on by that little philly you've got upstairs."

Jones' fear turned to anger. "Don't you dare touch her."

Whitman smiled triumphantly. "So that *is* it." He waved his hand. "No matter, our quarrel isn't with some waitress from the wrong side of the tracks. It's with you."

"Do anything you want to me, just leave her out of it."

Whitman's smile spread. "Our employer, or should I say, *my* employer, wants nothing to happen to you. You have proven yourself unreliable, therefore you will no longer be considered for future assignments."

Jones felt relief sweep over him.

"I see that was what you wanted, regardless."

Jones nodded.

"Good. You will be allowed to keep your money and jewels and you are of course sworn to secrecy. You will be monitored from time to time, and should any breach be discovered, you and your loved ones will be eliminated. You yourself have carried out several of these executions over the years, so you know my employer is sincere."

Jones went cold again, nodding as the images of the dead flashed before his eyes.

"But there is one thing, Mr. Jones."

"What?"

"My employer, your *former* employer, is not an individual, but an organization that never dies, and never forgets."

The Assembly.

"And as such, at some point in time, you, or one of your descendants, may be asked for a favor."

"One of my…"

Descendants?

"You are to write a letter for your children, confessing to your crimes, and to how you acquired your wealth. You are to make no mention of our employers, beyond indicating that should they be approached, they must cooperate, or we will eliminate your entire lineage."

"But…but…" Jones wasn't sure what to say. His entire lineage? What did that even mean? Did he mean they would kill his children and grandchildren?

"I see you understand, Mr. Jones. You will write the letter tonight. Someone will collect it tomorrow and it will be held by us until such time as it is needed."

"Wh-what might they ask them to do?"

Whitman shrugged. "I have no idea, Mr. Jones. It will depend most likely on what type of people your children and their children become. Perhaps your son will follow his father's footsteps and join the military. His skills could prove useful to our employer. Or perhaps your daughter will work for a newspaperman, and she'll be asked to plant a story." He smiled. "The possibilities are endless, and their needs diverse."

"But they won't be harmed."

"Not if they cooperate, Mr. Jones, not if they cooperate." He leaned forward. "Which is why you should make that letter as compelling as possible. Because should they not, the consequences will be dire, as you well know."

Jones nodded, his heart pounding, the blood rushing through his ears almost drowning out the noise surrounding them.

"And should I not have any children?"

Whitman's eyebrows popped up slightly. "Why, then your family would be spared." He flicked a wrist toward the apartment. "But I hardly think a woman as lovely as young Miss Margo would be satisfied without children."

He was right. She wouldn't. Which left him with only one choice.

"And if you're thinking of killing yourself, Mr. Jones, I would advise against it. My employer has instructed me to eliminate Miss Margo should you attempt such a course of action."

Jones' shoulders slumped as his eyes closed, the blood draining from his face.

"Face it, Mr. Jones," said Whitman as he retrieved a cigar from his pocket, biting the end off and spitting it out the window. "If you had only done your job, none of this would have happened. Our employer is generous and only expected one thing. Loyalty." He lit the cigar, taking several hard puffs, the cherry glowing brightly. He jabbed the air between them with the cigar. "Mr. Jones, your actions have condemned you and your family."

Jones nodded and opened his eyes. "For how long?"

"Three generations."

He felt his chest tighten, not sure if he was pleased with the answer or not. "Three?"

"Should nothing be asked of your grandchildren, then nothing further shall be asked of your family, and our employer will consider your debt paid."

Jones' head dropped onto his chest.

"But that could be a hundred years."

Moscone Convention Center, New Orleans
Present Day

"That is why we need to take a firm line when it comes to Russia's newly aggressive tone. If Russia continues to go unchallenged, we risk returning to the days of the Cold War, where the entire planet teetered on the brink of nuclear holocaust, where two sides were in an arms race that neither could let up on for fear of an imbalance that might lead one side to think they could win, triggering an unthinkable retaliation."

Command Sergeant Major Burt "Big Dog" Dawson scanned the partisan crowd through his Oakley Standard Issue Ballistic sunglasses, their dark lenses preventing the audience from seeing who he might be looking at from one moment to the next. The key was to keep the head movement to a minimum. Watch the crowd out of the corner of your eye and you were more likely to catch a suspect who thought he was in the clear.

There had been several dozen threats against his assignment going into tonight's speech, though most had been dismissed as harmless, yet in today's day and age it simply didn't pay to not be careful. It was a partisan, pre-screened crowd, but that didn't mean much.

And this guy was controversial, to say the least.

Which might be why he was so wildly popular.

Yet one threat had made it onto the radar and Delta had been requested to provide a four-man team to assist with the security, the threat coming out of Russia.

One country that had shown it was willing to kill to further its agenda.

"We nearly came to full-scale global nuclear war in 1962 but fortunately a firm military response by President Kennedy forced the Soviets to back down. And today we face a similar crisis. Many think it began in the Ukraine, but it didn't. Before Ukraine there was Chechnya, Georgia and Moldova. Threats against Poland, the Czech Republic and now the Baltic States, all NATO allies, could lead to the very all-out war our children's generation never thought possible, it now twenty-five years since the Soviet Union was a threat."

The man was right, though Dawson kept his politics to himself, it discouraged among serving members of the military to be political. Their job was to execute the orders issued by their elected Commander-in-Chief, whether they agreed with them or not, as long as they weren't illegal orders.

Illegal orders.

It had been a few years now since the fiasco that had led them from Peru to London, the death toll disturbingly high.

All innocent.

Because the President and his inner circle had fed them false intel, leading him and his team to believe they were targeting a domestic terrorist cell.

Instead it was innocent students and their professor.

And an ancient organization almost two thousand years old.

I'll be happy if I never hear of the Triarii again.

His eyes paused on someone reaching into an inner pocket, Dawson's finger twitching.

A handkerchief was produced just in time to smother a sneeze.

His eyes moved on.

"If I become President, should I be fortunate enough for the American people to bestow such an honor upon me, I will fight back against the schoolyard bully in Moscow rather than kowtow to him. I will strengthen the sanctions, provide weapons and training to the legitimate government of the Ukraine, and station more troops in the Baltic Republics to make certain the Russian government understands that their belligerence, their violation of international law, will not be tolerated under my administration."

About damned time someone told it like it was.

He exchanged a slight nod with Sergeant Carl "Niner" Sung who stood on the opposite side of the stage, sit reps coming in steadily over his comm.

All clear.

Niner was one of the most reliable men in The Unit, though that perhaps was a slight disservice to the others since they were all incredibly reliable—you didn't make The Unit if you weren't. But Niner was so gung-ho he seemed to infect the men of Bravo Team with his enthusiasm, it spurring them all on when things looked their bleakest.

And he was a funny sonofabitch too.

And that sense of humor had earned him the right to be the only man in The Unit to have chosen his own nickname, though Dawson had shortened it over time. They had been enjoying some brewskies when some rednecks took a dislike to Niner's Korean heritage, hurling insults at him. Niner had responded with a string of his own, much better Asian slurs, including the pièce de résistance, "Nine Iron".

His challenger hadn't taken too kindly to the bar laughing at him and swung.

At a Delta Operator.

It hadn't been a wise move.

Niner had insisted his new nickname be "Nine Iron" and the team had agreed, not really wanting to challenge him when so full of adrenaline. Dawson had kept the tradition of the nickname being "assigned" by shortening it to "Niner" which he had readily agreed to, probably more in shock that his request was being honored.

And relieved to rid himself of his old nickname.

Beaver.

Dawson smiled slightly. Niner had been so excited about making The Unit that all it had taken was someone calling him an "eager beaver" at a barbecue for the name to stick.

And like most nicknames given to you by someone else, he didn't like it.

Especially when he was forced to watch a Leave it to Beaver marathon one night, duct taped to a chair while everyone else drank beer and ate pizza around him.

Good times.

"It is time for America to be strong again, to not allow renewed Russian aggression to set the tone for our future, to not allow an increasingly militaristic China to increase its sphere of influence unchallenged. It is time for America to stop agreeing for the sake of agreeing. We have abandoned our traditional allies like Israel and Canada, and instead are appeasing Russia and Iran. Why? Are we a nation of cowards?"

Boos filled the room, fists thrown in the air.

"I didn't think so. And under my administration, America will be strong again. We will stand up to the bully, stop the proliferation of nuclear weapons and the territorial expansion of Russia and China, and bring the full force of the American military to bear on Islamic fundamentalism. Under my watch, America and her allies will be the policeman of the world, the firemen of the world, the paramedics of the world, because the world needs strong leadership once again. No longer will America apologize for being the greatest nation on Earth, no longer will we be made to feel guilty of our accomplishments, no longer will we feel shame for our success. Remember, come election day, a vote for me is a vote for a strong, secure and prosperous future! It's time to take America back!"

The crowd, whipped up into a frenzy by now, erupted in cheers, the rallying cry of the campaign, "Take America Back!" chanted by the hundreds gathered. Camera bulbs flashed, the effect almost strobe-like, this the time the sunglasses really paid off. He stepped forward, as did several others of the detail as the candidate began to glad-hand with the crowd, leaning over the stage to shake outstretched hands. His aide, Russell Saunders, whispered in his boss' ear and the man straightened himself, waving to the crowd, shouting out a goodnight before exiting stage left, Dawson and Niner leading the way, Sergeants Leon "Atlas" James and Will "Spock" Lightman covering the rear.

They made their way with purpose through the cleared path to the rear exit and were inside the armored limousine within two minutes of leaving the stage. The motorcade was underway immediately with Dawson in the front passenger seat of the candidate's vehicle, the rest of his team in an SUV behind them, a police motorcycle escort leading the way.

"Done for the day," sighed the exhausted man from the back seat, the partition down. "Thank God."

"It was a good day, sir," replied Saunders. "I think we picked up some votes."

"Let's hope so. My wife?"

Dawson could hear the concern in the man's voice, and for the first time in his life actually understood the concern a partner could have for their spouse. He had nearly lost the first woman he had ever truly loved in Paris only a few weeks ago. She was recovering well, yet it would be a tough haul for her.

To think you were going to break up with her!

When she had been shot he had decided in a moment of self-pity that it would be safer for her to be as far away from him as possible, yet in the end he had come around to realizing it would be selfish to do something so rash.

He had left the choice up to her.

And she had made it crystal clear she didn't blame him and felt closer to him than ever before.

"I love you, more than ever."

Those words, whispered from his beloved Maggie's lips after she had woken from her coma, had forced a lump into his throat that had made him realize how much he actually loved this woman. It was something he never would have imagined, he having resigned himself long ago to the bachelor life, not wanting to bring a woman, let alone children, into the life he led as a special operations soldier. He was the head of Bravo Team, a group of twelve operators in America's elite counter-terrorism unit, 1st Special Forces Operational Detachment – Delta, commonly known to the public as Delta Force. The Unit, as it was called, consisted of over one thousand personnel, the best of the best, and he would put any of them up against any enemy, any day.

Including on American soil. They were the only unit authorized to operate on home soil, the President authorized to suspend Posse Comitatus should it become necessary.

Today was just a protection detail and he honestly didn't expect any action, though expecting the unexpected was his job, so he never let his guard down, even now, his eyes scanning sidewalks, windows, pedestrians, even their escort vehicles.

Everything.

"Your wife is feeling better, sir, and is at the hotel waiting for you. Apparently it was just a case of exhaustion."

A relieved sigh of a husband who truly did seem to love his wife. Dawson had watched him dote on her the entire two days they had been here, he and his team only assigned yesterday morning after a fiery speech the night before where the presidential candidate had targeted Russia for the first time, deciding foreign policy was an area his rivals were weak.

It had lit up the Russian nationalists almost instantly, Homeland Security concerned enough to assign a Secret Service protection detail far earlier than the normal 120 day period leading up to the election. They had also asked for Delta assistance, the country still on edge after the Black Stone incident only weeks ago.

Dawson was only too happy to have been assigned, he and his team out of the rotation the past few weeks as they were fully debriefed on the events in Paris, Yemen and Saudi Arabia. Their Commanding Officer, Colonel Thomas Clancy, had reactivated them only two days ago. He had to admit he had felt a little guilty leaving Maggie, but she was in good hands. She was back at her apartment now and several of the wives in The Unit were taking shifts being with her, Maggie well known to them not only through her recent relationship with Dawson, but also the fact she had been the kinder, gentler face of Clancy, serving as his personal assistant for several years now.

Personal Assistant.

It had taken him over a year to figure out her job title, and he had managed to learn it through a Clancy tirade rather than having to sheepishly ask her after all this time. He had known what she *did*, he just hadn't known what the hell it was called. His mother had been a secretary for years and seemed to do the same work, yet he knew enough to know calling someone a secretary was somehow insulting now, though he wasn't sure why.

Mom was always proud of her job.

Clancy's tirade had been expected, and understood, the man not actually mad at Dawson, just concerned about a woman he thought of as a daughter, and the fact a team he had assigned to Yemen had been disavowed. Dawson had simply been the first person involved that he had been able to vent at.

He didn't take it personally.

The Colonel was the best CO he had ever had. A man who always had their back, as he had proven with the recent incident. A soldier's soldier, he passionately believed in the principal of 'no man left behind', no matter what the brass might say. Officially the team had been disavowed, but Clancy hadn't let that stop him from working the back channels and calling in favors.

It had saved them all.

"She's been trying to keep up as best she can, but she shouldn't be. I told her the American people would understand if she wasn't by my side at every event. She's recovering from chemo for Pete's sake."

"She's a good woman," said Saunders, softly.

"Too good for me."

There was a break in the conversation and Dawson turned to look at those seated in the back. "Sir, any changes to tonight's itinerary?"

"No, I'll be in for the night with my wife. We'll dine in the hotel room so your men should be able to take it easy. Any plans? Getting into some trouble?"

Dawson grinned. "We're not Secret Service, sir."

There was a grunt from the Secret Service driver.

A roar of laughter responded as Saunders' iPhone rang. A whispered conversation ensued then he ended the call. "Mr. Quaid wants to meet with you tonight, sir. He says it's urgent."

"Fine, no rest for the wicked."

Dawson's eyes narrowed. "Quaid? He's not on my list. I'll have him vetted by my people."

Saunders shook his head. "No need. He's one of our biggest donors."

Dawson nodded as they pulled up to the hotel, the security detail swarming out of their cars, a team already in place, along with hotel staff, forming a cordon from the limousine to the main entrance. "Okay. My team will hand over to the Secret Service team as soon as you're in your room. We'll take over again in the morning."

He climbed out and looked around, the usual press contingent held back behind a barricade, curious onlookers, mostly hotel guests, gawking.

He opened the door and Saunders then his boss exited, the politician waving to the crowd, pausing a moment for photographs, ignoring the screamed questions from the press corps.

Dawson and his team led them inside, the din of the crowd cut off the moment the doors closed. They climbed aboard an elevator being held for them and a staff member twisted the key to turn it into an express, the car shooting up to the tenth floor where they were greeted by two Secret Service agents. Within moments they were inside the hotel room.

"My team and I are going off duty now, sir," said Dawson after quickly inspecting the room.

"Have a good night, Mr. White."

"You too, Mr. Jones."

Acton & Palmer Residence, St. Paul, Maryland

"This is a good steak," said Milton, pointing at it with his fork. "Very tender."

"The key is the marinade," replied Acton as he sliced off a piece then chewed, the steak melting in his mouth. "Damn, I'm a good cook."

"If you do say so yourself," winked Laura, the rest of their dinner guests chuckling with the exception of tiny Mai Lien Trinh, she still attempting to learn the household's odd combination of American and British humor, her life in Vietnam ending only months ago. She had been exiled for her part in helping embarrass her country when she helped Acton, Laura and Niner escape Vietnamese and Russian authorities. In thanks for doing so, she had been granted asylum in America and a job at the university where she could earn money and complete her studies.

Acton smiled with pleasure as he saw young Tommy Granger lean sideways and bump shoulders with Mai, eliciting flushed cheeks from the shy girl. The two had been spending a lot of time together, and if they both weren't so meek, he was certain they'd be a couple by now.

All in good time.

Tommy was a computer whiz that had been instrumental in helping save Laura during the Blood Relics incident, Mai as well, her aptitude for computers newly discovered as she finally had access to the tools available to her that Americans took for granted.

"So when will we know if the painting is authentic?" asked Milton before shoveling some garlic mash into his mouth.

115

Acton shrugged. "It won't be soon. I've sent some emails out to several art experts and the chatter has already started. There's no hiding this now, that's for sure."

Laura put her fork and knife down, dabbing the corners of her mouth with a napkin. "I'm arranging to have it sent to the Smithsonian. We've got experts there who can't wait to get their hands on this thing."

"Where is it now?" asked Tommy. "It sounds valuable."

"Locked in one of the archeology department vaults," replied Acton. "It should be safe there, I can't see anybody wanting to steal it. Not in the next few days, anyway. Hardly anybody knows it exists yet."

"How are you going to transport it?"

"Armored car, I think. It's too valuable to just drop in the mail."

Laura picked up her utensils. "I wanted to drive it there, but James wouldn't let me."

"Hey, you'd be so nervous and distracted driving it, you might get into an accident. And I'd hate to see anything happen to a work of art." Laura's jaw dropped in mock offense. "A work of art such as yourself, of course." Acton grinned, raising his hand..

Milton high fived him, his wife Sandra snorted. "Nice save, Jim."

"Good thing you know how to cook, otherwise such talk might be grounds for divorce," said Laura as she took another bite of her steak. She swallowed. "Though it *is* good steak."

Sandra leaned forward. "Now Laura, all he did was marinade it—"

"Actually, I did that," interrupted Laura.

"Oh, then all he did was slap it on the grill and flip it once or twice?"

Laura smiled. "Come to think of it…"

"Hey, but these mashed potatoes are fantastic. And that garden salad was terrific," said Milton, leaping to his friend's defense.

"Actually, I made those," replied Laura, leaning back in her chair and looking at her husband. "In fact, for about ten minutes you had Greg working the grill while you did something inside." Her eyes narrowed. "Did you actually do anything?"

Acton huffed. "Well, duh, I did the most important thing there is to do."

"What's that?"

"I lit the barbecue."

"Ooh, what a man!"

Mai snickered.

She got that one.

Acton swallowed his last piece of steak, noticing he was the last to finish. He had been talking a lot, but he had also been given the largest piece at Laura and Greg's insistence. He was pretty sure Tommy was a little disappointed but knew the young man wouldn't dare object.

Something twigged as the Sirius XM station they were listening to in the background began to play Start Me Up, the vocals barely audible, it turned down so low. He tossed his chin toward the nearest speaker. "So for you Stones fans, I stumbled upon a little tidbit that you might find interesting."

"Stones?"

Acton turned to Mai. "As in the Rolling Stones."

She shook her head. "Is this a band?"

Acton's jaw dropped. "Only one of the most famous rock and roll bands in history!" He turned to Tommy. "You need to do a better job at educating her."

Tommy shrugged. "I've heard of them. Weren't they named after that magazine."

Milton groaned. "I feel so old."

Acton shook his head. "The youth of today. We're doomed."

"Hey, I'm sure you had no idea who your parents listened to," said Tommy defensively.

Acton laughed. "No, I knew *what* they listened to, I just didn't *like* what they listened to for the most part at the time. Now I actually like a lot of the classic rock from the sixties and seventies that my dad listened to."

"Including the Stones?"

Acton nodded. "Including the Stones." He leaned back in his chair. "Now, first, to correct one thing, Rolling Stone magazine was named after several things. The Rolling Stones, which came *before* the magazine, the song Rollin' Stone by Muddy Waters—"

"Ooh, Muddy Waters," said Sandra, "I love them."

"Him."

"Him?"

"Him."

"Umm, maybe I'm thinking of the Moody Blues."

"Maybe."

"And the third thing?" asked Milton, patting his wife's knee.

"The Dylan song 'Like a Rolling Stone'."

Tommy leaned forward. "Dylan?"

"I give up."

Tommy grinned. "Just kidding."

Mai giggled.

Acton pursed his lips. "I'm not sure you are," he said, doubt lacing his voice. "But let's give you the benefit of the doubt."

"Okay, you said you had some tidbit?" prompted Laura. "Now, remember, the Stones are from my side of the pond, so it will take a lot to impress me."

"Well, did you know that in high school Mr. Jagger played basketball?"

"No, I did not," replied Laura. "And that's this great big secret you discovered?"

Acton chuckled. "Patience, my dear, patience. Did you also know that his bandmates at the time felt his voice sounded too uppity to be singing the blues?"

"Uppity?" asked Laura. "You mean upper-class?"

"Yes."

"Odd. I never got that impression," said Milton. "Sounds pretty down to earth to me."

"Well, there's a reason for that *now.*"

"Oh, do enlighten us, oh great one!"

Acton jabbed a finger at Milton. "Hey, great one is reserved for Gretzky." He stuck his tongue out slightly, tapping the tip. "At a basketball game, he ran into another player and bit the end of his tongue off, and in the confusion, swallowed it."

"Eww!" cried Sandra and Laura together.

"Glad you waited until after we were done our medium-rare steaks," said Milton, his nose turned up.

"I pick my moments."

"So what does this have to do with him no longer sounding uppity?"

"Well, he wasn't able to talk for a week, and when he finally did, the shape and size of his tongue had changed so much that he no longer sounded upper-class, and his singing voice had completely changed."

"That's incredible!" cried Sandra, her eyes suddenly narrowing. "Wait, is this true, or are you just pulling our legs?"

Acton smiled. "Nope, completely true. If Mick hadn't made a tasty treat of his tongue, the Rolling Stones may never have been."

"Cool!" Tommy stretched and put his arm over the back of Mai's chair, prompting her to lean forward. He started to turn a little red and Acton felt sorry for the guy.

Mai leaned back.

Acton exchanged a glance with Laura as Tommy let go the breath he was holding.

"So back to this painting," said Sandra. "You really think it's possible that it was stolen off the Titanic as she sank, by someone who was on board a military boat?"

"Ship," interjected Acton.

"Huh?"

"If a navy guy caught you calling his ship a boat, he might toss you over."

"What's the difference?"

"Doesn't seem to be much agreement though some people say ships can carry boats, boats can't carry ships."

Laura laughed. "My granddad always said that if your ship is sinking, you get in a boat. If your boat is sinking, you get in the water."

"As good a definition as I've heard," smiled Acton. "Anyway, the theory makes sense, especially with that security alert."

"So it's not just insurance fraud?" asked Sandra.

"I don't think so. If it were fraud, how would some US Navy captain end up with it? It just doesn't make sense. What I think the real question is, is if it weren't fraud, how *did* a US navy captain end up with it?"

Laura leaned over, putting an elbow on the back of Acton's chair. "And if he weren't acting under orders, why would the Navy cover it up?"

"What do you mean?" asked Sandra.

"The security alert. Clearly they know he was involved. Didn't Steve Wainwright say he had his father's record but part of it was redacted? And it was when they started asking questions about that portion of the record the Navy shut them down?"

Acton nodded. "But do they actively know, or is it just something put in there from long ago? Classified missions are not unusual, so a redacted personnel record isn't anything new and no one would even think about it when printing it off. It obviously wasn't Captain Wainwright's file being watched, otherwise the security alert would have been triggered when the initial file was printed for his grandson. It wasn't until they asked about him in relation to the Titanic that the alert was tripped."

Milton frowned. "Which means somebody absolutely knows why."

Acton pursed his lips. "Can we say that? It could be some security alert programmed in years ago. Just a code on a file that the system says, anytime I see this code, I trip an alert."

Tommy shook his head. "You're forgetting one thing, Professor."

The table turned toward Tommy, the computer expert at the table. "What's that?"

"Someone had to choose the keywords that would trigger that alert."

"Meaning."

"Meaning that someone had to program the system, either specifically, or through a keyword database, to have an alert triggered when someone searched for Wainwright *and* Titanic together. And those systems are modern. Nobody involved with the Titanic would probably have been alive when those systems were programmed."

"So what you're saying is—"

"Somebody in the past twenty or thirty years programmed the system to make sure if anybody searched for information on that redacted mission, an alert would be triggered."

"But there's one thing I don't understand," said Sandra. "If it was programmed to watch for that, then who programmed it? Everyone

121

involved would be dead by now. Wouldn't putting a security alert in the system just let people know there was something they were trying to hide? I mean, I would assume the data isn't in the computer if they're trying to hide it, so if no one knows about this, then why create an alert in the first place? Aren't you just waving a big red flag saying 'look at me, I've got something to hide'?"

Acton felt his stomach churn a bit. "So what you're saying is that somebody *today* is actively monitoring that alert."

Tommy jabbed a finger in the air at Acton. "Exactly! That's what I've been trying to say. Somebody, somewhere, received that alert, because they were waiting for it. And I'm willing to bet you it wasn't the Navy."

Laura squeezed Acton's hand tightly.

"If not them, then who?"

Assembly Covert Communications Facility, Moscow, Russia

"The infection appears to be spreading."

Ilya Mashkov frowned. He was still getting used to the idea that The Assembly thought extremely long term. Both forward and back. They rigorously protected the secret of their existence, and would do whatever it took to preserve it, though this was the first time he had ever seen the distant past become an issue. And with the Titanic barely a century ago, it wasn't exactly the distant past for this organization.

The full truth had yet to be revealed to him.

As each year passed, and he found himself ingrained deeper and deeper into the organization, he was granted access to more of their files. He knew at least centuries were involved, what he didn't know was whether or not it was millennia. He had been provided an impressive amount of information on other organizations, from the Triarii to the Order of Mary, many millennia old. He had the sense it was to impress upon him the fact that organizations like this did exist today, and had been around for thousands of years. He assumed it was to prepare him for the revelation that he too was now part of an equally ancient organization, something he would have had serious doubts about believing.

But not anymore.

He just wanted to know the truth.

He had been given the file on the Titanic operation as soon as it had become an issue. All members were provided with all relevant information for any current crisis. After all, once one became a member, one was trusted.

Certain death was the alternative.

The Assembly could never risk a security breach from within, and the benefits of being part of the organization made it almost unfathomable that someone would betray it.

The wealth and power were intoxicating.

As far as he knew, not a single member had ever knowingly betrayed the organization, though from what he understood several had done so inadvertently in the past and were eliminated so the "infection", as they called it, couldn't spread.

"Our monitoring of Internet traffic suggests an increase in searches on a painting thought lost on the Titanic. Some of this is originating in the same geographic region as Congressman Mahoney's constituency office," explained the digitally altered voice, this man the longest serving member of The Assembly—which meant he knew who every single one of them were. This man was the only truly anonymous member of the organization.

Who kills him if he's the one who betrays us?

He doubted anyone knew who he actually was, he only known as Number One. Apparently The Assembly had forgone any names because of a previous security breach that had threatened to expose their identities, it now forbidden to use anyone's name, only their designation.

I wonder if I'll ever be Number One.

"I've invited our operative to bring us up to date."

A screen flashed and the image of an incredibly beautiful woman appeared, her cheekbones sculpted, framed by short raven hair, her skin a healthy light brown from the sun, her green eyes piercing in their intensity.

His breath was taken away.

"Thank you, sir. As you already know, interrogation of the records clerk yielded the name of the individual requesting the information on Captain Wainwright, Congressman Bill Mahoney. This interrogation also led us to believe at least one other person was involved. In questioning the

Congressman, we were able to determine it was Captain Wainwright's own grandson, a Steve Wainwright, that had requested the records search. Apparently some records were found in the Captain's basement recently including a painting supposed to have gone down with the Titanic. We are currently on route to pick up Mr. Wainwright and determine who he has spoken to."

"What is your contingency if he has spoken to others about this?"

"I have a plan to take care of it, assuming your orders are still to eliminate anyone involved."

"They are."

"Then you have nothing to concern yourselves with. The entire family will be eliminated should it become necessary."

"Very well, keep us posted."

The screen flashed and went blank, the beautiful woman gone, Mashkov determined to find out who she was, suddenly infatuated with the desire to have her as his own.

The intoxicating delirium of absolute power.

It was a wonderful feeling to know he could have anything, or anyone, he wanted.

Whether they were willing or not.

Money. Drugs. Both.

There was always a way.

Though he preferred willing.

In his home base of Moscow he had dozens of willing women, concubines for the lack of a better term, throwing themselves at him whenever he desired. He never had to resort to pressure.

Except with his wife.

Though they barely spoke anymore.

His wife and children lived in Saint Petersburg and he rarely saw them, which was fine with him. His two daughters were ungrateful, spoiled little brats that had turned against him long ago, his attempts to purchase their affections only making things worse. His son had rejected the family money and instead changed his name and joined the Russian Navy, determined to make a name for himself on his own.

Mashkov was immensely proud of him, though heartbroken he never saw him.

Give it time.

He had every confidence his son would come back to him once he had made a man out of himself, though if he were to interfere, to call in a favor to help his son climb through the ranks or get a plum assignment, he would never see him again should his son find out.

So he kept his distance, though a watchful eye was ever present.

He flinched as he realized someone was talking.

"…most disturbing. I think it's time we spoke with him, do you not agree Number Twelve?"

Oh shit, what did he just say?

He tried to replay the conversation but it was a total blank from the moment the alluring woman had finished her update.

"Of course," was all he could think of to say.

"Excellent. I took the liberty of arranging a meeting with our point man and Mr. Jones. I'll leave the rest in your hands."

"Thank you."

JW Marriott Hotel, New Orleans

Christopher Jones lay on his bed, eyes clothes, still in slacks and a dress shirt, though his tie was lying on the back of a nearby chair with his suit jacket. His wife Constance lay beside him, the only light in the bedroom of their suite from the alarm clock's LCD display and a sliver from under the door, activity still happening on the other side.

"I want you to head home tomorrow morning. I'll finish up here then join you."

He felt his wife roll over beside him. "No, I'll be fine. I should be there with you."

He turned on his side and reached out to find her in the dark, gently squeezing her arm as he felt her hand touch his chin. He kissed her fingers. "No, you've overdone it this time. The doctors said it would take months for you to recover your strength. It's only been weeks. This was a bad idea and you're paying the price."

"But I want to."

He shuffled closer and pushed an arm under her neck, pulling her closer, her arms wrapping around him. "I know you want to, hon, but it's more important that you get better."

"But this is a once in a lifetime opportunity. We can't let this pass us by because I was sick. People want to see a husband and wife together on stage otherwise they begin to ask questions."

Jones smiled, squeezing her a little tighter. "People only ask questions when there's no explanation. Besides, if the public won't choose me because my sick wife isn't at my side, then they don't deserve to have me as their President, and I wouldn't want to lead them anyway. But I don't think our fellow Americans are like that at all. I think they'll understand as long as we always tell them the truth."

She squeezed. "You'll get the sympathy vote for sure."

His eyes burned and he closed them, feeling a tear threatening to spill out. He held her tighter as the memories of almost losing her flooded back. It had been the worst year of their lives, the brave face he had to always wear exhausting, yet nothing compared to his wife's exhaustion, the poor woman not only suffering chemotherapy, but enduring the press hounding them at every step of the way, despite his pleas for privacy. The mainstream media mostly respected their wishes, it was the paparazzi that seemed to revel in the misery of others, as if the consumers of their filth thrilled at the sight of a politician's wife dying.

Sometimes freedom of the press goes too far.

He had seen a movie years ago called Paparazzi that he couldn't remember being good or bad, though the premise seemed particularly satisfying now, the victim of greedy paparazzi dishing out some vigilante justice.

Maybe when you're President you can have a few of them taken out.

He chuckled at the thought.

"What's funny?"

He laughed a little harder as he pushed back from her, running his hands through her thin, short hair, the drugs to save it unfortunately not working on her. "Just thinking of what I'd like to do to some of the press."

"You're thinking of that movie again, aren't you?"

"You know me so well." He moved closer and gave her a peck, it missing slightly, catching only half her mouth.

There was a knock at the door.

"Sir, Mr. Quaid is here."

"Give me a minute!"

He gave his wife another quick peck. "No rest for the wicked."

His wife rolled over and turned on a lamp, flooding the room with a gentle yellow glow. "I don't like him," she whispered. "Sleazy."

Jones rolled out of bed, slipping his feet into his shoes and tightening the laces. "I had him vetted. He's clean but ruthless when it comes to business. Unfortunately we need him. His pockets run deep. Once we're on the ticket, we won't need people like him again." He stood and debated putting on his tie. *You better.* He grabbed it and flipped his collar up, his wife coming up from behind, turning him around.

"Let me. You never tie it tight enough."

He smiled then raised his chin, giving her space to work. "You spoil me."

"Don't you forget it."

"Not a chance." He felt the knot tighten then a pat on his chest.

"There you go."

He turned and looked in the mirror. "Perfect as usual."

She helped him into his suit jacket then gave him a peck on the cheek. "Go get 'em. I'll be out in a minute."

He returned the kiss, shaking his head. "No, you get your rest. This shouldn't take long."

She smiled her thanks, her face so haggard it broke his heart. She had aged at least ten years it seemed, the bright, vibrant woman he had celebrated twenty-five years of marriage with just a year ago, gone.

He pushed the thoughts out of his mind as he drew a deep breath then opened the door, stepping out into the living area. "Pete, so good to see you."

Peter Quaid turned from his position at the window, gazing out at the city streets below. He smiled, closing the distance between them with a few quick strides, his hand extended the entire way. "Mr. Jones, I appreciate you seeing me on such short notice."

"No problem at all," said Jones, motioning toward a nearby chair as he took a seat of his own. "To what do I owe the pleasure?"

Quaid looked at the others in the room. "What I need to discuss can only be said in private."

Jones had learned long ago to hide any look of surprise, instead merely looking at Saunders. "Clear the room, please."

Saunders wasn't as practiced, the surprised look on his face almost one of hurt at being excluded. Within moments the few staff members had left, leaving him alone with Quaid. "Now what is so important my most trusted staff can't hear it?"

Quaid chuckled. "I'm sorry about all the cloak and dagger, trust me, it's more for your protection than anything else. And by protection, I mean protection of your integrity."

Jones already didn't like where this was heading. He knew from past experience that he was about to be asked to compromise his ideals. In previous instances he had stood his ground, his principles remaining intact, yet never had so much been at stake. This was his moneyman. Yes, he was one of many, but he was his largest donor, and had brought several other deep pockets to the table, promising even more if the campaign grew.

And it had. He was now the clear front-runner, running away with it in the polls, voters on both sides of the political spectrum actually responsive to his message of rolling back the increased surveillance of Americans and instead focusing on the real enemies.

And polling had told him his own distrust of Russia was shared by a majority of his fellow citizens, resulting in his latest foreign policy speeches that apparently had pissed off Moscow.

Like I give a shit.

Russia was a joke now, to call itself a democracy was an insult to its people, yet unfortunately its people were as well informed now as they were under the Communist regime, the vast majority of their media once again state controlled, the rest too scared to print the truth. Opposition party leaders were jailed and murdered, and now the Kremlin had just signed a law allowing them to shut down any "undesirable foreign organization" to further silence the truth.

Jones draped his arm across the back of the couch. "Please, tell me what's on your mind."

Quaid leaned forward. "I need you to tone down the rhetoric on Russia, specifically the sanctions."

Jones' eyebrows popped slightly, his practiced control failing him for a split second. He wasn't sure what he had been expecting, but it wasn't that. "I beg your pardon?"

Quaid smiled slightly, the sleaze his wife had referred to oozing out. "I need you to stop talking about Russian sanctions."

"But why? They're a vote winner, and I happen to personally believe in them. Russia's renewed aggression needs to be stopped, and next to military action, the next best option is economic."

"I'm afraid your benefactors must insist."

Jones felt his blood pressure rising, his face flushing. "And I'm afraid I don't care. If you choose to pull your financial support of my campaign, then so be it. I'd hate to lose you, but like I told you from the get go, I won't compromise my ideals for your money. All it does is buy you access to my ear, not my pen. We're going to win, Pete, and people want to back a winner. Replacing your money won't be a problem."

Quaid's smile never wavered, it one he had used himself in the past—when dealing with a useful idiot, their naïveté so obvious it was painful to listen to.

And Jones was no idiot.

"I don't think you understand the situation, Mr. Jones." He pulled an envelope from his breast pocket, removing a sheet of paper. He unfolded it and smoothed out the creases, pushing it across the table toward him. Jones glanced at it without picking it up, recognizing it as a list of his major campaign donors, all but a few highlighted in yellow. "Every single one of those highlighted are backing you because of *me*. If *I* pull out, they all pull out. And they will make certain their friends hold on to their wallets as well. Mr. Jones, you are burning through cash at an incredible rate. Running for President is a billion dollar proposition now. People with that kind of money talk to each other, and if so many names pull out now, publicly, your campaign will find itself out of money before the month's end."

Jones rose, his fists clenched.

Calm down!

He took a slow breath. "I refuse to believe that." He motioned toward the door. "I'll kindly ask you to leave."

Quaid rose, his smile finally turning into a frown. "I see we'll have to do this the hard way."

Saunders looked at his watch. It had barely been five minutes, yet it felt like an eternity. He hated being out of the loop, though he was pretty sure that would be temporary, Jones always filling him in on everything.

If I can't trust you, who can I trust?

The words had meant a lot to him when Jones had first said them, and he had done his best to deserve that trust, though sometimes it had proven difficult, politicians at times their own worst enemies. But he had run a good campaign—an excellent campaign—and they were most likely going to win the ticket, and he was confident, ultimately, the Presidency.

It was incredibly exciting to think about, and he found himself lying awake at night in his bed, usually in some overpriced hotel, fantasizing about what it would be like.

It was easy to forget that *he* wasn't running.

Eventually.

He was young and had been made certain assurances. A life in politics was definitely in his future, and if he played the game right, with the right backers like Jones had now, the sky was the limit.

Just keep the backers happy.

The elevator chimed to his right, his pacing halted as two Secret Service agents positioned themselves at the doors to see who was arriving. The doors opened and several popping sounds were heard, the agents dropping in heaps. Somebody shouted, a scream, then six men exited the elevator, their weapons raised and firing.

Saunders stood frozen for a moment then ducked behind one of the volunteers, a young woman from Oklahoma named Kitty. She took a shot, falling backward into him, and he held her up as a human shield as the attackers eliminated the agents at the far end of the hall.

A loud crack of gunfire from behind erupted and he dropped to the ground, Kitty collapsing atop him. One of the attackers went down but the others responded with a hail of muted gunfire. He turned to look behind him and saw the two Secret Service agents down, all resistance eliminated within seconds of their arrival.

He struggled to get out from under the deadweight that was Kitty but before he could one of the attackers stood over him, his expressionless face more terrifying than any gangsta sneer.

He fired, a sharp pain radiating from Saunders' chest as the door to Jones' room opened, Mr. Quaid standing there calmly.

"Let's get this over with, quickly."

"Yes, sir."

Quaid felt himself drifting away as somebody grabbed him by the pant leg, dragging him out of the hallway.

Tammy Clavin sipped her venti-sized Starbucks Iced Mocha Cookie Crumble Frappuccino, a 600 calorie monstrosity responsible for her pants being a little too tight these past few weeks. They were terrible for her, but she was sucking down three or four of them a day when on the road, which seemed to be almost every day now. She had never had a sip of coffee before joining the campaign—actually, that wasn't true. She had *exactly* a sip of coffee before joining. One sip. It was all she needed to know she hated coffee.

But she had to stay awake. She hated anything carbonated and energy drinks like Red Bull scared her.

Everyone drinks coffee, so it must be safe.

It was logic that worked, yet she couldn't get over the taste, and knew she never could.

Until she had seen Kitty with one of these delicious iced creations from the barista gods.

She had become addicted almost immediately.

It wasn't until she had to lie on her bed, battling to get her skirt done up, that she found out how many calories were in the darned things. It was Kitty who had mentioned the count.

It had stunned her.

Yet it hadn't stopped her.

I'll stop when I get home.

She looked at herself in the mirror, stifling a yawn.

Come on, do your magic!

She took another sip.

Then another.

She looked at her watch and jumped.

Where's Kitty?

The lineup at the Starbucks across the street had been longer than expected, but Kitty was supposed to collect her when Mr. Jones was ready and she hadn't yet. Which was odd, Kitty always very punctual, and it now about five minutes past when she had expected the final meeting of the day to start.

Maybe I'd better go up myself.

She took one last glance in the mirror, frowning at the slight midriff bulge, putting the hideous concoction on the dresser, resolving to lose the weight, starting now.

She frowned, eyeing the drink.

You're so weak!

She grabbed it and her bag, heading for the door.

Tomorrow you go down one size on the coffee. Wean yourself off, girl, wean yourself off!

She never ceased to amaze herself at how she could rationalize bad habits.

Or bad boyfriends.

Ugh. Men!

She was in the wrong business for meeting nice men. It wasn't that they were bad, it was just that almost everyone she met was so driven to succeed, that they were either entirely focused on their career, so had no time for a relationship, or entirely focused on their career, so looking for a wife that could make them look good to the public ten or twenty years down the road.

She wasn't going to be arm candy.

She pressed the button for the elevator, looking at herself in the brushed chrome doors, the blurred image somehow slightly more satisfying than the real thing.

She eyed the coffee.

Caffeine pills?

She shook her head as the doors opened.

No way am I becoming a pill popper.

She saw it too often, especially among the younger staff like herself. The lifestyle was too alluring, too many wanting to work the long hours then take advantage of the social life as well, leaving little to no time for rest.

Pop a couple of pills, problem solved.

Not really.

The doors opened to Jones' floor, Tammy stepping out.

That's odd.

The usual Secret Service detail wasn't at the doors, nor were they at the opposite ends of the hallway like normal. In fact, the hallway was completely empty.

She felt her chest tighten.

This isn't right.

Her steps were tentative, unsure, as she slowly crept down the hall toward Jones' suite, listening intently, hearing nothing but the rush of elevators and a dull drone of the HVAC system.

No voices, no laughter, no snoring, no coughing.

She was about to knock on the door when she stopped, instead pulling out her cellphone.

She dialed Saunders' number.

On the other side of the door she heard his America the Beautiful ringtone.

So they are here.

She knocked as she held the phone up to her ear.

Nothing.

She knocked again and tried the door as the call went to voicemail.

She killed it, knocking again, this time harder.

Something's definitely wrong.

She stepped back from the door, suddenly afraid of what might be on the other side.

What do I do?

She inched down the hall, never taking her eyes off the bottom of the door, watching for some sort of shadow from the other side.

That was when she noticed the drag marks on the hallway carpet, coming from various directions, all leading into the room, all in sets of two.

Heel marks!

She ran.

Dawson looked at his cards. It was a shit hand. A pair of deuces and nothing else to build on.

"Three." He tossed the cards on the pile, Niner dealing out three new ones from the well-worn deck, this particular set more travelled than most people, it having seen action in most of the world's hellholes.

"Three for the Big Dog, looks like he has a shitty hand."

Dawson picked up the cards, one at a time.

No help.

No help.

Ahh!

Another deuce. Three of a kind. Three of a shitty kind, but three of a kind nonetheless.

Why oh why are nines always wild when Niner deals?

Atlas took two and Spock sat pat with what he was dealt.

Bastard. Watch the eyebrow.

Spock's tell when he was excited was the eyebrow creeping up just a hint.

It wasn't creeping.

So he's not excited.

Or he's figured out his tell.

Dawson looked at Atlas, his muscular frame betraying him, his jugular pulsing a little quicker than normal.

He's got something. Poor bastard should wear a turtleneck.

He glanced at Niner with his tacky starfish Hawaiian shirt only half-buttoned, cigar jammed in one side of his mouth—unlit since smoking wasn't allowed in the room—dark sunglasses hiding his eyes, a tacky Las Vegas lime green croupier visor completing his ensemble.

I think he does it to distract us. At least I hope that's why.

Nickels started to be tossed into the pile, the bets quickly up to the massive twenty-five cent limit within moments.

"Too rich for my blood," said Spock, tossing his cards after the last raise, apparently having nothing after all.

Niner lowered his sunglasses slightly, giving the man a look. "We seriously need to discuss your finances."

"Hey, don't judge me. Maybe I'm just a penny pincher."

"Penny pincher my ass. I've seen your new car."

Atlas' impossibly deep voice joined the conversation. "Maybe *that's* why he can't afford a high stakes game like this."

Niner grunted as he eyed his cards. "Yellow Camaro convertible. *Please* tell me you don't have that lame Transformers decal on the back."

Spock said nothing, leaning back in his chair as he took a swig from a can of Diet Pepsi.

Niner shook his head. "Christ, you do, don't you?"

Spock shrugged. "I bought it used and it was already there. I didn't want to mess up the paint job trying to take it off."

"Bullshit!" coughed Atlas, he doing Iceman proud.

Niner threw another quarter onto the pile. "I think I'm going to start calling you Bumblebee."

"As you wish, Beaver."

Atlas snorted, Dawson stifling a laugh. "Forgot about that one," the huge man rumbled. "Beaver. Yeah, maybe I'll start calling you that too."

Niner folded up his cards and placed them on the table. "You know, looking through that sight can be pretty confusing at times. I'd hate to put a round in someone's ass."

Dawson smiled. "I think we'll leave them as Niner and Spock." He nodded toward Niner's cards. "And now that Niner's out, it's just you and me, Atlas. I call."

"Hey, I wasn't folding!" protested Niner, grabbing his cards.

Dawson shrugged. "Hey, you put them on the table. You know our rules."

"Yeah, but they're not *the* rules."

"Hey, you're the one who came up with it. You were sick and tired of waiting for Mickey to come back from the pisser. What did you say that day?"

Atlas leaned forward. "If you can't hold'em, you fold'em."

Niner frowned, tossing his cards onto the pile. "Fine. But I've got starving cousins back in Korea to feed, and you guys just took away next week's groceries."

Everyone groaned. "South Korea, man, South Korea. If your parents were from North Korea, you'd never have made The Unit," said Spock, watching as Atlas revealed his cards.

"Pair of Aces and Kings. Read 'em and weep."

Dawson's eyebrows raised slightly, his head bobbing in appreciation of a decent hand. "That's good, damned good. I hate to say all I have is this pair of deuces"—he revealed the pair of twos—"and their friend." He dropped the third and Atlas groaned.

"Are you kidding me? I lost to triple deuces?"

Dawson leaned forward, scooping the pot toward him. "Never underestimate the underdog."

"Or the Big Dog!" added Spock.

"Arf! Arf!" barked Niner as he grabbed the cards. "Time to win my money back. This time no cheating."

Somebody pounded on the door. "Hello?" cried a female voice from the hallway.

"Sounds like another pissed off girlfriend," said Spock, checking his watch.

"Must be for you," said Atlas, smiling at Niner.

"Ha ha. I'll have you know I leave all my women very *disappointed*, not angry."

"Help! Please!"

"Okay, jokes over," said Dawson, nodding toward Spock who was closest to the door. Spock rose and looked through the peephole, waving off the weapons. "It's one of Jones' staff." He opened the door and stepped back as Tammy Clavin burst in, her face ashen, her eyes wide with terror.

"You've gotta help me!" she cried, her eyes flitting from one operator to the next, finally settling on Dawson.

"What's wrong?" he asked, donning his shoulder holster as the others did the same.

"I was supposed to be in a meeting with Mr. Jones and the senior staff but no one is answering the door, and I think I heard somebody moving

140

inside, but I'm not sure. I saw drag marks on the hallway carpet." She took a large sip of her coffee. "I think something's wrong!"

Dawson holstered his weapon and stepped forward, taking the coffee. "I think you've had enough of that," he said, placing it on a table. "You stay here, we'll check it out. Don't open this door unless it's one of us, understood?"

She nodded, looking about as if not sure what to do. Dawson directed her toward a chair by the phone. "Sit here. Wait for us. If we're not back in fifteen, call 9-1-1. Understood?"

"Y-yes."

Dawson shoved the comm piece in his ear, activating it as they left the room. "Sawhorse this is Deacon One, come in, over."

Nothing.

He tried again.

Still nothing.

"Comms are working but no reply." He pointed at Atlas and Spock. "You two take the west stairwell, we'll take the east."

Niner took point as the others sprinted down the hallway to the other exit. Dawson activated his comm again. "This is Deacon One to anyone on this frequency, do you copy, over?"

Niner opened the door cautiously, peering up and down the stairwell before proceeding, Dawson following as again his communications attempt failed. They covered the flights quickly, soon at the tenth floor where Jones and his core team were staying. Niner peered through the small window and shook his head.

"Nobody."

Dawson frowned. "Not good." He activated his comm. "Deacon Zero-Two, Deacon Zero-One, in position, over."

Atlas responded. "Zero-Two in position, over."

"Zero-Two, Zero-One, proceed in three… two… one… Execute."

Niner pulled the door open and Dawson stepped through, checking left and right then advancing, Niner slightly behind him, Atlas and Spock pressing toward them from the other end, the floor empty the entire way.

Dawson paused, something on the floor catching his eye, a wet spot on the carpet. He knelt down and dabbed a finger in it.

Blood.

He showed it to Niner then wiped it on his pants as they continued. The two teams met at Jones' door, Dawson pointing at the drag marks on the floor, the others acknowledging with a nod. Clearly something was wrong. There should have been six Secret Service agents on the floor and the marks on the carpet definitely looked like bodies had been dragged.

But the only blood was the few spots near the elevators.

Maybe they were forced to surrender.

He looked at the carpet, there easily half a dozen distinct sets of drag marks.

Then why wouldn't they have just walked?

He held an ear to the door and heard nothing. Standing to the side, he knocked three times. "This is Agent White, please open the door!"

Nothing.

He knocked.

Harder.

There was a faint sound, as if someone was yelling against a gag.

Dawson pulled the keycard for the room and swiped it, the light turning green as a click sounded. Niner pressed down on the handle then pushed the door open, shoving a boot in to hold it as Dawson burst through followed by Atlas and Spock. He quickly swept the room, left to right, ignoring the ten bodies on the floor.

142

"Clear!" he shouted as he advanced on the closed bedroom door, Spock at his back. He threw open the door, revealing a darkened room, then reached over and flicked on the lights, the room empty. He advanced around the far side of the bed, looking behind the curtains as Spock checked the ensuite bathroom.

"Clear!" called Spock as he returned to the bedroom.

Dawson turned to leave when he heard a whimper. He froze, raising his fist and cocking an ear. He pointed to the bed, aiming his weapon, Spock doing the same.

"Come out from under the bed now, hands first."

"O-okay, d-don't shoot."

He recognized Constance Jones' voice immediately. "Mrs. Jones, is that you?"

"Y-yes."

"It's okay, it's Agent White. I'm part of your husband's security detail. It's safe, you can come out."

"O-okay."

The woman was terrified, that much was clear. A hand appeared from under the low hanging bed covers, a moment later the other. The frail woman slowly emerged and Dawson helped her to her feet, directing her to the sit on the bed. "Are you okay?"

She nodded.

"Did they do anything to you?"

She shook her head. "No, I just heard the shouts and I crawled under the bed. I heard the door open then someone walking around, then it closed again. That was it until you came in."

"Did you see them?"

She shook her head. "No, just his shoes."

"His. So it was a man?"

She shrugged. "Or a woman with huge feet."

Dawson smiled. "You never know."

"They're coming to," said Atlas from the door, his deep voice causing the woman to flinch.

Dawson nodded then turned back to Constance. "You stay here, I'll be right back."

"My husband?"

He glanced at Atlas who shook his head.

"We don't know yet," said Dawson. "But there's no evidence that he's been hurt so let's not jump to any conclusions." He put a hand on her shoulder. "Give me a few minutes, okay?"

She nodded, her shoulders slumping.

Dawson stepped back into the suite, everyone's bonds and gags removed, some still out cold, others in various stages of recovery.

"What took them out?" he asked.

"Looks like tranquilizer darts," said Niner, holding one up. "Nobody's been hurt."

"And the blood?"

"I shot one of them," said a groggy agent. "I know he went down. They opened up on us and after that"—he shrugged—"I have no clue."

"How many?"

"I saw six I think."

"Yeah, six," said another agent, pushing himself to his feet. "They came off the elevator, opened fire on Larry and Marsha and before we knew what was happening they had taken out Tom and Arnie at the west position. The only reason they didn't get us right away was because some of the staff were in the way, but once they were down that was it, they had clear shots as soon as we did." He frowned, shaking his head. "They were quicker."

Dawson twigged on something. "Why were the staff in the hallway?"

"We were asked to leave."

Dawson turned to find Russell Saunders sitting in a chair, his head dangling between his knees. "Explain."

"Mr. Jones had a private meeting—"

"Mr. Quaid."

"Yes. He wanted to talk to Mr. Jones alone so we cleared the room."

"How long after did the hostiles appear?"

Saunders' eyebrows narrowed. "Huh?"

"The bad guys."

"Oh, umm, five minutes maybe?"

"At most," said the Special Agent in Charge, McCarthy, one of the last to wake up, he evidently taking more shots than the others. "Have you called this in?"

"Not yet. Comms are down and we've just secured the room."

"Understood. Status?"

"Mr. Jones and Mr. Quaid appear to be the only ones missing. Mrs. Jones is in the bedroom, she hid under the bed but saw nothing of use. Everyone was taken out by what appear to be tranquilizer darts. Tests will confirm it."

"Okay, I'll call it in." McCarthy pulled out his phone and stepped into the hallway. Dawson nodded toward Atlas. "Go bring Miss Clavin up here."

"Yes, sir."

Atlas followed McCarthy out, Dawson turning to Spock and Niner. "You two cover the hallway until backup arrives. Shoot anything that doesn't immediately cooperate." Niner grinned. Dawson held up a finger. "Try to wound them." Niner pouted, Dawson pointing at the door with a "get out now" expression.

"What's on your back?"

Dawson turned to see everyone looking at Saunders as he rose. "Turn around."

Saunders did a bit of a spin, trying to see his back like a dog chasing his tail, but Dawson had seen enough, shouting at Niner. "Stop that phone call!"

Niner sprinted into the hall, shouting at McCarthy to hang up as Dawson stepped over and pulled off a paper taped to Saunders' back.

Tell anyone and he dies.

Acton Residence, St. Paul, Maryland

Acton jammed his thumb down on the top of his Corona, tipping it upside down, watching the lime slowly rise to the bottom.

"Does it really make a difference?" asked Sandra Milton, watching the display for probably the thousandth time in their friendship.

Acton shrugged, slowly tipping the bottle upright, the lime wedge's journey complete. "I've been doing it since college, why stop now?"

Milton cleared his throat. "We did a lot of things in college that we don't do now."

Acton took a swig, the distinct tang of the fresh lime making all the difference. He rested the bottle on his knee. "Name one."

"Umm…"

Acton winked at Sandra. "See, either he's lying or what he used to do in college is too embarrassing to say in front of his wife."

"Umm…"

Acton put his arm across the back of Laura's chair. "I think I win." He turned to Tommy. "Now, back to what we were talking about. You said that someone would have been monitoring the computers for that search phrase. Is there any way we can find out who?"

Tommy shook his head. "There's no way *we* could find out, but somebody probably could if they had access."

"Access to what?"

"The Dark Web. Specifically the Dark Web probably used to monitor this system."

Acton's eyes narrowed. "What the hell is the Dark Web?"

Tommy smiled slightly. "You all of course know what the Internet is."

"I may be dumb but I'm not stupid."

Tommy laughed, waving his hands. "No, I don't mean it that way. What I mean is, you know what the Internet *is*."

Acton frowned, now feeling dumb and stupid.

"Okay, I'll take it from the stunned silence that nobody is willing to admit they don't know what it is. Well, I won't bore you with the details because you won't understand it without the technical knowhow, but essentially it is a communications network. It passes data back and forth either completely unencrypted, or sometimes encrypted with accepted protocols, bouncing around between servers all around the world sometimes, before it reaches its intended destination. It's completely decentralized so that in the case of a major outage in one area, it will still work everywhere else."

Milton poked the air with his finger, leaning forward. "That's right. I read about that somewhere. DARPA designed it years ago to be able to survive a nuclear war."

"Gold star for the Dean!"

Milton gave Tommy a little look.

Tommy blushed, discovering how much rope he actually had to dangle from.

"But I read the web was invented in Switzerland, at that CERN thing where they have that collider thingy," said Sandra.

"That's the World Wide Web. Completely different thing. The Internet is a communications platform, the World Wide Web is an interface. Everything you see on your screen is just data, whether it's text or images, it's just data, which is broken down into bits that are transmitted across the Internet. The basic tech of the backbone hasn't really changed that much in decades; it's just become faster and more widespread. And in some cases, more secure."

"The Dark Web?"

"Exactly. See, some people learned long ago that the Internet was just too public for their liking. They dubbed it the 'clearnet'. To allow themselves to take advantage of the infrastructure, but protect themselves from the prying eyes of the public and law enforcement, they created darknets, which are networks that run on top of the Internet, but require specific hardware or software to use them. Some even use the Internet as a gateway to an entirely separate, private network that can be global in itself."

Milton whistled. "Sounds like spy stuff."

"It is in some cases. So if I have a special darknet interface in my home, I send my data through it, it goes onto the public network, but only someone with the same software or hardware can access that data. To anyone else it's just gibberish. Or, I can send my data to a specific device on the public Internet, encrypted of course, and then it can be a jumping off point to send that data, and any replies, across a separate, private network without anyone ever knowing."

"Sounds sinister," said Laura as Acton took another swig of his beer. "And this is legal?"

"Sure, the tech is legal, what you do with it might not be. Child pornographers live on the darknet, so do piracy sites, arms dealers, you name it. But it's also used for innocent things like anonymous Bitcoin transactions or just the paranoid conspiracy crowd who don't want 'the man' monitoring them. Like any technology, it can be abused."

"And you think this darknet or Dark Web is how they're monitoring this?"

"Possibly. What I do know is that we need someone with a lot more access than we have in order to check this out."

"Any suggestions?"

"Know any spies?" asked Tommy, laughing.

Acton, Laura and Milton all exchanged glances.

"What?" asked Sandra, suddenly noticing.

"Nothing," replied Milton a little too quickly.

"Nothing," said Acton, draining his beer.

It might be time for some Kraft Dinner.

Unknown Location, New Orleans, Louisiana

Christopher Jones sat at a table, the chair he was in quite comfortable, though his trip here hadn't been the most pleasant. He had been led out at gunpoint and taken via the freight elevator to the basement where he was put into the back of a black SUV with heavily tinted windows. Once clear of the hotel a hood had been placed over his head and they had driven for less than fifteen minutes where he found himself placed in a chair after a brief elevator ride, the hood removed.

A large wall filled with flat screens came to life, a dozen silhouetted faces appearing.

"Show him the letter," said a man's voice, distorted, the effect disturbing enough to send a shiver up and down his spine, his heart already pounding with fear.

A fear he was keeping hidden from his captors as best he could.

Quaid stepped out of the shadows, producing an envelope. He held it up, showing the scrawl on the front.

To my family.

Jones' eyes narrowed as Quaid removed a single piece of paper from inside, unfolding it gently before handing it over. Jones took it, his eyes narrowing further as he read it.

To whom it may concern,

My name is Brett Jones. For several years now I have been under the employ of an organization that is tremendously powerful and ruthless. When I met the love of my life,

Margo, I decided I had to leave this organization in order to have a life with her. Unfortunately as part of this, I betrayed the organization and was discovered.

In exchange for letting me and Margo live, I was forced to write this letter, committing any future children and grandchildren to fulfill any demand this organization might have in the future.

If you are reading this now, then they have for some reason decided to make good on their threat.

I'm truly sorry for this.

Please do not ignore them. These people are ruthless and won't hesitate to kill you and the ones you love.

May God forgive me for what I did. I never realized the ones I would hurt would be the ones I loved.

Yours,

Brett Jones

Jones re-read the letter, his skepticism growing, not sure what to make of it. He recognized the name of course, Brett Jones his grandfather, dead many years ago, but who was he talking about, and why would he possibly think his children and grandchildren would have to repay some debt of his a century later? It was preposterous.

He handed the letter back, saying nothing.

"Do you have any questions?" asked Quaid.

Jones shrugged. "No."

"So you'll cooperate?" Even Quaid sounded skeptical.

Jones nodded toward the letter. "I don't know what you expect me to say. You've shown me a letter that *might* be from my grandfather, who's been dead for almost forty years. What could possibly make you think I would pay any attention to it?"

This seemed to be the response Quaid had been expecting. He smiled, that same, "you're so naïve" smile that Jones wanted to wipe off his face every time he saw it. "Mr. Jones, I'm going to explain something to you, so listen carefully. The employers your grandfather referred to are from an organization so powerful, you couldn't possibly comprehend. This organization is eternal, has been around for longer than the country we both love so dearly, and are the ones financing your campaign because they believe in you and your policies." He held up a finger. "For the most part." He smiled, as if there was room for humor in this situation. "These people also do not tolerate dissent or failure, and when one agrees to work for them, one makes a commitment. A long-term commitment. In your grandfather's case, the price for leaving the employ of the organization, with the wealth he had stolen, was the next two generations of his family."

Jones looked at Quaid. The man clearly believed every word he was saying, and the fact he himself was here suggested at least part of what Quaid was saying was true. Clearly these people had power and money and were ruthless.

Yet so were criminals.

"That's ridiculous."

Quaid's smile broadened slightly. "What did your grandfather do for a living?"

Jones was about to blurt out a reply when he stopped himself, thinking back on the family stories. His grandfather had been in the military at one point, but other than that, he had no real clue. He had just been "grandpa", and nothing more. They had always been fairly wealthy. Nothing insane, just very well-to-do. "I-I don't know."

"Your grandfather was in the military. Did you know that?"

Jones nodded.

"He was dishonorably discharged, but his skill level was very high so my employers hired him."

"Your employers weren't alive then."

Quaid shook his head gently. "You're failing to grasp the situation. The organization we work for is ancient. No, the people behind me did not hire your grandfather, but those in power at the time did. And your grandfather betrayed their trust, and failed to fulfill his final mission, instead stealing a substantial amount of money and gemstones, along with a priceless painting that risked compromising the mission."

"I know nothing of that."

"Of course you don't. Your grandfather's silence was guaranteed when we threatened to kill the woman he loved, your grandmother Margo."

He remembered her. She was so full of life, always with a smile, always baking pies and banana bread. He closed his eyes, trying to picture the two of them together.

They were so happy.

"I still don't understand what that has to do with me. What my grandfather might have agreed to is irrelevant today. He had no right to commit his children or grandchildren to anything. What you're implying is ludicrous."

"It would be if it were anyone else demanding it, however the organization we work for made a deal. Your grandfather's services were no longer reliable, however his progeny's might be. None of his children had skills that the organization needed, so they were never called upon. But the next generation did have one person who possessed a set of skills that the organization considered valuable."

"You mean me."

"Of course."

"And those skills?"

"Charisma. Ambition. You showed a desire to enter politics from the moment you ran for class president and won. From that point forward we have manipulated things to make sure you won each step of the way, either through financing you or discrediting opponents. Whatever it took to make sure you rose in prominence. All to bring us to this point in time, where you have a legitimate shot at becoming the next President of the United States."

"That—that makes no sense. I won all those elections, fair and square. There were no tricks."

Quaid chuckled. "Yes you did win, but sometimes with a little help. Didn't you ever wonder why any serious challenger you ever faced either dropped out due to some scandal or from funding problems? You won every time, sometimes on your own merits, other times with a little help from us."

Jones' shoulders slumped as he quickly ran through the elections he had been involved in. In college he had won in a landslide when his main opponent was accused of rape, a girl coming forward just days before the election, then recanting and disappearing days after. He had run for city council, his opponent discredited because of personal financial troubles, the bank inexplicably calling several business and personal loans, Jones then capitalizing on the fiscal mismanagement angle.

And his first shot at congress his opponent had died.

His jaw dropped.

"You didn't kill…" He couldn't finish the sentence.

Quaid laughed. "No, that was just luck. Besides, you were going to beat him anyway. I see you're starting to realize that everything you have now you owe to us. We were content to let your grandfather's agreement lapse with your generation should you continue to follow our wishes, but your refusal tonight has forced our hand."

"The Russian sanctions."

"Yes."

Jones shook his head. "I don't understand. If you're so powerful, so ancient like you claim, what do sanctions matter?"

"Sanctions threaten to destabilize the Russian economy. With a megalomaniac in power, it could lead to war, a war we do not desire, nor should you."

Jones inhaled slowly. It was his firm opinion that the Russian leadership had no stomach for a war with a real enemy, nor would they have any hope of winning such a war, their military still formidable, yet no longer the threat it once was despite recent efforts at modernization.

And with an army that still relied upon conscription to fill its ranks, he was certain the volunteer armies of NATO could handily defeat them.

Yet Quaid was right. He didn't want war. Nobody wanted war.

At least on our side.

"If you don't want war, then why wouldn't you want sanctions? Russia is invading and threatening its neighbors. They have to be stopped."

Quaid gave that smile again. "You need not worry about war with Russia. We have contingencies in place to prevent it."

Jones' eyebrows popped. "Such as?"

"None of your concern. Let us just say we have zero concerns."

"Then why?"

Quaid looked at one of the screens with a numeral '1' in the corner. "May I?"

The shadow nodded.

"It is time to rebalance the world."

Jones eye widened. "Excuse me?"

156

"Throughout history the threat of war, and war itself, have driven scientific advancement, bettering mankind. But with modern weaponry, war has the potential to become too destructive, which was why the Mutually Assured Destruction doctrine worked so well for so long. Both sides didn't want war, as they knew they both would be completely obliterated in a nuclear exchange. However, both sides were forced to continually advance their weaponry, and their prestige programs like the space program, to maintain that deterrence balance. But with the collapse of the Soviet Union progress slowed and a new enemy had to be found."

"Terrorism."

"Yes. We've been steering China in the right direction, and they are nearly there, but Islamic fundamentalism unfortunately filled the void. Without the Soviet Union and the Warsaw Pact to focus on, the West turned its attention toward what had been a minor annoyance, and really still is, despite recent events. If the West truly wanted to crush Islamism, it could, but it doesn't. It just wants to keep it contained so it stops killing innocent people. From a technological standpoint, they aren't a challenge, which means there's no scientific development. Iraq and Afghanistan advanced some technologies, but not enough, though there have been some interesting medical advances."

Jones pinched his nose, stifling a sneeze, the air dry. "So what you're saying is we need an enemy that is technologically advanced to compete against."

Quaid snapped his fingers. "Exactly! With Russian oil financing their military development, they have been able to begin modernizing their military, and even have new weapons development programs that are rivaling our own. But that's because we never had the incentive to keep moving forward. The enemy we were fighting used AK-47's and IEDs, slept in caves and didn't have a navy or air force, so why focus on those technologies. Instead we've developed new and better ways to spy on individuals and entire populations, monitor our own citizens, and slowly chip away at the freedoms once enjoyed in the West."

Jones allowed himself a slight chuckle. "You're preaching to the choir on that one."

"I know, which is one of the reasons you've gone so far with us."

Jones straightened in his chair, breathing deeply as he squared his shoulders. "And I think we've gone far enough. If you know me at all, you know that I am a man of principles, and I *cannot* compromise them. No matter how convincing an argument you may make, I personally believe that a weakened Russia is absolutely necessary for world peace. Belligerent powers must be put in their place, otherwise it encourages more belligerence." He shook his head, looking at the screens. "I'm sorry, but I cannot continue this relationship, even if it ultimately costs me the Presidency."

Quaid smiled. "I told them you would say that."

Images suddenly began to flash on the screens, dozens, hundreds, photographs and video clips showing his family, his parents, his wife, their children, his nieces and nephews. Everyone he had ever met related to him, everyone descendant from his grandfather.

Everyone.

Suddenly it all stopped, the screens all black, then a flash as a single image filled them all, spread across the entire wall of panels.

He gasped at the video.

It was his granddaughter Kaitlin, on a swing, her mother—his daughter—pushing the little girl.

All seen through what appeared to be a sniper scope.

He suddenly spotted the red dot dancing on her crisp white Hello Kitty t-shirt, the innocent little girl who cried if she stepped on an ant, who had never hurt a soul in her life, now at the mercy of some madman.

"You wouldn't," he whispered. But he knew they would. Everything he had heard told him these people didn't care about human lives. Or did they? What Quaid had told him suggested they seemed to care about the advancement of human kind as a species, but not the individual. Individuals could be sacrificed for the greater good.

"Please, Chris, these people are serious. They *will* kill your granddaughter, and every single member of the Brett Jones line. Their promise to him was that his entire lineage would be wiped out should their wishes not be fulfilled."

A lump formed in Jones' throat as bile filled his mouth.

"I-I..."

"You *will* cooperate, or they will *all* die."

"N-no, I c-can't. I can't hand the presidency over to you people. You're crazy."

Quaid stood back and pulled his phone out, speed dialing a number. "Take the shot."

"No!" cried Jones, jumping to his feet. "Please, no!"

"Hold on," said Quaid, the image on the screen still showing his daughter pushing little Kaitlin, the two of them laughing and talking. Quaid looked at him. "Do you have something further to say?"

Jones nodded, collapsing in his chair.

"I'll cooperate."

JW Marriott Hotel, New Orleans

"Why am I not making this call?"

Dawson looked at Special Agent in Charge McCarthy as he stormed into the room looking none too pleased. Dawson held up the paper that had been taped to Saunders' back.

"Shit," muttered McCarthy as he took the paper by the corner. "Now what do we do?"

"I see two choices."

"They are?"

"We sit tight and hope Mr. Jones is returned safe and sound."

"I don't like that one. And number two?"

"I use the resources at my disposal to find him."

McCarthy dropped into a chair, waving the paper. "And their warning? What makes you so special that you can ignore it but I can't?"

Dawson smiled. "You wouldn't like what I'd have to do to you if I told you."

McCarthy's jaw dropped in realization. "Ahh, you're one of those guys. I had a feeling. White, Green, Brown and Silver? Come on guys, a little less obvious next time."

Dawson smiled. "I'm sure I have no idea what you're talking about." He wiped the smile off his face. "Now, am I making that call?"

McCarthy thought for a moment then nodded. "Absolutely, but from this moment on we're locked down, understood. All cellphones are turned off and turned in, nobody talks to anybody. We can't risk them finding out we're breaking the one demand we actually have from the kidnappers."

The door opened and Atlas appeared with Miss Clavin, the young woman rushing forward and into the arms of another. "Kitty!" The two sobbed for a moment as Dawson made a mental note to make sure caffeine was kept away from her for the duration. He stepped into the hall, Atlas and Spock guarding either end, no backup on the way.

Atlas joined him. "What's the word?"

Dawson pulled out his phone. "We found a note that said if we told anyone they'd kill him."

"That's a good sign. Means they don't plan to kill him right away unless we don't follow instructions." Atlas nodded at Dawson's phone as he dialed. "What are you doing?"

"Not following their instructions."

Hanauma Bay Nature Preserve, Oahu, Hawaii

CIA Special Agent Dylan Kane kicked with his legs, slicing through the water, his breath held, his snorkel mask providing a spectacular view of the tropical fish in the Hanauma Bay Nature Preserve. Schools of yellowfin goatfish and blueline snapper surrounded him and Leiko, a half-Hawaiian half-Japanese lovely he had met a couple of days ago on Queen's Beach.

It was paradise.

Hawaii was probably his favorite state though he'd never admit that to his parents. His mom would be heartbroken to hear that home wasn't his favorite place to visit. It wasn't that he didn't like where he had been born and raised, it was simply that when he wanted to decompress after an assignment, he preferred laid-back locales where the pace of life was different than the hustle and bustle of modern day America.

Enter Hawaii.

The mainland way of life hadn't completely taken over here yet, and from the Hawaiians he had met over the years, he doubted many of them would let it.

It was the perfect place to fully recover.

And it was his last day.

He had been taken down hard by food poisoning a few weeks ago, his strength totally sapped. It had taken everything he had to suit up and help out Bravo Team when they had been railroaded by Washington, and after he had rescued them, he had pretty much collapsed, exhausted.

He didn't bother returning to Fiji, instead deciding to hit Hawaii and be surrounded by English and modern plumbing with safer kitchens.

But he had milked it long enough, he good to return to work a week ago, but Leiko had delayed that, her delights demanding his attention.

And what delights.

He looked over at her and gave her a thumbs up. Her eyes widened, conveying her happiness, she reaching out and squeezing his hand. He could feel his lungs reaching their limits and pointed up. They kicked toward the surface and Kane gasped for air as he pulled out his mouthpiece, Leiko barely out of breath.

"I don't know how you do it," he said, treading water as he pulled her tightly against him.

"Practice, practice, practice."

Kane laughed. "I thought that was how you got to Carnegie Hall?"

She shrugged. "I don't know about that. But I can tell you where it *will* get you." She leaned in and placed a kiss on him that not only had his heart thumping hard in his chest, it guaranteed he wouldn't be walking out of the water any time soon.

He felt a slight shock on his wrist.

Shit.

His CIA issue watch appeared to be like any other watch. And it was. Just with a few custom upgrades, one of which was a discrete messaging system that would give him a slight tingle to tell him a message was waiting. It allowed him to covertly get intel without anyone else in the room knowing, the jolt strong enough to wake him if necessary, and once removed from his wrist, the pulse wouldn't activate. And should someone else put it on, unless they knew the sequence to press to activate it, it would never signal again.

He didn't give Leiko any indication something was wrong, but he had to get a moment of alone time to check the message.

He broke the kiss.

163

"Let's take this back to the room," he said, running his hand through her hair, her golden brown skin the softest he had felt in a long time, this gorgeous local having all the right curves for his liking.

She nodded, wrapping her legs around his waist and grinding against him, causing him to moan. "I'll race you." She let go, lifting her knees up then pushing off his chest with her feet, diving backward and flipping over, swimming hard for the shore as Kane recovered from the shock, sputtering to clear his pipes from the sucked in water.

Recovered, he took after her, his swimming skills excellent, but this lovely girl had grown up on the water, and there was no beating her.

She climbed out of the water first, turning to watch as he reached the shore, stepping out after her. She looked down at his crotch and giggled.

Damn.

He pulled off his mask and held it at waist level as she grabbed his hand, dragging him toward the hotel parking lot. There were a few snickers, mostly from young guys who he was sure were secretly envious, Leiko a vision with a brain, her day job a marine biologist. He had to admit he had learned more over the past week about what they were seeing under the water than he had in a lifetime. A learning vacation.

Never thought I'd enjoy that.

But if he had teachers half as gorgeous as Leiko in high school, he probably wouldn't have needed Chris Leroux to tutor him so much.

His watch shocked him again.

Yeah, yeah, I'll get to you.

They were at the hotel in minutes and he excused himself, locking the bathroom door and relieving himself as he entered the coded sequence, the watch immediately displaying an alert that one of his private messaging servers, one he kept secret even from the CIA, had received an urgent message.

And there was barely a handful of people who it could be from.

All of whom were more important to him than a roll in the hay.

He stepped out of the bathroom and grabbed his cellphone. "I just need to check my messages."

Leiko popped her bikini top off.

Something else popped.

You're killing me!

He pulled up the secure app and logged in with a thumb scan, the message appearing.

Uh oh.

It was his old professor, a man he had reestablished contact with only recently, Professor James Acton and his new wife magnets for trouble, he having to get involved on more than a few occasions to help them out. But they were good people, and as he read the message, his chest started to tighten slightly.

This could be serious.

And he couldn't help in person, he leaving for an op in less than 24 hours. But he knew people who could.

"I'm sorry, beautiful, but I just got an urgent message from work. I have to deal with something, something confidential—you know the insurance business. Can we meet in say an hour, then I'm all yours?"

Leiko's pout would be genuinely heartbreaking if it weren't for the fact she followed it up with a grin. "No problem, sweet cheeks," she said, picking up her bra then smacking his ass. "I'll be in my room. Call me when you're done."

He stepped closer, pulling her half-naked body against his. "I'll make it up to you."

She reached down and squeezed. "You bet you will. My vacation ends tomorrow too. I am *not* going to have my last night ruined by some insurance investigation."

Kane kissed her, hard, his free hand gripping the back of her head, pulling it tightly against him as he leaned her back slightly.

Then he broke it off, leaving her gasping, her eyes wide.

"Take that to your room," he said with a wink. "We'll be down soon."

"We?" She looked down and giggled. "Oh, *we*." She grinned. "*We* will be anxiously awaiting your arrival."

She put her bikini back on then glided from the room, leaving Kane momentarily distracted.

She's incredible.

He shook his head, trying to rid himself of the image, then dialed.

Operations Center Charlie

The Unit, Fort Bragg, North Carolina

"This is Bravo Zero-One, I need to talk to Control-Actual."

Master Sergeant Mike "Red" Belme jacked in, his eyes narrowed slightly at his best friend's unexpected call. Dawson's team was supposed to be off duty, the Secret Service taking control of the op until morning, but Colonel Clancy had ordered a minimal staffing of the Op Center just in case something went wrong.

Things rarely did, yet no one wanted to be caught with their pants down on an op with an unmanned Op Center.

"Go ahead, Zero-One, this is Control-Actual."

"We've got a situation here."

"Explain."

"Our primary has been kidnapped by at least six hostiles."

Red snapped his fingers, everyone suddenly alert. He hit the mute on his mike. "Make your calls, I want us fully staffed immediately." The two others in the room with him leapt into action as he removed his finger from the mute button. "Any demands?" he asked.

"Negative, except a note was left behind saying they'd kill him if we told anyone."

"Status on the security detail?"

"All were taken out by what appear to be tranquilizer darts. They were dragged into Mr. Jones' room then bound and gagged."

"Is he the only person missing?"

"Negative. The person he was meeting with isn't here either. A Mr. Peter Quaid. He wasn't on our list to vet so I'll need you to check him out. He's apparently the moneyman for the campaign."

Red pointed at one of his team who nodded, already running the name. "Local law enforcement?"

"Negative, we managed to contain the situation for now. Nobody knows he's missing except us."

"What do you need from us?"

"Tap the surveillance video, try to find out what happened, see if you can trace where they went."

"Roger that, we're on it. I'll get back to you in fifteen mikes with an update."

"Roger that."

The call ended and Red picked up the phone. "Time to wake the Colonel."

"Sergeant, we're going to have a problem."

"Why's that?" asked Red, pressing down on the switchhook.

"DC has this operation wrapped up tight. Everything we do is routed through the Secret Service op center, even when we're in control. Some new civilian oversight protocol when operating on home soil after what happened during the coup attempt. If we do anything, they're going to know, and they're going to want to know why. And if there's a leak, the hostiles might hear about it."

Red pursed his lips, thinking for a moment. They needed to be able to access satellite and hotel footage, and probably traffic cameras. On any other given day it wouldn't be a problem, but with the op actually being on American soil, the rules were different. He didn't have a problem with that, it his duty to follow orders, and civilian oversight a good thing.

But not today, not when that very oversight might get their man killed.

Then a thought popped in his head and he smiled.

"Get us our friend at Langley."

Chris Leroux and Sherrie White Residence
Fairfax Towers, Falls Church, Virginia

"You're bad."

"I know. And you like it."

Chris Leroux grinned, eyeing the naked form of his girlfriend as she paraded back and forth in front of the television. Yet she wasn't completely naked. She *was* wearing a hat.

"You like?"

Leroux nodded emphatically. "Me like."

"But you're not even looking at the hat," pouted Sherrie.

"You've got a hat on?"

She pulled it off and whipped it at him like a Frisbee. "You're so mean to me!"

He laughed, tossing it back to her, his throw short, it falling on the floor.

I was never good at Frisbee.

Or any sport for that matter. Leroux considered himself a geek. An introvert for the most part, women something he only fantasized about until he had met Sherrie. They had fallen in love quickly, shoved together by his best friend, Special Agent Dylan Kane, a high school buddy he had tutored for several years. Kane was the jock, the popular kid, but had struggled in high school. Not because he was stupid, but because he had spent too much time enjoying himself rather than applying himself and had fallen behind.

Leroux had been on the list of math tutors in the guidance counsellor's office, Kane picking him for a reason that actually had made Leroux almost cry when it had been confessed to him much later.

170

"I knew you had no friends so you wouldn't have anyone to tell that I was stupid."

At that point they had become friends, and it had made it sting even more. Their friendship through high school had thrived, though it was mostly a secret, Kane coming over to get tutored several nights a week, the two rarely doing anything outside. It wasn't until Kane showed up for his tutoring lesson one night that things changed completely. A particularly nasty bully named Darcy had humiliated Leroux in class, yanking down his pants and boxers in front of the entire English class. In his panic he had tried to run rather than pull them up, causing him to trip over his pants and fall flat on the floor, naked from the ass down.

The laughing and taunting had been merciless.

He had struggled to his feet and pulled his pants up, tears running down his face as he shuffled out of the class, running home and locking himself in his room, swearing to never come out again.

He could hear Kane and his mother talking through the open window but he wasn't sure what was said. Moments later there was a gentle knock on the door. "Hey buddy, can I come in?"

"Go away!"

"Come on, let me in. Tell me what happened."

Leroux reluctantly got up and unlocked the door, leaving it closed. He returned to his bed, shoving himself into the corner, his knees drawn up to his chest as he hugged them.

The door opened and Kane stepped inside, closing it behind him. He grabbed the small office chair from the computer desk and wheeled it to the bed, taking a seat. "Tell me what happened."

Leroux said nothing, instead burying his head deeper behind his knees.

"Listen buddy, I'm your friend. Tell me so I can help you."

Leroux felt a desperate rage grow inside him, finally erupting with a horrible tirade against his one and only friend. "It's people like you who are always picking on me! You jocks think you're so cool, you think you can pick on people like me and it's funny. Well it's not! We have feelings too, you know! Just because we're not popular doesn't mean you get to pick on us all the time. I hate all you jocks! I hate you!"

He had immediately regretted those last few words, the hurt look on Kane's face causing him to nearly vomit. Kane had never made fun of him, never picked on him, even before they had met. In fact, though Kane was a jock, one of the most popular kids in school, he was nice to everyone, including the dorks, geeks, nerds and spazzes.

"I'm sorry, Dylan, I didn't mean it."

Kane had smiled at him, covering up his hurt quickly. "I know you didn't, buddy. Why don't you tell me what happened?"

He did and the rage he saw in his friend was unlike anything he had ever seen before. He rose from his chair, cursing Darcy, swearing he'd get even with him.

And he did.

The next day before school started Leroux arrived to find Darcy duct taped to the flagpole, naked, one of the teachers trying desperately to free him as the entire student body looked on, laughing, Darcy himself in tears.

Darcy had switched schools, and Kane made it crystal clear to everyone that messing with Leroux meant messing with him.

Leroux was never touched again. It didn't mean he suddenly had friends, it simply meant he was no longer terrified of school.

They had drifted apart after high school, Kane ahead of him by a couple of years. Kane went to college then joined the Army after 9/11, Leroux going to college as well then recruited into the CIA as an analyst. He didn't know that Kane had been recruited out of the Delta Force and was essentially a spy for the CIA until a chance encounter in the cafeteria. Their friendship had been renewed, though with Kane's lifestyle, it meant they rarely saw each other.

But now Sherrie filled the void that had always been there. She was gorgeous, way out of his league, yet she had fallen for him while on assignment. Assignment to test his loyalty to the CIA, to test his ability to keep his mouth shut about the things he knew when faced with the greatest temptation possible.

Her.

And he had passed.

She had asked to be reassigned before the ultimate test, the feelings she had developed unexpected, but she had been refused. When he had discovered the truth, in a rather embarrassing fashion, he hadn't wanted to ever see her again.

But Kane had brought them back together, and the rest was history. They were now living together and their relationship continued to grow, despite the ever-watchful eye of their security detail made necessary by their involvement in foiling an attempt by an ancient organization called The Assembly to start a war with North Korea.

It had been stopped, yet at great cost, and the end of their private lives.

It was only when they were alone in the apartment they could be themselves.

And God did he love it.

Sherrie turned around, bending over to pick up her hat, her buttocks making the perfect shape of a heart, reminding him of the purported true origin of the heart symbol now known the world over.

Something stirred, Sherrie looking back at him, still bent over.

"See something you like, big boy?"

He grinned sheepishly. "Umm, yeah, Game of Thrones is starting. You're blocking the screen."

She looked at his crotch. "I don't think you're one hundred percent committed to the television. She spun around, doing a little dance with the hat covering her most private parts.

Leroux turned off the TV.

His phone vibrated.

He glanced at it, his eyes narrowing. "It's work."

"Awww!"

Sherrie plopped on the couch beside him as he flicked his finger across the screen.

"Hello?"

"Hey boss, priority tasking. We need you."

Leroux sighed, recognizing Marc Therrien's voice, a member of his staff working the night shift. "Okay, call in the team, I'm on my way."

"Hope I didn't interrupt anything too important. See you soon."

Leroux ended the call, looking down at what Sherrie was gripping.

No, it wasn't too important. But gawd it was bad timing.

"Sorry, hon, but I've got to go."

She squeezed harder.

"Hon, you're just making this harder than it has to be!" he pleaded as he texted the security detail outside.

"That's the idea, silly!" He gave her the stink eye and she laughed, letting go. "Okay, but you're going to be frustrated all night." She struck a suggestive pose. "Quickie?"

His pants were off in seconds.

Acton & Palmer Residence, St. Paul, Maryland

"Wow, that was fast!"

Acton pointed at the phone and mouthed, "Dylan". It hadn't even been half an hour since he had sent the emergency message to the number Kane had given him, stored in the phone under his reversed initials, KD, or Kraft Dinner. Kane had been an average student when he had taught him, he genuinely interested in archeology, though not sure of what he wanted to do with his life.

That is until 9/11.

Then he knew for certain.

The young man had sought his counsel and he had been happy to give it, he himself former National Guard. He had encouraged the man to follow his heart, it his opinion that a military career was always an excellent choice.

He had never envisioned him becoming a spy for the CIA however, and had been shocked to learn the truth.

Yet thankful he had, his help proving invaluable on numerous occasions.

Including, perhaps, tonight.

"You caught me between assignments. I read your message and I'm a little concerned. It's probably nothing, this Captain may be a thief or an opportunist, who knows, but that security alert is what is setting off my alarm bells."

"Yeah, that's what I was concerned about as well. Can I put you on speaker? Laura, Greg, Sandra, Mai and Tommy are here. I trust them all."

"Go ahead, Doc."

Acton placed the call on speaker and put the phone down on the table. "Okay, you're on speaker. Is there any way to trace who received the alert?"

"Probably, but it will take some doing."

"Someone with Dark Web access?"

A chuckle came through the speaker. "Where did you hear about that, Doc?"

"From Tommy Granger, he's one of our whiz kid grad students."

Tommy blushed, Mai looked almost proud.

"Granger? The one who hacked the DoD mainframe?"

"Umm, yeah," mumbled Tommy, now definitely embarrassed.

"You've got skills, bro. Let's just hope you put them to good use from now on."

Tommy's chin dropped to his chest. "Yes, sir."

Mai squeezed his hand.

Tommy brightened.

Wow! There's definitely something there.

The hand darted away.

"So, Dark Web, huh. Well, it's possible, and if whoever set this up is using it, then it will be much more difficult to trace, but not impossible. The problem is you might just trace it to a dead end. What they'll sometimes do is have their data sent to a specific IP address, the customized hardware at that location will then grab that data, reroute it somewhere, perhaps through a hard line not even connected to the Internet, and then at the receiving end someone is notified. Once used, they never use it again, scrapping the hardware or wiping the software. It depends on how covert they want to go."

"We're assuming pretty deep. This seems to be a conspiracy going back a century that someone still cares about."

"Perhaps, but sometimes the simplest explanation is the most obvious. The Navy might have had a legit reason for monitoring for that particular search. Maybe it had nothing to do with Wainwright and was just the word Titanic that made them curious. It could be as simple as the system thinking he was using it for unauthorized purposes, just trolling the records, and clamped down on him."

Acton's phone vibrated on the table with a news alert, the notification bar at the top of the screen giving the first few words.

Congressman Mahoney Dies in Car Accident.

"Jesus," muttered Acton, grabbing the phone.

"What?" asked Kane.

"You remember in the message I told you that Steve Wainwright had met with his Congressman, and it was *he* who had called the records office?"

"Yeah, why?"

"Congressman Mahoney just died in a car accident. I just got the news flash on my phone."

"Okay, Doc. That changes everything. Do you have a gun?"

Acton felt his chest tighten, the mood of the entire table immediately changing.

"Yes."

"Get it. I'm sending help."

Operations Center Charlie
The Unit, Fort Bragg, North Carolina

"Hey BD, I've got some intel for you."

Master Sergeant Mike "Red" Belme scanned the screen as he fed the executive summary to Dawson. "We ran this Peter Quaid for you on a separate network. Born April 7th, 1962, both parents deceased, only child, inherited his father's business at age twenty-eight, a microchip design company named Silidev. Looks like they make chips for all the big boys like Boeing, GE, Lockheed, NASA, the big three."

"Any red flags on the file?"

"Just one that I can see. He apparently has significant investments in Russia."

"Christ, I knew I should have run him."

"Hindsight's always twenty-twenty. He's their biggest financial backer, how the hell were you supposed to know?"

"If anything happens to Jones, tell that to the inquest." He could hear Dawson sigh on the other end. "Any unusual banking activity? Anything that might suggest why he might be kidnapped with Jones?"

"I don't have that data yet. Langley's coming online now. I'm hoping to have some more intel for you shortly. Anything on your end?"

"Negative. We've confirmed that one of the hostiles was shot, but there's no body so either he walked out or was carried out. Check the local hospitals, but I doubt you'll find anything."

"Descriptions?"

"Yeah. All white males, around six feet tall, all athletic builds with short hair, dark suits and sunglasses."

178

"So no use."

"No. The civilians only saw the guns, two agents were down in seconds, the other four down a few seconds later. This op was executed quickly and effectively. These were pros who risked their own lives to not kill their target. They could have come out shooting with SMGs but they didn't."

"But wouldn't they know their target was in his room?"

Dawson grunted. "Only if they have someone on the inside."

"Do you think they do?"

"There's huge money and huge stakes here so nothing would surprise me. I've confiscated all cellphones just in case."

The door to the Op Center opened and Colonel Clancy entered, his eyes scanning the screens then coming to rest on Red. "Colonel's here, I'll get back to you in fifteen."

"Roger that."

Red ended the call, turning to the Colonel. "Sorry to disturb you, Colonel."

"Sergeant, you just saved me from an evening with my sister-in-law. If it weren't against protocol, I'd kiss you so hard you'd forget you were married."

Red grinned. "Thank God for protocols, sir."

Clancy nodded toward the screens. "Report."

Red began to bring the Colonel up to date as the screens slowly started to flash over to the Langley feeds.

Let's hope Leroux can come through for us!

Operations Center Four

CIA Headquarters, Langley, Virginia

Leroux entered the Operations Center, completely relaxed and free of tension, a smile on his face. It had been the true definition of a quickie, almost reminiscent of his first couple of times with Sherrie. Almost. This time he was pretty sure she had gotten something out of it too other than the realization she was dealing with a rank amateur in the boudoir.

Have fun super stud!

He stifled a grin at her parting words.

"Report."

Therrien stepped forward, remote control in hand as he flashed through the briefing describing the non-lethal attack in New Orleans and the kidnapping of the current front-runner for the Presidency, Christopher Jones. "Any leaks?"

"None yet. Press and local LEOs seem quiet. Secret Service had the floor sealed off anyway so hotel staff aren't allowed on without permission. Mr. Jones had no more appointments for the day so until tomorrow morning, no one will be missing him."

"Family?"

"Wife was with him and safe. He has three kids, one grandchild. Secret Service is moving to secure them as we speak."

Leroux nodded toward the screen. "What have you got so far?"

"We've just tapped into the hotel security cameras. Watch this."

The door opened and they all turned as their boss, Leif Morrison, the National Clandestine Service Chief, entered the room.

"What's this I hear? Christopher Jones has been kidnapped?"

Leroux's eyes popped. "How did you find out?" Morrison gave him a look, sending Leroux's proud nads into hiding. "Sorry, sir, I mean, how, umm, did you find out? I was just told we had no leaks."

"It's my job to know," replied Morrison who then gave Leroux a wink. "I'm notified when emergency requests for Op Centers are made."

Therrien cleared his throat. "Sorry, boss, I, um, forgot to mention that I briefed the Director after I called you."

Leroux waved his hand. "That's fine, I was just worried there was a breach we didn't know about." He pointed at the screen. "What are we looking at?"

"Hotel footage that we've pieced together. Here you can see two black SUVs—we're running the plates now—entering the underground parking garage. Six men exit, go up the elevator, exit on the tenth floor, quickly dispatch the security detail and civilians in the hall." He paused the video. "You can see here one of them is wounded in the shoulder. The unconscious bodies are dragged into the room, but watch this." The video zoomed in as best it could on one of the doors, the angle sharp. It opened without anyone knocking or using a pass. "See that? It was opened from the inside." They all watched as the bodies were dragged inside, then moments later the door opened again and Jones along with another man were led out and to the elevators, where they rode in silence, a gun clearly in Jones' back, but not the other man's. "You can see it looks like the other man we've identified as Peter Quaid, a major contributor to Mr. Jones' campaign, seems to be going with them voluntarily." The two SUVs were loaded, the last footage of them clearing the parking garage and disappearing into the city streets.

"Any traffic camera footage yet?"

"We've just tapped the local feeds. We're running through it now."

"Satellite?" asked Morrison.

"There was a bird over the area during the event, we're pulling the footage now."

"When did this all go down?" asked Leroux.

Therrien looked at the clock on the wall. "The kidnapping took place exactly sixty-two minutes ago."

"I've got something," said Sonya Tong, waving her hand then pointing at one of the screens. It flipped over to a satellite feed. "I've got the two SUVs going under the overpass, but neither coming out."

Leroux and Morrison stepped closer to the screen. "Run it again, from about thirty seconds before they enter until about a minute after." The two SUVs disappeared under the highway, along with two other vehicles right behind them. Leroux mentally counted, the other two vehicles reappearing as expected, the SUVs nowhere to be seen. Another vehicle disappeared then moments later reappeared, followed by two large sedans. He snapped his fingers at the screen. "That's them. Grab their plates and run them. See if you can follow them."

"Yes, sir."

"And notify the team in New Orleans. They'll want to check out that underpass."

Wainwright Residence, Collette Court, Odenton, Maryland

Nadja Katz opened the rear door of the house, a standard upper middle-income home in a newer, upscale neighborhood, her intel suggesting the home was worth nearly a million dollars, the Wainwrights obviously doing well in retirement. Her file said he had bought the first local McDonalds franchise decades ago and parlayed it into a decent sized restaurant empire, owning several dozen by the time he sold off a bunch of them for his retirement, divvying the rest up for his children.

They had money.

And a piss poor security system.

It had been easily bypassed after she had confirmed the house was empty, the Wainwrights at his sister's place for dinner, no doubt eagerly discussing the painting they had found. After Congressman Mahoney had peed his pants, he had spilled everything he had known.

Coward.

The beating was enough to break most men, though she had encountered a few in her career that hadn't. That was when the families were brought into play. And for those few who still held out, she felt nothing when the bullet tore open the target, the called bluff never a bluff.

Not with her.

She was good at her job because she was ruthless when necessary, and in her line of work, too often that was necessary. She had stopped counting how many people she had killed, certainly many dozens, if not over a hundred. It didn't matter, they of no consequence to her. She found the emotions portrayed by her targets curious at times, especially when a loved one was killed in front of them due to their lack of cooperation.

She felt nothing.

For anything.

Life was a job. You did it until you could do it no more. Why cloud things with emotions, relationships, family? Her parents had been killed by a drunk driver when she was five, she herself suffering head trauma that the doctors later told her had damaged her prefrontal cortex from which she might never recover.

She felt fine, though at times, including her parent's funeral, she had to fake her emotions, the tears for the delayed service forced for the benefit of those in attendance.

None of whom had taken her in. Ten years in a foster care system that had her ferried between alcoholics and pedophiles were probably easier on her than the others, her emotions dulled to the point nothing bothered her, even a fat old bastard sodomizing her three times a week.

Yet he had been the last. Something inside had snapped one night when she lay face down on the bed, her foster "father" preparing for his latest "lesson". Something inside had finally said no, said enough is enough. She had reached over, grabbed a pencil from her nightstand and spun around backhanded, plunging it deep into his ribcage, just missing his heart, though puncturing a lung.

It had been a lucky shot, the assault over.

She had dressed and walked out as he gasped for breath on the bed, his naked, hairy girth jiggling from the effort.

She had never bothered checking to see if he had died that day.

Several years on the street had toughened her up even further, then she had fallen in with Dietrich, a man thirty years her senior, who taught her the trade. A former Stasi spy, he took her in off the street when he caught her stealing from his store, a small repair shop in a back alley of a dingy street in what was once East Berlin.

He had caught her and taught her, giving her a purpose. And for the first time in her life she found she was actually interested in something. She found it somehow fulfilling, learning how to repair things like watches and electronics, while also learning how to put those skills to work picking locks, cracking safes, and defeating alarm systems.

And when she had become adept, he had put her to work.

And she had excelled, the old man apparently never having really left the spy business, his skillset for hire to anyone who could pay his fees, fees that he happily gave her a cut of, he treating her like a daughter, he the closest thing to a father that she could remember.

When he died she had felt little, his still body lying in bed, he having died peacefully in his sleep of what she assumed were natural causes, though in his business one could never be certain. She had called it in anonymously, taking anything of value that she could carry.

Including his cellphone.

A cellphone that kept ringing with jobs.

Which she began to fulfill, working her way up in the business until one day she received a call that changed everything. Within weeks of that first, strange meeting, she was working exclusively for an organization she knew nothing about, except that they were extremely well-funded and the jobs were challenging, global and quite often violent.

Something she had no problem with.

At all.

She casually searched the house, not bothering with most of the drawers, what she was looking for specific. The computer had been hacked earlier in the day, all data already pulled, somebody reviewing it for anything of value. From what she could tell Steve Wainwright had stumbled upon a family secret a century old, and unfortunately for him it meant the end of a successful life.

But not yet.

Not tonight.

Everything had to be done in its proper order otherwise the infection could risk spreading. Already there was another problem in New Orleans that might require her involvement, though for now this was her primary task. Stop the infection in Maryland from spreading any further. In order to do that, she needed to know everyone he had told.

And in order to make a man like that talk, she needed leverage.

She opened a kitchen drawer near an old style rotary phone and felt the corners of her lips turn up slightly.

An address book.

You gotta love senior citizens.

She flipped through it, jammed with handwritten names and addresses including a hefty listing of Wainwrights across the nation.

She had her leverage.

Now it was time to find out how much farther the infection had spread.

Gentilly Boulevard, New Orleans, Louisiana

Niner brought the SUV to a halt, blocking the lane, the emergency vehicle lights integrated into their government issue vehicle flickering off the walls of the underpass, the dim lighting, coated in road grime and exhaust pipe soot casting a dull glow over the area. Dawson exited the vehicle with the others, approaching it cautiously, weapon raised. He fully expected both to be abandoned, yet they couldn't take any chances.

"Federal authorities! Come out with your hands up, now!"

Niner and Spock swung to the front of the two vehicles, Niner shaking his head when he had a view through the windshield. Atlas took the passenger side of the rear vehicle, Dawson the driver side, confirming it clear as well.

"Check for booby traps."

Dawson wasn't expecting any lethal surprises, the method in which the security detail had been taken out earlier suggesting killing law enforcement officers wasn't their intention. The team, experts at this, quickly cleared the exterior of the vehicles and did a visual inspection through the windows.

Dawson ordered the others back then tried the unlocked door of the rear SUV, deciding against getting out the rip kit as time was their enemy. He winced slightly as he opened it.

No explosions.

Niner did the same on the lead vehicle and soon all four were searching. Dawson went through the usual haunts up front, as Atlas took the rear. There was nothing in the glove compartment beyond registration papers that matched what they already knew.

Avis rentals, Red already running down who had ponied up for the vehicles.

"I've got blood!"

Dawson stepped out of the vehicle, looking to where Spock was searching. Spock pointed at the back seat. "Blood on the back of the rear seat. Not much so I'm guessing they got the bleeding stopped."

"Okay, take samples for DNA. The keys are in this one—"

"Same here!" called Niner.

"Let's lock them up and save it for the Local LEOs when we invite them in." He pointed to Niner. "And put a couple of tracking devices on these, just in case someone decides to move them."

"Roger that," said Niner, returning to their own vehicle to retrieve his bag of tricks.

Dawson's phone vibrated in his pocket. He answered it with a swipe. "Hey, BD, it's Red. We've got a possible location on your guy. We traced the vehicles to an office tower not too far from you. I've sent the details to your phone."

"Just a second." Dawson brought up the secure text then tapped the location, a map appearing with an automatic routing displayed. Ten minutes away. "Got it, ETA ten minutes." He slammed the doors on his side shut, the others doing the same, then locked it with the fob as he climbed into their vehicle. He held up his phone to the others as he put it on speaker. "Red traced the vehicles to an office tower about ten minutes from here. Let's go."

Niner put the vehicle in gear and pulled out into the light traffic, it slowed by the lookyloos, as Dawson punched the address into the onboard navigation system.

"Do you want us to send backup?" asked Red.

"Negative, too many guns, we can't risk the candidate."

"Roger that."

"Do you have eyes on the building?"

"Negative, no birds are over the area at the moment."

Niner took a sharp right, Dawson pretty sure his side of the vehicle actually left the pavement. He gave him a look. Niner grinned. "What can you tell me about the building?"

"Constitution Tower. Mostly financial firms, but get this, the first two floors are reserved for those corporate image packages, you know, where small companies share facilities."

"Got you, anything standing out?"

"We're running the companies now, but we won't know anything before you get there. ETA?"

Niner glanced at the phone. "If BD wasn't giving me the stink eye constantly, five minutes, but probably seven."

Red laughed at the other end.

"Good hunting."

Unknown Location, New Orleans, Louisiana

The screens flicked off, one by one, Christopher Jones not sure what would happen now. Peter Quaid still stood in front of him, that infuriating smile still plastered on his face, and in the shadows he knew there were at least several of the gunmen that had brought him here.

"You won't be seeing me for a few days as I have business in Moscow. But we'll meet when I return."

Jones glared at him, his stomach still churning, his heart still pounding, his entire body drenched in sweat, he not yet recovered from the very real threat to kill his granddaughter.

And his entire family.

"Why, Pete, why would you get involved with such people?"

The smile slowly faded and for the first time he could have sworn he sensed a hint of regret in the man's eyes.

And a little fear.

"Sometimes you wake up one day and realize the life you once thought was your own, actually isn't, and maybe never was. Much like you've just been woken up." He sat in another chair Jones' hadn't noticed in the darkness before. "Listen, my friend, I'm sorry this had to happen to you. But don't blame me, I'm just the messenger here." He jerked a thumb over his shoulder at the blank screens. "Even *I* don't know who they are. I work for them, just like you do. Unfortunately for you the choice was made for you a century ago by someone you barely remember. Your grandfather made a stupid mistake betraying these people and now you're paying the price." He leaned forward. "But think about it. What price? You're going to be the most powerful man in the world very soon. They *will* make that happen. You *will* be sitting in the White House, and almost every decision you make will be yours. But in some cases, a few cases, they won't be." Quaid shrugged. "My life is mostly my own, but occasionally I have to do things like I did today. I've learned to live with it, and so will you."

Jones gripped the arms of his chair. "You and I, sir, are apparently two very different people."

Quaid frowned, immediately picking up on the implied insult. "Perhaps we are. Or perhaps we once were very similar, and in time, will be again." Quaid rose, extending his hand. "Until we meet again."

Jones ignored the outstretched hand.

Quaid shrugged. "In time, Chris, you'll realize I saved your life tonight." He leaned in, his voice low. "Whatever you do, don't tell anyone what happened here tonight, or they *will* kill you. No matter how well protected you think you are after tonight, they will *always* find a way to get to you. And your family." He rose. "Your story is this: you and I were kidnapped by unknown assailants. You were brought here, you don't know where they took me. They threatened your life if you didn't stop talking about the Russian sanctions, then they left."

Jones' eyes narrowed. "Doesn't that defeat the entire purpose?"

Quaid smiled that infuriating smile again. "The truth is the best lie to tell. You will, however, be deeply affected by this, and will over the coming days tone down your rhetoric, and eventually, when you are in power, will drop the sanctions as a goodwill gesture. The minutia will be figured out later by people smarter than us. For now, just remember you were yelled at a lot then left alone. You don't know who they are, what happened to me, and just want to move forward. As far as you're concerned, the case is closed. Got it?"

Jones nodded and Quaid slapped him on the shoulder, walking away.

"What do I do?" asked Jones, turning in his chair.

"You wait."

"For how long?"

Quaid chuckled.

"Not long, my friend, not long."

Assembly Covert Communications Facility, Moscow, Russia

"The infection continues to spread," said Number One, Ilya Mashkov sipping his tea, it now five in the morning in Moscow. He had been woken by his butler, Dimitri, a trusted man provided by The Assembly.

Urgent business.

It's always urgent with them.

He didn't trust his butler as far as he could throw him. He was an Assembly man which meant his loyalties were to them, not him. Though he never had any intention of betraying them, there was always the chance he could screw up one day, and Dimitri would be there to catch him.

And report back.

Then he'd most likely be dead.

It meant he never felt comfortable in his own home, which sort of defeated the purpose of being "all powerful". He was trying to ignore the man's background, and at times he was able to forget, and perhaps eventually he'd put his foibles behind him—after all, The Assembly seemed to be all seeing, all knowing, so if he were to screw up, then there'd be no way they wouldn't find out, butler or no butler.

He took another sip of his tea, a brilliant concoction from Dimitri that was one of the many reasons he wished he could trust the man, he spectacular at his job.

"What is it this time?" asked Number Two.

"Our agents are reporting increased Internet traffic involving the painting."

"Is it still localized to the same geographic region?"

"Negative, it's now going global. We have significant search traffic originating from St. Paul's University and the surrounding area, as well as the Smithsonian and several other academic institutions and museums around Europe."

"And there's no chance this is simply a coincidence?" asked Mashkov, almost instantly regretting it, all the silhouettes freezing for a moment as if in stunned silence at his stupidity. "What I mean is, are we sure there hasn't been some new reference to it in a movie that may have spurred a temporary blip. I would expect that after the release of the James Cameron movie and the recent hundredth anniversary, search related traffic would have spiked. Perhaps that's all we're seeing now."

Number One decided to humor him. "I don't believe so. Our NSA sources have provided us with copies of several emails sent from St. Paul's University and a residence in St. Paul where a professor claims to have the painting in his possession, and means to authenticate it posthaste."

Mashkov frowned. "That's unfortunate."

"Indeed. A forgotten painting, unknown to all but a few, is suddenly a hot topic among academia. And should this painting actually be authenticated, it could be a disaster for us. Too many questions will be asked."

"Do we know who this professor is?"

"Yes. Professor James Acton."

Mashkov's eyes narrowed. "Why does that name sound familiar?"

"You might remember him from the report on our two CIA headaches, Dylan Kane and Chris Leroux. Professor Acton was Kane's teacher at university, the one who apparently encouraged him to join the Army."

"I thought we had ordered Leroux and Kane eliminated?"

"We did, but it has to appear as an accident and unfortunately that has proven difficult with Kane being a deep-cover operative and Leroux constantly accompanied by a CIA security detail."

Mashkov pursed his lips, nodding slowly. "Perhaps we need to draw Special Agent Kane out."

"How do you mean?"

"With a little bait."

Constitution Tower, New Orleans, Louisiana

Niner pulled into the office complex, the visitor parking out front mostly empty, only a few stray vehicles in view, though to the right there were ramps that lead to underground parking. As he slowly drove up to the front of the building Atlas cursed.

"Is that who I think it is?"

Dawson turned to see what Atlas was looking at.

A large black sedan matching the description of the vehicle that had left the underpass earlier.

"Can you see the plate?"

"Not from this angle."

"Park."

Niner nodded, swinging into a spot. The sedan drove past, the license plate light giving them a nice view.

"That's them," confirmed Atlas, holding up his phone with the plate numbers. Suddenly the car surged ahead, careening sharply onto the road.

"Gee, boss, do you think we've been made?" asked Niner as he hammered on the gas, jumping a curb and ending the useful life of two small pine trees. Niner glanced in his rearview mirror before cranking the wheel and flooring it. "Good thing Marty didn't do that, hey?"

"Huh?"

"Would they have called it No Pine Mall?"

Niner hammered the brakes, taking off some speed as he made another sharp turn, his mad skills getting them closer.

"Are you on your damned movie references again?" asked Spock as he rolled down his window, prepping his weapon.

"When do we ever leave them?" asked Niner as they continued to gain, the engine in the government issued law enforcement vehicle impressively tuned. "So, if Marty McFly had run over both trees with the DeLorean, what would Old Man Peabody have named the mall?"

"You datin' anyone?" asked Atlas as he leaned out the window.

Several gunshots rang out, Niner not bothering to swerve, the ballistic windshield able to withstand most small arms fire. "No, why, your sister single?"

"Neeever gonna happen, little man."

"Hey, easy there, big fella. I've showered with you so I know stereotypes are bullshit."

Atlas' eyes shot wide open. "What are you trying to say?"

"Taking out the tires," said Dawson, ending the verbal castration. He took a bead on the right rear tire and opened fire as the sedan skidded around another corner, three quick shots, two finding their mark, the tire shredding within seconds, sparks flying from the steel rim as the car rapidly slowed then came to a halt, all four doors bursting open as those inside jumped out in a hail of gunfire.

Niner skidded to a halt, positioning the vehicle directly behind the hostiles as he drew his own weapon, he and Dawson opening fire on the gunmen as Atlas and Spock in the rear threw open their doors, stepping out and joining in.

It lasted only seconds, all four gunmen down, all four Delta operators unscathed.

"Don't shoot!" shouted someone from inside the car.

"Come out with your hands up!" ordered Dawson as he opened his door and stepped out, using its reinforced skin as a shield.

"Okay, I-I'm coming out."

A pair of hands appeared, then a foot followed by another, Peter Quaid finally appearing, shaking like a leaf. "M-my name is Peter Quaid. I was kidnapped with Christopher Jones, you know, the man running for President?"

Dawson motioned for Atlas and Spock to advance, the two men immediately rushing forward, weapons aimed at Quaid. They quickly cleared the vehicle, then patted down the still quaking civilian.

"He's clean," said Atlas, stepping back, the first sirens of local police sounding in the distance.

"Where's Mr. Jones?" asked Dawson, stepping forward.

"I-I don't know. I haven't seen him since they took us from the hotel."

"Did you both get in the same vehicle?"

The man hesitated for a moment. "Umm, yes."

"And after the switch?"

"I-I'm not sure, we had hoods on. I think so, maybe. I-I just don't know!"

"BD, if we're going to keep a lid on this, we better book."

Dawson nodded. Atlas was right. "Okay, take him with us. Let's get back to that office tower, see what we find."

Atlas and Spock each grabbed an arm and half carried, half walked the man to the SUV, helping him into the back before climbing in themselves. Niner quickly pulled a U-turn, guiding them around the light evening traffic that had been caught up in the mess, casually turning down a side street as onlookers gawked.

Onlookers who had cellphones out, recording everything they saw.

"Shit!" muttered Niner.

"I guess there's no keeping a lid on this now," said Atlas.

This just turned into a Charlie-Foxtrot.

Unknown Location, New Orleans, Louisiana

Lights flickered on, the entire room bathed in a sudden harsh, white light, startling Christopher Jones from his reverie of self-pity. He turned to see a janitor backing into the room, pulling his cart, earbuds entertaining him during his lonely shift.

Jones looked around. It appeared to be some sort of hi-tech conference room, a long, oval table in the center with a bank of monitors filling one entire wall, empty chairs ringing the table.

Empty chairs.

He breathed a sigh of relief, pushing himself up from his seat then straightening his tie and jacket, running his fingers through his hair before he squared his shoulders and walked out a door at the opposite end, the janitor not noticing him.

He saw a sign for the elevators and walked toward them as calmly as he could, realizing he was doubtless on security cameras. Pressing the button, the elevator immediately chimed, probably left there by the janitor. He stepped on, hitting the button for the main lobby.

As the doors closed, he ran through his story in his mind, still not sure if he wanted to go through with it.

They're going to kill Kaitlin if you don't.

Bile filled his mouth and he took a quick breath, realizing he had no choice. He had to follow their instructions.

Then when he became President, he'd devote every resource he had to finding and destroying this organization.

Starting with Peter Quaid.

The doors opened and he stepped out into the lobby of what appeared to be a Class-A building. To say any of this was what he expected would be a mistake. Before the janitor's arrival, he had visions of a James Bond super-villain lair, or an abandoned warehouse in a seedy part of town.

Not what appeared to be a modern office building.

A security guard behind the desk nodded to him. "Good night, sir."

"Ah, g-good night," he stammered, not sure of what to do. Should he order a taxi? Call the police? Call the Secret Service?

Not the police, they'll ask too many questions.

He could call the Secret Service, though he wouldn't even know how to begin without raising suspicions.

Call the room at the hotel?

That seemed to be the wiser idea. By now for sure the Secret Service would be there.

And his wife.

Constance!

He had totally forgotten about her in all this. What had happened to her? Was she okay? He had seen the bodies dragged into the room before he was taken—staff and agents. Did they kill her as well?

He had to know.

"Can I borrow your phone?"

The guard nodded, lifting the phone up and placing it on the counter. "Dial nine for an outside line."

"Thanks."

He lifted the receiver and hit 9 when tires squealed outside and headlights beamed into the lobby. He looked toward the door, the guard rising as four doors of an SUV were thrown open and men piled out.

Men with guns.

He slowly backed away from the door as the men advanced on the main entrance.

"I've got a situation here!" shouted the now panicking guard, his weapon drawn, a radio in the other hand pressed to his mouth. "Four armed gunmen!"

The lobby was still well lit which meant those outside had a clear view of the two of them. One of them raised his hands and reached into his pocket, producing a wallet. He held a badge up against the glass and shouted, his voice muffled.

"Federal authorities! Lower your weapon!"

And Jones recognized the voice immediately.

Agent White!

"Th-they're with me!" he cried excitedly, motioning for the guard to lower his gun. Jones raised his hands and rushed toward the doors as White and the others entered, their weapons aimed at the floor, though still at the ready as they cleared the lobby. The Asian one disarmed the guard, leading him back to his chair, the poor man still shaking.

"Are you okay, sir?" asked Agent White.

"Y-yes. How d-did you find me?"

"Satellite footage. We traced the vehicles. Are they still here?"

"I don't think so." He looked over his shoulder, toward the elevators. "I think they all left about ten minutes ago."

"Okay, let's get you to a secure location," said White, taking him by the upper arm and leading him toward the doors, the others covering their exit. As they left the climate controlled building into the sticky evening air, sirens rapidly approached, flashing emergency lights flickering as a stream of police cars raced down the road, turning into the parking lot and screeching to a halt, the officers jumping out, weapons drawn.

"We're definitely not keeping this one quiet," said the large black man to his right.

They're going to kill everyone I know!

Constitution Tower, New Orleans, Louisiana

Detective Isabelle Laprise parked, stifling a yawn. She had caught the call near the end of her shift and had volunteered to take it.

Why go home to an empty apartment?

Four dead, gangland style shootout. It had at least sounded interesting, especially when she heard all four were Caucasian wearing suits. It didn't fit the normal profile.

"Are you going to be able to stay awake for this?" asked Detective Ray Salinger as they exited the vehicle. "You *do* know the night shift could have taken this?"

Isabelle shot Salinger a look. She had known him for a about a year but it had only been a few months since they found themselves working together. After the plague incident a couple of years ago where New Orleans was ground zero, she had bounced between partners far too often, none really meshing, most complaining to the LT that they wanted out of the partnership, she too hardheaded.

It didn't bother her that much, though it did a little. The problem was it wasn't really her, it was this façade she had created when on the job. Outside of work she was as nice as could be—or at least that's how she felt. Perhaps that wasn't the way others perceived her, then again, if she thought about it, she didn't have much of a life outside of work.

Another reason her partners seemed to keep deserting her.

She volunteered too often.

Those with families almost always wanted out, but Salinger was single, new to the city, and didn't seem to mind the long hours.

Except for tonight.

"Hot date?"

He blushed. He was a young pup in her eyes, at least ten years her junior, yet that hadn't stopped her before.

Dylan!

Dylan Kane had been a CIA operative sent in to help track down the source of the virus that had threatened to wipe out half the planet. Their time together had been brief but passionate, it still firing her fantasies to this day. And there wasn't a day that went by that she didn't enter her apartment hoping she'd find him there.

I can't believe I still miss him.

There had been a couple of men since then, though none could compare to the fantasy she had built up around Kane, she really not knowing anything about him other than he was a talented agent and a talented lover. She was chronically single, she not wanting to date within the department, and most men too intimidated by her job.

Besides, she never had time to meet anybody *because* of the job.

The job.

She loved it, yet it also kept her from being loved.

It was frustrating.

Yet it didn't seem to stop everyone from finding someone special.

"My sister set us up. Blind date," explained Salinger as they walked toward the office tower entrance, a black SUV parked directly in front of the doors, four men standing around it in fairly casual attire, one taking it to the extreme with a Hawaiian shirt and Bermuda shorts. All had shoulder holsters filled with weapons.

Must be the Secret Service agents.

"I've been on one blind date. Never again," she replied as the officer in charge of the scene approached. "Good enough looking but my gawd was he self-absorbed." She stopped, looking at her younger partner. "Want a little bit of free advice."

"Sure."

"Let the poor girl get a word in edgewise." She turned to the Sergeant. "Hey Bill, what've we got?"

"We're treating this as a secondary crime scene. You've seen the primary, I assume?"

She nodded. "Just came from there. Four guys dead, shot by these guys"—she nodded toward the SUV—"I presume?"

Sergeant Bill Labelle nodded. "Yeah, they've admitted to it. Apparently the perps had kidnapped two people from the Marriott. They were traced here. When the agents arrived, a vehicle was leaving that matched one of their suspect vehicles. They gave pursuit, the suspects opened fire on them so they took out their tires. Suspects then exited their vehicle and opened fire, the agents eliminated the targets, rescued one of the hostages, then returned here when they received intel from the hostage that the second one might be here. He walked out of the lobby just as they arrived."

"Huh?"

"Yeah, that's what I said. Apparently they put him in a conference room, yelled at him, then left him alone. He wandered out a few minutes later."

Isabelle chewed her cheek. "Any idea why they were kidnapped?"

"Well, get this. The guy they found here is Christopher Jones."

Isabelle's eyebrows leapt. "Seriously? The dude running for President?"

"Yup. And between you, me and the lamppost, he's got my vote. 'Bout time someone stood up to the Rooskies."

"Damned straight," agreed Salinger. "I'd vote for the guy too. My problem is I think he's too good to be true. Something's gotta come out at some point, it always does."

Isabelle looked at Salinger. "I never realized you were so cynical."

He shrugged. "You just gotta get to know me."

She looked at Labelle. "So young and already so jaded."

The silver-haired Labelle pushed his lips out, nodding. "You should hear my teenage son. The entire world is run by some secret organization of one-percenters that controls the government, police and courts for their own benefit." He grunted. "In my day one-percenters were bikers, not Wall Street."

"Now that's a rumble I'd pay to see," grinned Isabelle, the three of them laughing.

One of the Secret Service Agents stepped forward and she held up a hand, stopping him. He didn't look pleased. She turned her back on him. "Anything else I need to know?"

Labelle shook his head. "We're still canvasing both areas. We haven't turned up anything here but are pulling the security camera footage. We've got lots of cellphone footage of the shootout, but I think that's pretty clear cut. These guys did it, and were probably in their rights to do it."

"Agreed. I think the question now is who were the perps and why did they do what they did." She lowered her voice. "Is he still behind me?"

"Yup."

"Pissed?"

"Oh yeah."

She grinned. "And I wonder why nobody likes me." She turned and walked toward the man, tapping the shield on her belt. "I'm Detective Laprise. You are?"

"Agent White, Secret Service."

"What can you tell me?"

"Not much. Just that there was a non-lethal attack at the hotel, Mr. Jones and Mr. Quaid were taken here. Mr. Quaid said nothing was asked of him, but Mr. Jones said he was yelled at a lot about Russian sanctions, then left alone. Mr. Quaid was taken with them when they left which is when we intervened. We eliminated the hostiles, took Mr. Quaid into our custody, returned here based on intel from him, and found Mr. Jones in the lobby. We took him into custody and were about to return to a secure location when your people stopped us."

"I'm going to need to talk to them."

"Of course, but not here. The hotel is secure—"

"It wasn't before. And come to think of it, why am I hearing about this for the first time? We had no reports of an assault at the Marriott."

"They left a note indicating Mr. Jones would be killed if the police were brought in."

"Then how did you find them?"

"We traced the vehicles."

"How?"

"That's classified."

"Uh huh."

"Am I free to secure these men?"

Isabelle looked through the tinted windows, the faint shadows of two men inside. "Like I said, I'll need access to them."

"Absolutely." Agent White handed her a business card. "That's a switchboard. Ask for the security detail at the Marriott, they'll put you through."

Isabelle looked at the man then the others, their manner of dress suggesting the entire detail had been caught with their pants literally down. Her eyes rested on an Asian man with a lime green visor. "You guys don't look like Secret Service."

White chuckled, the Asian man whipping the cap off and giving her a toothy grin. "We were off duty."

208

"Uh huh. We were supposed to be too. Shit happens."

The man smiled, his head bobbing. "Indeed it does."

She tapped her watch. "I'll be by later. Don't leave the hotel."

White nodded and the four men climbed into their SUV as she waved for the cruiser blocking them to be moved. She turned back to Salinger. "So, where do *you* think we should start?"

"Primary crime scene?"

"You read my mind."

Outside Acton & Palmer Residence, St. Paul, Maryland

CIA Agent Sherrie White parked down the street, turning off her lights but leaving the engine running as she carefully observed the neighborhood. She had received the call from Kane only minutes after Chris had left for work and jumped at the opportunity to do something, even if it was off the books.

She chewed her lip as she surveyed the area, finding it hard to believe anything sinister could possibly happen here.

Peaceful.

It was the type of neighborhood she hoped to live in one day with Chris, perhaps have a couple of kids, though if they did, it would effectively kill her budding spy career. There wasn't officially any policy against deploying women with children to the field, but she wasn't sure how she felt about actually putting her life on the line when she had a kid back at home.

Then again, thousands upon thousands of women did that every day in the military and police, so why should she be any different?

Because with the CIA you expect to die, then are happy when you don't.

Her boyfriend's best friend—and possibly only friend—Dylan Kane, had talked to her about what it was like to be deep undercover. His philosophy, one she hoped she never would adopt, was to assume you were already dead, then party hard when you found out you weren't. She didn't think it was any way to live, but Kane was different. Different than anyone she had ever met.

A polar opposite to the man she loved.

She never really understood how they were friends until she had learned over the past couple of years about how horrible Chris' school years were until Kane came into the picture. She understood how Chris worshipped the slightly older Kane like an older brother, and she could see how Kane felt like that older sibling, having looked out for him for several years, and now again helping him out.

Especially with this Assembly business.

I'm so sick of them!

And she had no idea who 'them' were. Chris was the one in real danger and he had been assigned an escort since the first attempt on his life, though now that they were a couple, too much of her life was spent being watched.

I guess I know who watches the watchers.

It was sort of ironic that she was a spy, and hated being spied upon.

Or was that hypocritical?

Either way she didn't like it, but she loved Chris and didn't want anything to happen to him. She just hoped that someday they'd figure out who The Assembly were and put an end to them once and for all so they could dump the security detail and move on with their lives.

I wonder if Chris will ask me to marry him.

Probably not. Not that he wouldn't want to someday, but he was too painfully shy to ever put himself out there like that.

I'll have to drop some serious hints so he knows what the answer is in advance.

She smiled at the thought.

Mrs. Sherrie Leroux.

She frowned. She had lost both parents in a car accident when she was sixteen, and wasn't sure if she wanted to drop the name, keeping it honoring their memory in a way.

Mrs. Sherrie Leroux-White?

She turned the engine off, spotting what she had feared she might find.

211

A car, farther down the street, two people sitting inside, water from the air conditioning system draining toward the curb.

Rookie mistake.

It was a hot, muggy evening, it threatening to rain at any moment. She could understand why they were running the air conditioner for some relief. It made the stakeout more comfortable, and also kept the windows from fogging up.

Now, how to get rid of them?

She smiled.

Easy peasy!

She pulled out her phone, dialing 9-1-1 to report two suspicious men with guns.

Then hung up as the two people leaned together and kissed.

Wrong car.

She shook her head, chuckling as she killed the call. She opened her door, stepping out into the thick heat, window rumblers and central air units groaning away as the buttoned up houses of modern America denied reality.

A shoe scraped behind her and she could almost sense something about to hit her.

She ducked, spinning around as she reached for her shoulder holster.

But it wasn't enough.

The impact was shocking, excruciating, the thud audible as whatever it was smacked her squarely on the back, the force all the indication she needed that she was now in a fight for her life.

She dropped to the pavement, rolling twice as her hand gripped her Glock, the sight of two men advancing on her, one with a crowbar, the other with a gun, sending her heart racing even faster. The gun was their backup should the silent crowbar not do the job.

Kane was right. They are in danger.

Her only hope to save them was to warn them. She tried to pull her weapon but they were on her before she could draw it completely.

I have to warn them.

She squeezed the trigger.

"Did you hear that?" asked Acton as he leapt for the basement window facing the street, moving the curtain aside slightly. He looked outside but could see nothing out of the ordinary.

Laura joined him. "Sounded like a gunshot to me."

"Me too." He looked at the others, all perched on various seats of his future man cave, the basement reno a project that never seemed to gain any traction. "I'm going to check it out. Whoever Kane is sending might be in trouble."

"I'm coming with you."

Acton shook his head at Laura. "No, you stay here with them." He motioned toward the Glock in her hand. "And don't be afraid to use that. When I come back, I'll knock on the basement door a two-one-two pattern, got it?"

She frowned. "You need backup."

"She's right," said Milton, wincing as he stood, his back starting to act up, it way past his bedtime. They had been holed up here since Kane's warning, help apparently an hour away.

And an hour had passed.

He could see it in the eyes of his houseguests that they were all terrified. The guns he and Laura were gripping made them even more so, especially the fact they actually knew how to use them, holding them properly, loading them properly, Laura's former SAS security team training them well.

If there was to be gunplay tonight, it wouldn't be the first time.

For either of them.

Acton frowned. "Okay." He nodded toward the phone. "If you hear anything, you call 9-1-1. And don't let anybody down the stairs." He pointed at the spare Glock sitting on the table. "Anyone know how to use that?"

Nobody said anything, then Mai rose, picking it up. "I do."

Acton smiled. "You're just full of surprises."

"My brother was a criminal. You pick up a few things."

Tommy's eyebrows leapt. "You never told me that."

Mai blushed. "It's embarrassing."

Acton headed for the stairs then stopped, looking at his friends. "Be careful."

Milton smiled. "That's what we should be saying to you." His lips pressed tight together. "Take care of yourselves."

Acton nodded then rushed up the stairs, Laura on his heels. "Back door," he said as they emerged into the hallway. "They might be watching the front."

Another shot rang out.

Laura pushed him from behind, urging him toward the patio door. "Let's go!"

The first shot had ricocheted off the pavement, causing both men to pause, though only for a moment. The man with the gun raised it, taking aim as Sherrie leapt to her feet then over the hood of a parked car. He held his fire as she hit the pavement hard, her ribs cracking as she smacked into the concrete curb.

She gasped.

Pain is just weakness leaving the body!

Her instructor's voice barked at her, memories of Quantico flooding back as she pushed herself to her feet, looking for her opponents. The gunman was rounding the vehicle to the left.

But where's crowbar boy?

A reflection in the car window caught her eye and she dove backward, firing her weapon where she guessed he might be.

And missed.

But he didn't.

The crowbar caught her in midair, in the midriff, knocking the wind completely out of her, her already tender ribs causing her to cry out in pain, her weapon falling from her hand and onto a perfectly manicured lawn.

She hit the ground on her back and twisted, the follow up blow about to land, the hooked end of the crowbar embedding itself in the soft turf.

She grabbed it and kicked up, catching the bastard in the balls.

He doubled over in pain, she pretty sure his Adam's apple had a pair of nuts for company.

"Drop your weapons!" shouted someone from across the street. Her assailant with the tenderized gonads reached for his own gun.

"Federal agent! Shoot them!" she shouted as the man swung around with his weapon.

Three quick shots rang out, overlapped by another three shots from a second weapon, her man jerking with each hit then collapsing on top of her. She struggled against the deadweight, her cracked ribs not helping.

"Clear!" shouted a man's voice, the announcement echoed by a female, and she knew immediately who had saved her.

Professor James Acton and his wife, Professor Laura Palmer.

Footsteps on pavement rushed toward her and she immediately recognized them from the file photos, Acton reaching down and hauling the body off her.

He looked down at her. "Were you sent to save us?" he asked with a wry grin.

She laughed then winced, grabbing her ribs. "Yes." She extended her other hand and he hauled her to her feet. "Dylan sent me." She nodded toward the dead man at her feet. "Just in the nick of time by the looks of it."

"Let's get inside, there might be more."

Sherrie nodded, bending over to pick up her weapon.

She gasped in pain.

"I'll get it," said Laura, easily retrieving the weapon and handing it to her. She grimaced a thank you then limped toward the house, the two professors—the two civilians—covering her as porch lights turned on and curtains were pushed aside by neighbors wondering what was going on in their quiet little suburb.

"Grab just what you need. We're leaving here immediately," she said as they entered the house, Laura closing and locking the door behind them.

"We've got four people in the basement."

Sherrie stopped. "What? Who?"

"Guests, friends of ours. They were here when Dylan said to hole up."

Shit!

"Okay, so we're seven then. That means two vehicles. Not good, but we don't have a choice." She gasped as a pain shot through her chest. "Get them up here."

Acton nodded and rapped out a pattern on a door then opened it. "We're okay. I need you to come up now. If you need it, don't leave it."

There was a shout of acknowledgement and the sound of footsteps on bare wooden stairs. Acton pointed farther into the house. "Get Greg's wheelchair, he's going to need it." Laura nodded and disappeared for a moment, returning pushing what looked like a very expensive unit.

Jesus, seven of us, one in a wheelchair?

"We need to get to a secure location," she said as she returned to the front door, looking out the window, the first sirens now sounding in the distance. "And we need to get out of here before those police arrive."

A man stepped slowly through the basement door, holding his back. Laura pushed the chair over to him and he dropped into it with a sigh. "Thanks." He looked at her as three others appeared. "Shouldn't we wait for the police? Can't they protect us?"

"Not from a sniper round. We need to clear out of here before their backup arrives."

"Whose backup?"

Acton pushed his friend toward the door. "We shot two people outside. They were attacking—" He stopped. "I'm sorry, what's your name?"

Sherrie gripped the handle of the front door. "Agent Sherrie White, CIA, but tonight I'm a civilian."

"Got ya."

"We need two reliable vehicles. I came in one—"

"Our Jeep is new. We'll use that."

"Good." She nodded toward the man in the wheelchair. "Do you have any special needs?"

He shook his head. "I can walk, but why don't we take my van? It'll be a tight squeeze but at least we're all together."

Sherrie shook her head. "No, it'd be like driving a tank. We'd never be able to outrun anything if we had to." She looked at the group. "Who's the best driver?"

Acton squeezed the back of his wife's neck. "She is."

Sherrie's eyebrows popped and Laura explained. "I do some racing as a hobby."

"Then let's go. Professor Palmer, you drive your Jeep, take two of your guests with you, I'll take everyone else in my car."

"I'd like to go with my wife."

Sherrie shook her head. "I'm here for you—"

"I go with my wife."

Sherrie held her tongue. "Fine, there's no time to argue. You stay on my ass. I need to get you to a safe-house now." She reached into her pocket, pulling out a tiny round device and handed it to Acton. "Swallow this."

"Huh?"

"It's a tracking device in case we get separated. Swallow it."

Acton took the oval shaped device that almost looked like a gel capsule and eyed it for a moment before popping it in his mouth, swallowing it dry. "How does it work?"

"I can track you anywhere on the planet for the next thirty-six hours."

"Why only thirty-six hours?"

"Because by then, Professor, I'm going to assume you've had a bowel movement." She reached for the door handle. "Now let's go!"

"What about the painting?"

She sighed. "What painting?"

"It's what this is all about, isn't it? We have to get it."

"We'll discuss that when we're out of here." Sherrie unlocked the door and opened it slightly, it looking clear, the sirens suddenly much louder, neighbors now on their lawn. "Where's your Jeep?"

"In the garage."

"Okay." She pointed at the youngest two. "You two with me, casual, calm walk to my car. The rest of you into the Jeep through the garage. Pull out, hang a right"—she jerked her thumb in case there was any doubt— "and if I'm not ahead of you, I'll pass you. Go right at the stop sign and head for the highway. Got it?"

Laura nodded.

"Then let's go."

She stepped out on the porch, walking down the driveway and toward the road. A neighbor approached. "Are you guys okay?"

She nodded, slowing her pace, her conversation continuing over her shoulder. "Yeah, what happened here?"

"Two people were shot. I thought I saw Jim and his wife out here."

"They were, they heard the shots then went inside to call the police." She waved. "Sorry, gotta get these two home!" The three of them walked briskly down the street, Sherrie with one hand on her gun in her shoulder holster, the other gripping the key fob. She pressed the button, her vehicle chirping. "Get in."

Her two passengers climbed in the back seat as she noticed Laura pulling the Jeep out of the garage. The same neighbor ran up to the passenger side window and she saw Acton roll it down, words being exchanged as she started up the car. She did a shoulder check and pulled out, driving past the excitement as the first police car careened around the corner at the far end of the street.

"Everybody look at the bodies as if you're shocked but not scared. That means mouths open, eyes wide as if your dentist just squeezed your boob."

She glanced in the rearview mirror and almost chuckled.

Clearing the scene, she drove slowly past the police car as it locked up its brakes, shuddering to a halt. Another look in her rearview mirror showed the Jeep backing onto the road and following just as the two officers stepped out of their car.

She came to a stop at the end of the street, signaling her turn, Laura pulling up right behind her. She was about to pull out when the girl screamed from the back seat.

She turned to see a pair of headlights racing toward her.

Goodbye Chris.

"Jesus Christ!" exclaimed Acton as a large SUV slammed into the driver side of Sherrie's car, shoving it into the curb then up onto two wheels. It pulled back, the sedan dropping back onto all four tires as Acton reached for the door handle.

"Wait!" Laura slammed the car into reverse as a woman stepped out of the passenger side, machine pistol in hand. She aimed it at them and opened fire as Laura floored it, ducking behind the dash as Acton threw himself over her, the windshield taking several hits.

They hit something, hard, and the gunfire stopped.

He looked up to see Mai and Tommy being hauled out of the back seat and tossed in the back of the SUV, Sherrie pulled from the driver seat and thrown to the ground.

"No!" screamed Acton as he jumped out, pulling his weapon as the woman put two rounds into the young agent's chest.

"Drop the weapon!" shouted someone from behind him, but he ignored them, instead beginning to sprint toward the SUV as the woman and her accomplices climbed back inside. It started to pull away, the passenger side window lowering, a gun appearing, the muzzle belching lead.

Something slammed into his shoulder, sending him spinning to the ground, the gun clattering on the pavement as he lost his grip.

"Stay where you are!"

He looked toward who was shouting and saw two police officers rushing toward him, weapons drawn. He collapsed on his back, exhausted and in pain as Laura blew past the officers and to his side.

"James, are you okay?"

He nodded, grimacing. "Check on her, I'll be okay."

Laura's lips pressed together as she gave him a concerned look, then she jumped to her feet, sprinting to the end of the street as he was suddenly grabbed by the officers and flipped over onto his stomach.

Giving him a clear view of Laura beginning CPR on the young agent sent to save them.

JW Marriott Hotel, New Orleans

Christopher Jones rushed into his sobbing wife's arms, disappearing into their bedroom for a private reunion. The large suite was bustling with activity, a mix of Secret Service, FBI and NOPD spilling out into the hallway and other rooms commandeered for the emergency. The secret was out, but it didn't matter now. Jones was safe and they'd be leaving for Washington within the hour, the jet already fueling up, Jones' house being swept and secured.

And then our part is done.

NOPD wouldn't be happy, but the police chief had already agreed to allow the evacuation of their witness. Jones would be made available via video conference and if necessary in person at a later time, once things were secure.

Detective Laprise might insist upon that.

Yet that wasn't his problem or concern. His was to keep this man safe and he had failed. He should have split the team, two on, two off at all times, but no one had thought anything like this could actually happen.

And the Secret Service team was competent. He didn't really blame them, they were taken by surprise, and to be certain his team wouldn't have failed as well would be presumptuous.

At least in writing.

Unofficially, he did feel quite confident his men would have prevailed, though that was part of the training, to be able to react instantly to unexpected situations.

In the end Jones had been saved, but at what cost? The embarrassment to the Secret Service would be significant. Delta wouldn't wear it officially since they "didn't exist", and unofficially the pre-approved plan was for Delta to only be responsible for security outside of the hotel.

They weren't to blame.

But he still felt at fault.

"Okay, everyone, we've finished with the phones."

Special Agent in Charge McCarthy stepped back as the staff and Secret Service agents whose phones had been confiscated surged toward the table they had been collected on. Dawson smiled slightly, the crazed expressions shown by some revealing the withdrawal they had been suffering from these past couple of hours.

"Oh my God!" cried one, "The press is going crazy!"

"Twitter is on fire," observed another, shaking her head as her thumbs went crazy on the tiny display. Saunders reached into the fray, pushing several phones aside until he found his, a Blackberry. Dawson was about to turn away from the feeding frenzy when he stopped, something caught by the corner of his eye.

Did he just do what I think he did?

Dawson darted forward, grabbing Saunders' hand as he stepped away from the table.

"Hey, what's the idea?"

"Show me your hand."

The entire room turned toward the two men, Dawson an imposing figure, Saunders anything but.

Saunders went pale, his body starting to tremble. "N-no."

Dawson squeezed slightly tighter. Not enough to hurt the man, simply to illustrate a point. "I must insist."

Saunders tried to pull his arm away, but Dawson's grip wasn't to be broken.

Somebody knocked on the bedroom door, McCarthy stepping toward the exchange.

"What's going on here?" he asked, looking at the terrified Saunders then the dispassionate stare of Dawson.

"Is there a problem?"

Dawson looked to see Jones stepping out of the room, his eyes narrowing at the sight of Dawson holding the wrist of his senior aide.

"Mr. Saunders took two phones from the table."

"I-is that all this is about?" asked Saunders, his voice shaky. "I have two phones, one for business, one for personal."

"So do I," said someone else in the room.

"Me too."

Dawson nodded, his hand still clamped on Saunders' forearm. "I'm well aware of that. Six of you have two cellphones each, all your numbers provided to the security detail ahead of time. But Mr. Saunders only has one phone listed."

"I'm sure it's just an oversight," said Jones as he stepped toward his aide, his wife holding the doorframe, her face stained with fresh tears.

"Of course it is." Saunders yanked again. "Let me go!"

Dawson held out his other hand. "The phones, please."

Saunders looked over his shoulder at his boss. "Sir, please, tell him to let me go."

Jones looked at Dawson for a second then drew a deep breath. "Give him the phones, Russ."

Saunders' jaw dropped, his eyes popping wide. "But sir!"

Jones stepped forward, putting his hand on his aide's shoulder. "Listen, these men risked everything to save me tonight. I trust them and so should you. All they want to do is check the phones. You know I trust you, I know you've got nothing to hide. It's just routine. Let them do their job."

Saunders didn't seem convinced, his mouth closing, his eyes still wide. With fear.

This guy's definitely hiding something.

The question was what. The man was married. Was he having an affair and keeping a separate phone for it? Or was he secretly a Heisenberg, running a meth lab in his spare time.

The possibilities were endless, and regardless of where the truth lied, it was a security breach.

"Come on Russ, give him the phones." Jones sounded a little more insistent this time, his expression no longer bemused, but instead suggesting he was beginning to think there was more going on here than an innocent oversight.

"Fine," muttered Saunders.

Dawson let go of his grip and took the two phones, Saunders rubbing his wrist, clearly in discomfort. Dawson looked at the phones, an iPhone and a Blackberry. "Which is the phone you registered with us?"

"The Blackberry. They're more secure so we do all of our campaign business on them. The iPhone is just my personal phone. Only my family has the number."

Dawson looked at the phones for a moment, trying to figure out what his gut was trying to tell him. He held up the Blackberry. "So this is your business phone."

"Yes."

"And you never receive business calls on this one?" He held up the iPhone.

"Never."

"Then why, sir, did you receive a phone call from Mr. Quaid on your iPhone earlier today when we were coming back from the last speech of the day?"

Constitution Tower, New Orleans, Louisiana

Detective Isabelle Laprise entered the server room for the hi-tech building, Ray Salinger behind her, dozens of racks of tech far beyond her understanding hummed and flashed, the HVAC keeping the room uncomfortably chilly. She wrapped her arms over her chest, concerned her body might betray her, and there no need for the younger Salinger to get a cheap thrill.

"Where are you guys?"

"Back here, Detective."

Isabelle followed the voice to the back of the room, finding Randy and Lucas hammering away at laptops and keyboards, it appearing they had their own computers jacked into those belonging to the tower. The two were young. How young she wasn't sure, but if they were over twenty-five she'd be stunned, though it might just be the way they carried themselves. These were geeks. Uber-dorks of the first order, two who would fit perfectly into any episode of Big Bang Theory or the nearest Comicon.

Which was exactly what you wanted working your IT problems.

"What have you found?"

"Oh, they were hacked alright," replied Randy, pointing at gibberish on the screen.

"Explain."

"Well, that conference room your guy said he was held in was booked all day according to the building's concierge service head, but now it's showing it free all afternoon and evening."

"So someone cancelled. What's that tell us?"

"No, dude, you don't understand." Lucas caught himself. "Sorry, Detective, umm, dudette, umm." He paused.

If mankind's survival depended upon this guy getting a date, we'd be screwed.

"Cancelled. What don't I understand?"

"Oh, umm, yeah, well, it wasn't cancelled from inside, the IP address is showing it was somebody outside the building that did it."

"So, I can cancel meetings in Outlook using my phone. So what?"

"So this booking wasn't just cancelled, it was wiped from the record completely. There's no record of it ever having existed, and the IP address I'm pretty sure is spoofed."

"Pretty sure!" interrupted Randy. "Try absolutely. Unless our government is involved."

Isabelle's eyes narrowed. "What do you mean?"

"I mean the IP address that apparently did this belongs to the government."

"Which government?"

"Ours, dude, in Washington."

"I find that hard to believe."

"Exactly, dude, which means it was probably spoofed. Made to look like it came from Washington."

Lucas leaned back in his chair. "Whoa."

Isabelle gave Salinger a look, her eyes rolling slightly. "Whoa what?"

"Somebody just hacked into the system."

"Who?"

"I dunno, but they're pulling everything. Fast."

"Can you stop them?" asked Salinger, leaning forward.

"Yeah, I guess. Easiest way is to cut the hardline."

"No cutting, can't you just turn it off?" asked Isabelle.

"That's what I mean." Randy reached for one of the nearby racks. "Want me to?"

"Can you trace them?"

"Oh yeah, dude, sure we can."

"Then do it. There's nothing on here that we care about. And there's no way this is a coincidence."

The conversation quickly devolved into acronyms and insults as the two "men" attacked their keyboards, each either in a race with the other, or somehow collaborating, she not sure which, to trace the origin of whoever was trying to tap the system.

"Whoa."

It was said in unison, all typing stopping at once.

"What?"

Randy and Lucas both pointed.

Isabelle was getting frustrated. "What the hell am I looking at? Who's hacking the system?"

"The CIA."

"What? Another spoof?"

They both shook their heads in synch, as if sharing a single brain.

"No, for real this time."

Isabelle turned to Salinger. "What the hell is going on here?"

Suddenly something changed on the screens that had the boys excited again.

"What's going on?"

"They're gone," explained Lucas. "They've disconnected."

"What did they get?"

"Everything."

"Meaning?"

"I mean everything. They tapped every pipe coming into the building and just copied it all." Lucas shook his head, awe written all over his face. "These guys are good."

"The best," agreed Randy as he tentatively typed something, almost as if he were afraid to touch anything. "And they cleaned up after themselves. If we weren't here when it happened, no one would have ever known."

"And you're sure it's CIA?"

"Yes." Randy paused. "Unless…"

"Unless what?"

"Unless they've got a mole."

"Huh?"

"Someone on the inside, using their hardware." Randy shrugged. "I don't know, I doubt it, though you never know nowadays."

Isabelle frowned. "Well, that's above my paygrade. I'll mention it to the LT when we get back to the station." She nodded toward the screens. "Now you were going to show us some security footage?"

"Oh yeah! Almost forgot!" Randy hammered at the keyboard. "This is going to be so mundane compared to what just happened."

Sorry, "dude", but what just happened wasn't exciting to most of us.

A video appeared of the parking garage. "So they wiped all the cameras for the elevators and the conference room floor for the entire time they were here, which was less than half an hour apparently, but they forgot one."

"Which one?"

"Parking garage, third level," replied Lucas. He pointed at the screen. "See the angle? You can actually see part of the second level through those concrete columns. I'm guessing they figured they didn't need to wipe anything below the second level since they were never there."

Five men suddenly came into view.

"Do we have audio?"

Randy shook his head. "No, dude, this is all The Artist like."

"Just without the music!" laughed Lucas.

"Dude!" laughed Randy, fist bumps exchanged.

Society is doomed.

The men left the frame. "Play it back." Randy complied and Isabelle leaned forward, peering at the screen. "The one in the middle is the kidnap victim that the Secret Service rescued in the shootout. Mr. Quaid."

"Yup," agreed Salinger.

"Play it again."

Keys were hit.

Isabelle stood up straight. "What does it look like he's doing?"

Salinger pursed his lips for a moment, then his eyebrows popped. "He's arguing."

Lucas shook his head. "Dude's got Hulk-sized cajones, man! And look at them, it's like they're scared of him."

Isabelle wasn't sure she agreed with that assessment, though she did agree with one thing.

It took massive balls to argue with four gunmen.

And why did he seem completely unafraid?

JW Marriott Hotel, New Orleans

"One last time, what's the password for the phone?"

Once again Saunders refused to answer, his arms crossed stubbornly over his chest, as they had been for most of the half hour Special Agent in Charge McCarthy had been interrogating him.

"This is going to a lab as soon as we get back," said McCarthy. "We'll get into your phone. All you're doing is delaying things. And making things worse for yourself."

"What's going on in here?"

Dawson turned to see Detective Isabelle Laprise in the doorway to the hall, her partner behind her. She didn't look pleased.

McCarthy rose from his perch on the edge of a couch. "I'm interrogating a suspect. And you are?"

"Detective Laprise, NOPD." She flashed her badge. "And *you* are?"

"Special Agent in Charge McCarthy."

"Has this man been read his rights?"

"He's not under arrest."

"Then why are you interrogating him?"

"Because he had an unauthorized cellphone and refuses to give us access to it."

Isabelle frowned. "I wasn't aware he's required to."

Jones stepped into the room. "As a member of my staff, he's bound by his employment contract, which includes a clause that requires him to cooperate fully with any security protocols deemed necessary."

"And I deemed it necessary," said Dawson, pointing to the next room, pushing the conversation out of earshot of their suspect. "He's involved, that much is clear."

Isabelle lowered her voice. "I don't doubt it. This was an inside job if there ever was one."

Jones suddenly looked uncomfortable. "I don't believe it. I mean, Russ, he's been with me for years. He's the best. He's been in the business for twenty years." Jones shook his head. "No, I refuse to believe he's behind my kidnapping."

"Two of you were kidnapped today, Mr. Jones." Isabelle looked at him, hard, Dawson getting the distinct impression she had her suspicions about Jones himself.

This could be interesting.

"How well do you know Mr. Quaid?"

Jones shrugged his shoulders. "I'd call him an acquaintance rather than a friend. He's done a lot for my campaign, not just from donating his own money, but in gathering others to the cause. Outside of formal functions, though, I don't really know much about the man."

"So you're willing to take millions from a man you barely know, who will then have the ear of the President of the United States should you win."

Jones blushed, lowering his voice to almost a whisper. "It's just the way the game is played. If I win, I'll fight to bring in campaign finance reform, but until then, I can't even mention it. If the moneymen thought they'd lose their ability to buy their government, they'd pull their support in a heartbeat, and I'd never win."

Isabelle didn't seem impressed with his subdued campaign promise. "What exactly was said to you when you were held captive?"

232

Jones again seemed uncomfortable, Dawson an expert at reading body language.

And this man's holding something back.

"They wanted me to stop talking about Russian sanctions. To tone down my speeches about the Russians." He looked at the floor then away from them. "I don't know, maybe I've been a little harsh. Perhaps the best way to peace is appeasement at this point rather than sabre rattling that could lead to an all-out war."

Now I know something's wrong.

"Uh huh." Isabelle didn't seem to be buying it either. "That's quite the turnaround from the speech you gave earlier today."

Jones flushed bright red, but said nothing.

"And what happened to your *acquaintance*, Mr. Quaid, while all this was going on?"

Jones shook his head. "I don't know. I mean, we were taken from here together, but when we got to wherever it was they took us, we were separated. I didn't see him again until you guys showed up at the building." He looked around. "Where is he?"

"Being held down the hall," replied Dawson. Something had stunk about this entire situation from the get go and there was no way he was going to allow Quaid access to Jones until he knew the complete story. "He's being debriefed by one of my men."

Jones looked at Dawson. "You need to take it easy on him. He-he could walk with his money, then I'm ruined."

Isabelle snapped her fingers and her partner produced a laptop. "I think there's something you need to see." With a few swipes and clicks a video from a security camera began to play. He placed it on the table for everyone to see. "Tell me what you see there, Mr. Jones."

He shrugged. "I don't know. That's Pete by the looks of it, with some of the guys who took us."

"What else?" pressed Isabelle.

Jones shrugged, looking at her. "I don't know."

"You don't know?"

He sighed then suddenly snapped. "No, I don't know! Why don't *you* tell *me*, Detective? It's been a long night and I just want to get on a plane and go home, sleep in my own bed, and put tonight behind me! So why don't *you* tell *me* what you see?"

The tirade didn't seem to faze Isabelle at all.

This one has her shit together.

"I'll tell you what I see, Mr. Jones. I see a man who has no fear."

The wind seemed to be taken from Jones' sails as his voice dropped. "What are you trying to say?"

Isabelle pointed at the looping video. "I say this man Quaid knew his captors. I say he was in on it." She leaned closer to Jones. "And I say you know it."

Leaving St. Paul, Maryland

Nadja Katz looked at the two terrified people in the backseat, sandwiched between her men. They were young, definitely not her original targets, but her employers had ordered total rapid containment, there apparently a serious issue in New Orleans that she might be sent in to clean up once the Titanic infection had been put to bed.

She had to admit she was curious about this entire affair. The Titanic had sunk over a century ago. No one from that time was alive anymore, so why the concern? She wasn't privy to any details, except that she was to contain any references to a Captain Wainwright and a painting. Anyone who had been exposed to that information was to be tracked and eliminated along with anyone they may have had contact with that could have contracted the disease.

The disease being information.

Knowledge is power, she had always believed, but she also knew knowledge could sometimes mean death. In this case it was unfortunate, as these people weren't involved in actively seeking out state or industrial secrets, they had just stumbled upon something they were never supposed to know about. And even then, they didn't really know much.

But if they continue to pry...

And that was what her employers were terrified of, though *she* was attributing the emotion to them. Though she had never felt fear before, she assumed her reaction would be to do whatever it took to remove the cause of the fear, and with the leeway she had been given on this assignment, it was as if her employers were doing everything possible to remove their own fear.

The Asian woman was young, judging from her facial structure she'd guess Southeast Asian, possibly Vietnamese, most likely Mai Lien Trinh, one of Professor Acton's grad students. The other one was nobody to her, though clearly somebody to this young girl, she cradling his head, blood caking one side of his face where he had sustained some sort of injury.

"Your name?"

The young woman looked startled, terrified. And said nothing.

"Your name, now." She didn't raise her voice, simply changed the tone. There was no emotion, no impatience, it was simply a tone she had seen others use that elicited the response she needed.

"M-Mai Trinh."

Thought so.

"And him?"

"T-Tommy Granger."

"Who is he to you?"

"M-my friend."

"Not boyfriend?"

The young woman flushed.

Not her boyfriend. Yet.

"You are one of Professor Acton's grad students?"

Mai's eyes widened and she nodded.

"And him?"

"He's a student, but not one of Professor Acton's."

Nadja pulled out her cellphone and selected Professor Acton's cellphone number from the list. The bug planted at Steve Wainwright's house had paid off quickly, they returning home from their dinner full of conversation about the two professors who were helping determine if the painting was real, and about how they believed Captain Wainwright and his ship must have been at the scene of the sinking.

It was information her employers hadn't told her, and she would make certain they never knew what she knew, otherwise she herself could become a target. What her employers' involvement was with this she didn't know, but if it were true, that there was a US Navy ship on the scene that didn't render assistance, and her employers were behind it, she could see why they would want that kept secret.

What was more interesting to her was what the original mission of the ship was. It couldn't have been there by coincidence, it's too big an ocean. And if people had indeed gone on board like the Wainwrights were discussing, it certainly wasn't to steal a painting.

What could be so important that you would let so many die?

Especially a US Navy ship.

That simply didn't make sense to her. She couldn't imagine it happening today, though perhaps back then it was possible. The world was a different place, yet even so, it was just unfathomable to think military personnel of a modern democracy would allow innocent civilians, many from their own country, to die while they sat idly by, stealing something.

There was definitely something much bigger going on.

And you don't want to know what it is.

She tapped the number.

A man's voice answered after several rings. "Hello?"

"If you want to see your friends alive, Professor Acton, you will bring us the painting."

"Who's this? Who are you?"

"Who I am is unimportant. What I have, and what *you* have, is."

"I don't understand. What do you have? Are you the people who just shot that young woman and took Mai and Tommy?"

"Yes. And you, Professor Acton, can save their young lives by telling the authorities nothing. If the police become involved, they die."

"But they're already involved. They arrested Jim and Laura just a few minutes ago!"

Katz's eyes narrowed. "Who am I speaking to?"

"I'm not sure if I should tell you."

She shook her head. She had read the extensive file on Acton on her way to his house, her employers providing an impressive dossier on the man, his travels, his exploits.

And his friends.

"This is Dean Gregory Milton, isn't it?"

Somebody gasped.

A woman.

"Yes."

"And your wife, I presume."

"Yes."

"You will tell the police nothing about this conversation or not only will these two young students of yours die, so will your wife and daughter."

She ended the call, looking back at her two hostages.

They'll die soon enough.

Though not before the trap was set for much bigger prey.

JW Marriott Hotel, New Orleans

Christopher Jones sank into a nearby chair, his head dropping between his knees as he grabbed at his hair, unsure of what to do. *They know!* And if they know, then everyone he cared about would die. If his own aide was in on this, and his primary financial donor as well, then there was no one he could trust.

Or is there?

These people were new. Could this cabal that had threatened him earlier have brought in a New Orleans police detective so quickly? He doubted it, but then again, they had somehow managed to kidnap him and take him to a location that from what he had overheard was pre-booked. That meant the contingency of him not agreeing to Quaid's demands had been anticipated.

Which meant they could have also anticipated something else going wrong.

And that meant they might have had a detective ready.

No, he couldn't trust her.

His thoughts turned to Agent White, a name he knew wasn't real, the team of four he was with on special assignment. They could have been brought in by this organization as well.

But why would they have killed four of their own men?

That didn't fit, though he had read enough news stories and briefings to know that organized crime, especially mafias like the Russians, treated their muscle as commodities. Sacrificing four foot soldiers would mean nothing to them, especially if it were to make him trust them.

But the phone?

That made no sense. Why would this man White reveal Saunders involvement? Surely that wouldn't be of any benefit. Then again, it certainly would make him trust these men even more. Wouldn't it?

He wasn't so sure.

He liked to think he was a good judge of character. Quaid he had never trusted but needed his money. He had never thought he was a criminal working for the Russians, yet he was definitely someone he never trusted. Saunders was cutthroat when he had to be, and had crushed more than a few people in his path over the years. He was someone he would never consider a friend, would probably not associate with if he weren't the best at what he did.

And had come highly recommended to him by others.

I wonder if they were in on it.

It was frustrating. This entire experience had him questioning the loyalty of everyone around him, and everyone that had been involved in helping choose his team.

The only person he could trust was his wife.

He sat up, his eyes coming to rest on this Agent White, still not sure if he could be trusted. His gut told him yes, but his paranoid self was screaming no.

"I can tell by your reaction that I'm right," said the detective, pressing her advantage.

Jones felt his chest tighten.

No one can know!

"Can you clear the room please?"

The detective looked at him for a moment then nodded. "Everyone out!"

The room quickly emptied and he saw Agent White turn to leave.

"Not him."

White turned toward him, his face expressionless.

"What did you have to tell me?" asked the detective.

Jones looked at her, still not sure if he could trust her, but they were beyond that. He had to say something, enough to at least stop the incessant questioning.

And then it dawned on him.

If she were one of *them*, then she wouldn't be pressing him for the truth. There was no way they would want him to actually answer her questions. It was one thing to try and test him, but not in public in a room full of people. That made no sense.

He had to trust her. He had to trust White.

Otherwise he was totally alone, left to fight a cabal of people he knew nothing about, with extraordinary money and resources at their disposal.

The detective stepped closer. "You know that Mr. Quaid is involved, don't you."

He sighed, nodding at her. "You can't tell anyone that. They'll kill me, they'll kill everyone."

"Who?"

"I can't say."

"If you don't tell me, how can I protect you?"

Jones shook his head. "There's no protecting me from them. Nobody can protect me, especially not you."

Agent White stepped forward.

"She can't, but I can."

Anne Arundel Medical Center, Annapolis, Maryland

Sherrie White could hear the muffled tones outside her door, the doctor explaining her status to Milton and his wife. She was lucky. Damned lucky. Her business had taught her to be paranoid—or abundantly cautious—so she had been wearing a vest.

When Dylan Kane warns you it could be dangerous, you listen.

That man knew dangerous, his daily routine more dangerous than her most hazardous mission to date.

Though she did now have the distinction of being shot.

Twice.

At point blank range.

Remind me to send the inventor of the bulletproof vest a bottle of scotch.

She had two broken ribs, three cracked ribs, significant bruising and a reinflated left lung.

She felt like shit.

And she wished Chris was here.

At this moment, as far as she knew, he had no idea what had happened. Things had happened so quickly, she had just been wheeled into the recovery room less than ten minutes ago.

She looked through the window. She could see Milton's head, he obviously in his wheelchair, his wife at his side.

Where are the professors?

Her heart picked up a little speed, the monitor beeping to her left betraying her. She tried to sit up and gasped, the pain intense despite the painkillers she was on.

She collapsed back into her pillow.

I'm out.

"She'll need a couple of days rest here where we can monitor her, then she can head home. She'll need a couple of months before she's back to normal, though."

"Okay, thanks, Doctor."

Milton wheeled into the room, his wife behind him.

"Where are the professors?" asked Sherrie, not bothering with any small talk.

"They were arrested at the scene. Laura saved your life. Apparently your heart stopped."

Sherrie paused for a moment as she processed those words.

You were dead.

Yet another thing to add to her bona fides.

It scared her a bit. Not so much that she had died, the possibility of death never really bothering her that much. It was the thought of leaving Chris all alone that would haunt her. The poor guy was so shy he would hole up in his apartment and never put himself out there again. She would want him to move on, to find a new love to share his life with, but she knew he wouldn't.

And thoughts like that could make her a less effective agent.

So she kept them to herself.

She looked at Milton, recovering her train of thought. "Arrested? For what?"

"For shooting those two guys who tried to kill you, I guess. I'm not really sure, we haven't been able to find out much. Jim told us to go with you and make sure you were okay, so we did. But..."

"But what?"

"Well, I got a phone call."

Sherrie's eyes narrowed.

"From who?"

"I think from the woman who shot you."

Sherrie pushed herself up on her elbows, ignoring the pain, her heart monitor beeping faster.

"What did she say?"

"Well, she basically said she wanted the painting or she'd kill Mai and Tommy. She thought I was Jim. At least at first."

"What do you mean, 'at first'?"

"Well, I told her I wasn't Jim and she just instantly knew who I was. And Sandra too." He reached out and squeezed his wife's hand, the look of fear on her face obvious.

Sherrie began to feel a sense of foreboding grip her, almost afraid to ask her next question. "What did you tell her?"

"I told her Jim and Laura had been arrested."

"You told her?"

Milton nodded, his eyes widening slightly. "I didn't really have much choice, I thought she might hurt Mai and Tommy. Besides, Jim and Laura are safe at the police station." He paused. "Aren't they?"

Sherrie shook her head. "No, Mr. Milton, I think they're in more danger now than they ever were."

Annapolis Police Department, Taylor Avenue, Annapolis, Maryland

Nadja Katz strode up to the Desk Sergeant, flashing her Homeland Security ID, two of her men behind her, everyone in dark suits and sunglasses, earpieces in place.

They were the stereotype.

Because it worked.

"Special Agent Willow. We're here for the prisoners." She produced a sheaf of perfectly faked transfer orders. "Acton, James and Palmer, Laura."

"Christ, you people are fast. We haven't even booked them yet."

"When you kill a CIA agent, the wheels turn a little bit quicker."

"A CIA agent is dead?" asked the sergeant, alarms immediately tripping in Katz' head.

I shot her twice, point blank range. She has to be dead.

Unless she was wearing a vest.

Clever girl.

"That's the information I have, though things are still sketchy. She didn't die?"

The old sergeant shook his head. "No, she took quite the beating but I just heard that she's going to pull through."

"That's a relief. I guess the charge in her case will be *attempted* murder."

"Well, you've still got two dead regardless. I'm sure those charges will stick if it wasn't self-defense. That guy Acton was shot too."

So I did hit him.

"You mean he's not here?"

The sergeant shook his head as he rose from his stool. "Naw, just a graze. They treated him at the scene and then they were brought here for

245

questioning. He's in Interrogation Room Two, she's in Three. Who do you want to see first?"

"Acton."

He nodded toward a door to the right. "Check your weapon and I'll buzz you through. Down the hall, third door on the left."

Katz ejected the mag and cocked the action, showing the empty chamber, then handed her weapon to one of the officers manning the door. She turned to her men. "You two stay here, I won't be long."

If she couldn't have a weapon with her, she wanted her men out here to still have theirs.

Because she was quite certain within minutes there would be blood.

And it wouldn't be hers.

The Kahala Hotel & Resort, Honolulu, Oahu, Hawaii

Dylan Kane felt himself drifting off in a post-coital bliss, Leiko having worn him out completely, her appetite almost insatiable. She was fantastic. And memories of her would have to satisfy his carnal lusts for the next few weeks, there probably little to no possibility of a hookup where he was going.

Pakistan.

He hated few countries in the world, but Pakistan was one of them. Primitive, backward, stuck centuries in the past, with a population that seemed to hate anyone different, trusted no one, and was incredibly quick to take offence.

It was a Taliban paradise.

Word was a top al-Qaeda leader was in Peshawar to meet with local Taliban to discuss a response to the ISIS threat. Even al-Qaeda was scared of them, their brand of Islam even more perverted.

The Wahabists would be proud.

It was his job to determine if the man was indeed there, try to determine what agreements, if any, were reached, then direct a drone strike if the powers that be ordered it.

Just another day on the job.

He wasn't a big fan of drone strikes. They were too impersonal. It wasn't necessarily that he liked putting a bullet between someone's eyes, it was just that with a gun, he knew exactly who he was killing and that they deserved to be killed. With a drone strike it was everyone in the vicinity, and you weren't always sure if your target was dead, the explosion quite often large enough to make the body unrecognizable.

And on more than one occasion, a target presumed dead showed up weeks or months later, alive and well, perhaps missing an arm or leg that had been used to decide they were erroneously terminated.

Give me a rifle and a scope any day.

His watch vibrated with another message. Leiko was breathing deeply on his chest, the woman finally worn out herself as well. They hadn't left the hotel room from the moment he knocked on her door, food ordered in, the remnants on a cart in the hall.

They were both each other's desert.

He carefully extracted himself, doing the old Ross Geller hug and roll, and retreated to the bathroom.

Urgent from SW.

He frowned.

This can't be good.

He pulled out his encrypted phone, locking the door and turning on the shower. Dialing, Sherrie White almost immediately answered. "Hello?"

"It's me. What's your status?"

"I'm out of commission. The professors have been arrested, two of their students kidnapped, and I don't know what to do. I need help."

He could hear the disappointment in her voice. Nobody wanted to fail on a mission, especially a young agent trying to make her bones in the business, but it happened. Even he had failed once or twice.

Though he had always managed to clean up his mess.

"Are you secure?"

"I'm in a hospital recovering. I'll be fine. I've got a police guard but I'm off the books so I haven't notified Langley."

"Which means you haven't notified our boy."

"No, he doesn't know."

"He will soon enough. Better he hears from you. Why were the professors arrested?"

"They shot the two men who tried to kill me. I think the police are just sorting things out, but the woman who shot me called Dean Milton. She wants the painting or she's going to kill the two students that were with me. And she knows the professors have been arrested."

"Which means she knows where they are."

"Right."

"And if those two men were at their house and tried to kill you, then they were most likely there to kill the professors."

"That's my assessment as well."

"Okay. Sit tight. I'm going to call in some big guns."

"Okay, thanks Dylan. And I'm sorry."

"Don't be sorry. Just call Chris. Now."

"I will."

Annapolis Police Department, Taylor Avenue, Annapolis, Maryland

Nadja Katz knocked on the door then opened it, not waiting for an invite. The cop sitting across from her target looked at her, surprised. She flashed her badge. "Homeland Security. We're taking over the case." She jerked her head toward the door. "Give us a minute, would you?"

He didn't look pleased but he grabbed his pad and paper and left, Acton's back to her. She closed the door then rounded the table. Acton's eyes widened. She put a finger to her lips then pulled out a small device that looked like a cellphone. She activated it.

"This will allow us to talk in private."

"I've got nothing to say to *you*."

"So you recognize me."

"You're the bastard that killed Sherrie."

She forced a smile.

It was expected.

"You'll be happy to hear that she's alive and well. It's amazing what Kevlar can do these days."

Acton breathed a sigh of relief before his rage refocused. "What have you done with my students?"

"They're safe. For the moment."

"What do you want from me? From us? What have we done?"

Another practiced smile. "You've created headaches for my employers by asking the wrong questions publicly."

Acton's eyes narrowed. "What questions?"

"Questions exactly like that. You, professor, need to learn to shut your mouth."

250

Acton looked at her. "It's what I do."

Cheeky.

She forced a smile. "Right now all you're going to do is come with me, quietly, then take me to the painting."

"I don't think so."

"If you don't, your students will die, as will your best friend, Greg, and his lovely wife Sandra. And I *will* finish the job on your young CIA agent."

Acton glared at her. "What if I just tell the cops you're the one they're looking for?"

She smiled, it almost instinctual, as if some vestige of memory from her forgotten youth wanted to rear its former self. A rare occurrence. "If I'm not outside in ten minutes, my men have orders to kill everyone involved." She leaned forward, her knuckles pressing into the table, her bangs hanging in front of her eyes. "Or you can come with me, quietly."

Acton's glare intensified then broke, his shoulders slumping. "Fine." He rose. "I give you the painting, then what?"

"Then we part ways."

With a bullet to the back of your head.

Louis Armstrong New Orleans International Airport, New Orleans, Louisiana

Dawson stood by the door as Jones and his wife rushed up the steps. The staff would be taking commercial flights, this flight limited to Bravo Team members, a minimal flight crew, and two scared passengers.

No one else.

Niner and Spock were busy closing all the blinds on the windows to prevent any snipers from getting a good shot, and the Secret Service, not too pleased to be excluded from the op, were providing external security until the plane was airborne.

Atlas was last on board, one of the flight crew pulling up the stairs of the Learjet.

"Let's go!" shouted Dawson at the open cockpit door, the pilot already edging up the throttle, the sleek private jet beginning to taxi for the runway, the Secret Service having arranged for an immediate departure.

It was a rapid extraction, but necessary. Whoever they were dealing with had power and money, and though they hadn't killed, yet, clearly were willing to break the law. Jones hadn't told them much, his fear of harm to his family genuine. And probably justified. Langley had informed them of the hack on the Constitution Tower computers, masked to make it look like it came from government computers, the hacks actually originating out of Russia apparently, though that meant little. Organized crime and foreign powers set up secret cells in various rogue states so that anything they did could be blamed on the state they had taken up residence in. China had been the most popular, though now that Russia was back in the bad books, they were the preferred locale, it a lot easier to blend into the Russian mosaic than the Chinese homogeny.

The powerful engines shoved him into the back of his seat as the pilot lifted off, the emergency ascent approved to put them out of range of bullets or shoulder launched missiles as quickly as possible.

It was a terrifying experience he was sure for those on board not used to it.

The plane began to level out when he felt his satellite phone vibrate. "Speak."

"Hey, BD, it's me."

Dawson immediately recognized Kane's voice and smiled. Then frowned. "Okay, you never call to just say hi. What do you want?"

Kane laughed, though he sounded like he was trying to keep from being overheard. "You know me so well. I need your help."

"We're just wheels-up and airborne for two and a half hours."

"You're not in Bragg?"

"Negative. Just leaving New Orleans."

"Shit. Listen, the Professors are in a bit of trouble."

"Again?"

"Yeah, it never ends with them. We should start sending them a bill."

Dawson laughed. If the bill were actually tallied, the US government might come out owing the Actons after all they had done for them over the years. With Laura Palmer filthy rich, her money had helped save his men on more than one occasion.

The Feds might think they're owed, but Delta owes them big time.

Which was one of the many reasons he never hesitated to help when he could.

"What happened this time?"

"Not sure, it's a weird one. Apparently somebody found a painting that was supposed to have sunk on the Titanic, began asking some questions, and a security tap was triggered. It looks like they might have uncovered something to do with the Titanic—a US Navy ship might have been there and done nothing."

Dawson's eyes narrowed. "Are you kidding me?"

"Hey, it sounds like bullshit to me, but two people are dead, the agent I sent was shot twice, and two people were taken hostage."

Okay, not a joke. "Where is Acton now?"

"The professors were both arrested at the scene. My guess is they'll be released after it's shown it was self-defense, but here's the rub. Their friend Milton told the woman who shot Sherrie that they had been arrested."

"Sherrie? As in Sherrie White?"

"Yeah. Oh, that's right. I forgot you worked with her before."

"Yeah. Good agent. She's fine?"

"She will be but I don't think she's secure."

"What do you need?"

"Boots on the ground. I'm on the other side of the planet, heading into hell itself tomorrow, so I'm going to be out of the loop in less than twenty-four hours. I need to know this is being handled."

"Don't worry about it, I've got it covered."

"Thanks, buddy, I knew I could count on you."

"No problem. Next time *you* buy the beer though."

"You got it."

"For all of us."

"Are you shittin' me? I'm a public servant!"

"Hey, I've seen enough James Bond movies to know you've got some tucked away for a rainy day. Well it's about to start raining, my friend."

"You're a cruel, cruel man, Mr. Dawson. But you save my friends, you've got a deal."

"Consider it done."

"Hey, baby, who you on the phone with?"

Dawson chuckled, the sound of a woman's voice clearly audible on the other end. "Hell itself, I presume?"

"You're a sick, sick man. I'm letting you go now."

"Good luck in hell."

Annapolis Police Department, Taylor Avenue, Annapolis, Maryland

Katz looked up as the door opened, a man in a suit, probably a detective, stepping inside, two uniformed officers directly behind him. She picked up the jamming device, slipping it into her pocket.

"We're ready to go here," she said, but she knew immediately something was wrong, the two uniforms each with a hand on their holster.

"Can I see your ID please?"

Katz circled the table, pulling out her badge wallet and flashing her ID. "Special Agent Willow, Homeland Security. And you are?"

"Lieutenant Mitchell." He held out his hand. "And I'm going to need to see that."

"Why? What's going on here?"

"Special Agent Willow, we have reason to believe you're an imposter." He stepped forward, as did the two officers still in the hall. "Now I must insist. Your badge."

Katz looked at him for a moment, her mind quickly playing out what would happen over the next sixty seconds.

She liked the outcome.

Her hand darted out, her knuckles crushing the detective's windpipe almost instantly. As he dropped to the floor, grabbing for his throat, gasping for breath, she pulled his weapon from his shoulder holster and flicked off the safety, burying two bullets in each of the officers, then spun toward Acton.

"Let's go."

Acton stood, staring at the bodies for a moment until she reached out and grabbed him by the front of his shirt, hauling him out of the room. She fished out her cellphone as an alarm sounded.

"Get in here!" she shouted as soon as the call was answered, then shoved it back into her pocket as she hauled Acton toward the secure door. A door to her left opened, a detective stepping out to see what was happening. She put a bullet in his head then almost smiled when she saw who was sitting at a table inside.

Laura Palmer.

"Professor. On your feet, now!" She pressed her gun against Acton's head and the woman's eyes widened. She leapt to her feet and rushed into the hallway as the heavy thumping of MP5's sounded from the other side of the secure door. "In front!" She pushed the two professors ahead of her then reached down and grabbed a second weapon, turning around, her back to the secure door, as she opened fire on anything that dared look into the hallway.

A buzzer sounded and she heard the heavy clicks of the secure door unlocking. She glanced over her shoulder and saw two of her men enter the hallway, their MP5's raised as they aimed down the hall.

"Let's go!" She turned and grabbed the two professors by the back of their shirts and pushed them through the doors, her men opening fire, covering their six. They exited the building quickly, their SUV at the bottom of the steps, the doors already open, her driver revving the engine. "In the back!"

She shoved the married couple toward the open rear door, her men still firing at anything that moved, then climbed into the passenger seat, slamming the door shut. She pointed both guns at the entrance, emptying the magazines as her men dove in the back, the tires chirping as the driver floored it.

Not exactly as planned.

But it didn't matter. She dialed her phone, someone picking up immediately. "Jam them, now!"

"Done."

She looked over at the driver. "Slow down. Their frequencies are jammed, they don't know who they're looking for."

He nodded and eased off on the gas, expertly putting distance between them by avoiding any red lights that could delay them, always taking the turn before if necessary. Within minutes they were miles away. She turned to look at the two professors.

"Now let's talk about a certain painting."

Operations Center Four

CIA Headquarters, Langley, Virginia

"I might have something here, boss."

Leroux looked over at Randy Child, one of his top computer guys, his mad skills at tracing Internet communications unmatched. It had been a dream to get him on the team, Morrison only giving him the news last week. He was young, which Leroux liked, he still finding it difficult to not even be thirty and have some staff that could be mistaken for his parents, though in this case Child fit perfectly in with his insecure management skills.

"What have you got?"

"A possible jumping off point for that security alert."

Leroux smiled. "Awesome! Show me."

His enthusiasm seemed to rub off on Child, his underling beaming a smile. He quickly began explaining, Leroux fortunate enough to be able to follow the tech unlike Morrison, still in the room now that they had received word Sherrie had been shot, probably to back him up in case he couldn't continue.

But he was determined to.

Sherrie had called him and told him she was okay, then went into the details. He had lectured her on this method in the past after a bad experience years ago when he had been pulling onto the interstate. His phone had rung and the call display had shown it was his parents. They never called in the morning, they fully aware he would be on his way to the office, so he knew immediately it was an emergency.

"I had to take your father to the hospital last night."

"What!"

"Don't worry, he's okay."

"Mom! *That's* how you start this type of conversation! Tell me he's okay, then tell me what happened!"

She had learned her lesson.

"English, please."

Leroux and Child looked over at their boss. "Sorry, sir. Essentially we've found the piece of hardware that was used to leave the Internet."

"So you know where it is?"

Child cleared his throat. "Not exactly, sir. We know the IP address—the unique identifier for it. This was hardcoded into the security software almost twenty years ago by the looks of it. There's no evidence it's been changed since then, and with modern security practices when it comes to version control, any unauthorized change to the code would be caught. I think we're looking at something that was put here when the system was originally developed."

Morrison crossed his arms and tapped his chin. "Okay, if I'm understanding you correctly, you've found a number that identifies a machine that you don't know the location of or even if it still exists today."

"Oh, it exists."

"How do you know?"

"Because if it didn't then nobody would have known the security alert had been triggered."

Morrison nodded. "Good point. Okay, so it exists. Do we have any way of finding out where it actually is?"

"Given time we might get a general idea," said Leroux. He turned to Child. "Run that address against our database, see if it's ever been used before."

Fingers flew then the results appeared onscreen, Leroux gasping.

"Holy shit!"

"Our problem in New Orleans is growing."

Ilya Mashkov frowned. Things weren't going well for The Assembly. In the past twenty-four hours he had been called to more emergency meetings than the past year, and the news never seemed to be good, or if it was, it wasn't for long. His last briefing on what had been the major crisis, the Titanic incident, suggested things there might be soon wrapped up, most of the parties either in custody or soon to be. Once the primaries were eliminated, a fake copy of the painting, already being prepared, would be planted at Professor Acton's university to be found after his death. It would be tested by those already contacted, declared a forgery, and then quickly forgotten.

The records clerk was dead, which meant the infection had been stopped at the military end, the Congressman was dead and all indications were he had been too scared to tell anyone after the security protocols had ended his phone conversation, and the taps in Wainwright's house suggested the only people who knew in his family were his wife and sister. They had kept things quiet after their conversation at the university, it apparently shaking them enough to decide to keep quiet.

Once they and those at the university are dead, it's over.

But now there was a new problem.

New Orleans.

And it was his problem to deal with, the entire financial side of the Jones' presidency bid his responsibility, Quaid his man.

262

"A New Orleans Police Detective named Isabelle Laprise is holding our man Peter Quaid along with a minor operative, Russell Saunders," reported Number One.

"What do they know?" asked Number Seven.

Mashkov leaned forward, clearing his throat. "Saunders knows nothing except that Mr. Quaid is his contact. Even if he talks, all he does is implicate Quaid. Quaid on the other hand is of more concern. He has met with several of our senior operatives, and should he talk, our chain of command could be compromised." He already knew how his colleagues would want this handled, but he wanted them to ask it so he could prove to them his resolve.

"How do you suggest we solve the problem?"

"We eliminate both liabilities before the infection can spread, then send a new representative to continue in Mr. Quaid's place. Now that Mr. Jones knows who his true masters are, there's no need to replace Mr. Saunders."

Once again, kill them all.

Unknown Location within Arlington, Virginia

Acton blinked rapidly as the hood was yanked off his head. Someone shoved him from behind and he stumbled toward a group of chairs in the middle of a massive concrete expanse. As he gained his bearings he looked about. Steel girders and large glass windows surrounded them, it clearly a warehouse of some sort, a warehouse completely devoid of anything except two SUV's and half a dozen chairs. To his right there was what he assumed to be an office, perhaps with a bathroom, he suddenly noticing that he had to piss like a racehorse, the several beers he had partaken in earlier making their presence felt on his bladder.

He forgot all about that when he saw Mai and Tommy sitting in two of the chairs. He rushed forward. "Are you two okay?"

Mai was crying, fresh tears rushing over old stains as she leapt into his arms. Tommy though was more of a concern. His face was caked in dried blood and he seemed groggy.

"Professor," he mumbled.

Acton let go of Mai and redirected her to the loving arms of Laura, then knelt in front of Tommy, carefully examining his head wound. He turned to their captors. "He needs a hospital. Now."

"Not yet," replied the woman. "When we have the painting, then we will deal with your friend's wound."

"He's just a kid. They both are. Let them go and I'll cooperate fully with you."

"We both will," said Laura, holding Mai in her arms. "We won't resist. Just let them go, please."

Their words and Mai's sobs seemed to have no impact on the woman, her expression cold, her eyes dead. He hadn't seen any emotion from her beyond slight smiles that were so exactly alike he'd swear she was a cyborg if he thought they existed.

Could she be a psychopath?

She'd have to be a special bit of crazy to be doing what she's doing. It was one thing to kill for your country like Kane or the Delta guys did, but he could tell from this woman's eyes she intended to kill every last one of them, not for any emotional reasons, but simply because she felt it was necessary for her mission.

She not only intended to plug the leak, she was going to mop up anything that had escaped.

And it had already started, Congressman Mahoney dead in what he was certain was a staged car accident.

The woman looked at him. "Where is the painting?"

Acton quickly decided he needed to cooperate. Sherrie would be missed, he was sure of it, and they needed time for additional resources to reach them. He had swallowed the tracking device and it was still good for at least a day.

They would be found.

The question was whether they'd be found dead or alive.

And at this moment in time, he had no leverage over this woman, but she had three people he cared about, including one that was priceless.

He looked at Laura.

"At the university, in one of the archeology labs."

"Then, Professor, you and I are going for a ride."

Operations Center Four
CIA Headquarters, Langley, Virginia

"What?"

Leroux looked at the search result on the screen. There was only one other hit in their database, and the contact on the record was him. And he knew immediately what it was. "That's the message."

Morrison looked at him. "What message?"

"*The* message."

Morrison looked confused for a moment then his eyes popped wide. "Oh. Are you sure?"

Leroux nodded.

"Clear the room!"

Everyone looked at each other for a moment, puzzled, then jumped to their feet, the room emptied except for Leroux and Morrison within seconds.

"What are you saying?" asked Morrison as he sat in one of the now vacant chairs. Leroux dropped into the chair vacated by Child just seconds ago. After the BlackTide incident he had been tasked to try and find out who The Assembly were. He had found absolutely nothing until the New Orleans plague scare when all surveillance laws were suspended, automatically opening up Langley's taps to data sources they didn't normally have access to. During that incident his monitoring routines were still running and they found something. A single hit.

A single email.

Sent through the IP address in question.

Because the email was discovered by accident, and would have been illegal to obtain if it hadn't been for the crisis, Morrison had ordered it quarantined, not to be looked at, he concerned it could destroy any future case against those behind the North Korean incident. Leroux had understood the decision but it had driven him nuts since, his one piece of evidence forbidden fruit that might actually help lead him from the purgatory he found himself in, constantly under surveillance by a protective detail.

But maybe that was all about to change.

"The email you had me quarantine, our one lead to who The Assembly might be, went through this same IP address."

"You mean—"

"The Assembly is behind this entire thing, and this email might lead us to them."

Morrison leaned back in his chair, his lips puffing in and out. "So if we open this illegally obtained email, we might find out who is behind all this."

"Yes." Leroux bit his lip, stunned at what he was about to say, possibly causing his boss to stick with his original decision, a decision he sensed was about to change. "But the same was true all along. If I had opened it before it might have led to their discovery."

Morrison nodded. "But until now, we didn't have a corroborating piece of evidence. Am I right in assuming that now that you have this IP address, you would be running it against everything we have?"

"Absolutely. Actually, it's running now. That hit was just our own internal database."

"So it is conceivable that you would have found this email eventually."

Leroux knew what his boss wanted him to say, and his tone, with a slightly tilted head and ever-so-slightly elevated eyebrow suggested he was right.

"Yes."

Morrison smiled. "Then it is no longer fruit of the poison tree as far as I'm concerned. Open it."

Leroux hesitated, his heart pounding as he realized he was about to open what could be Pandora's Box.

Or spam for penis enlargement pills.

He clicked on the entry, entered his authorization code, and the email suddenly appeared on the screen. He switched it to one of the large monitors so Morrison could read it.

Eureka!

Morrison rose from his chair, mouth agape. "This is it," he whispered.

Leroux couldn't believe what he was reading. It was an email congratulating Ilya Mashkov on his acceptance into The Assembly and assigning him a designator of "Number Twelve" for all future correspondence. A simple reply at the top read, "Number Twelve thanks you, Number One."

We have a name!

Morrison snapped his fingers several times, pointing at the screen. "I want everything we've got on this Ilya Mashkov."

"Yes, sir." He paused. "My team?"

Morrison nodded. "Get them all on this. I want to know everything, fast, before they go to ground."

Saint Paul's University, St. Paul, Maryland

It was the dead of night, barely anyone about. Acton wasn't sure what time it was, his watch confiscated when he had been arrested, though he'd have to guess around three in the morning. His captor had parked their SUV at the rear entrance to the sciences building where the archeology lab was located and the two of them were now walking down a deserted hallway, their footsteps echoing on the hard walls, nothing being said between them.

He stopped in front of one of the doors. "This is it."

"Open it."

"I don't have the key."

The woman stared at him blankly. "Why not?"

"The police took everything when I was arrested."

"And you decide to tell me this now?"

He shrugged. "I honestly hadn't realized it until this very moment." The sad thing was it was actually true. Now he wondered if it would cost him his life.

The woman drew her weapon and he took a step back with his right foot, preparing to disarm her.

A slight smile appeared, almost genuine. "I'm not going to shoot you, Professor. Your training from Colonel Leather will do you no good here."

Christ, she knows everything about me!

She fired two rounds into the lock then kicked the door open, Acton breathing a sigh of relief as she holstered her weapon. She jerked her head toward the lab. "You first."

He nodded, stepping inside and reaching over to flick the light on. He looked about to make sure they were alone, though he wasn't sure why, there no possibility of anyone being there at this hour.

"Quickly, Professor. Somebody likely heard those shots."

He nodded, walking to a climate controlled storage room to the rear, his captor following at a cautious distance. There would be no surprising her. From everything he had seen, this woman was deadly. She wouldn't hesitate to kill, and there'd be no dramatic delays with flamboyant speeches before she killed him.

She'd just take the shot.

Leaving no time for someone to rush to the rescue at the last, climactic moment.

He opened the rear door, it a coded panel not requiring a pass.

The door hissed, there a slight positive pressure on the opposite side to keep contamination out. Stepping inside, he pointed at the painting, it laying on one of the examination tables, still slightly curled. "There it is."

The woman stepped over and grabbed it by one end.

Acton gasped. "Be careful with that, it's priceless!"

She looked at him. "You do realize, Professor, that this painting will be destroyed. No one can ever know it existed."

Acton suddenly forgot about his own life that hung in the balance, a piece of history now at risk. "Is that really necessary? Can't you at least preserve it so that one day, perhaps years from now, it can be shared with the world once again?"

She quickly rolled the painting up then grabbed the case it had been delivered in by Wainwright. She stuffed it inside then turned to Acton. "Professor, your idealistic vision of the world we live in is curious." Her eyes narrowed. "Does everyone think like you, or are you unique?"

It was an odd question, he immediately wondering if there was indeed a Terminatrix under that beautiful exterior. For she was beautiful. Gorgeous in fact, and if she wasn't pure evil, he might have actually allowed himself to acknowledge that fact. But beauty wasn't only skin deep. Beauty to him extended far deeper, into one's heart, into one's soul. And this woman had neither.

She was the ugliest woman he had ever met.

Yet her question made him wonder if she even knew how ugly she truly was. Or if she'd care.

"I like to think I'm your average guy."

She nodded slightly. "Interesting." She motioned with the case toward the door. "Let's go. Quickly."

He stepped outside the pressurized storage room when a flashlight beam suddenly blinded him.

"Professor Acton, is that you?"

Acton's heart leapt as he recognized the security guard's voice. "Tucker, get out of here!"

Two shots rang out from behind him, the beam of light suddenly broken.

"No!"

Poydras Street, New Orleans, Louisiana

"Homeland Security, FBI, CIA, NSA. They all piss me off. Who do they think they are?"

Isabelle looked over at her partner, understanding his frustration. Their case was being taken away from them, and right now they were a glorified escort to the NOPD transport van ahead of them. There was actually no real need for them to be there, but she didn't want to let these two men out of her sight until they were delivered into the hands of the FBI.

Orders from the Chief himself.

Apologetic orders, but non-negotiable as well.

"They're the Feds," she finally responded. "Nothing we can do about it."

"Yeah, yeah, it just pisses me off."

"Then join them."

"Huh?"

"Join them. Take the FBI exam, they'd be lucky to have you."

"And leave your pleasant company? What would you do without me?"

Isabelle chuckled. "Don't you worry about me, dear, there's been many before you and there'll be many after you."

"Careful, Laprise, taken out of context some might think you were casting dispersions on yourself."

"You're a pig, Salinger. You definitely need to get laid."

"I was trying but you decided to take this case."

"You really think you had a shot tonight?"

"Absolutely." Salinger paused. "Okay, probably not. Not at least tonight. At least I hope not. Who wants to get into a relationship with someone who'll sleep with you on the first date?"

Isabelle blushed slightly, thinking back on Dylan Kane and her impulsive actions.

God, that so wasn't me!

She smiled slightly.

But it was so much fun!

"What are you smiling about?"

She glanced over at her partner. "Nothing."

"Bullshit." His jaw dropped. "You slept with someone on a first date!"

"I did no such thing." Which was true. She hadn't. It wasn't a date.

Two SUV's whipped by them, the city streets almost empty, they having come out of nowhere.

"Jesus!" exclaimed Salinger. "Where's a cop when you need one?"

But Isabelle wasn't ready to chalk it up to a street race. She reached forward and flicked her emergency lights on.

Too late to do anything.

Both SUV's matched the transport vehicle's speed, one on either side. Someone on the SUV to the left, it travelling on the wrong side of the road, reached out from the rear window and threw something that stuck on the side of the van like a magnet, then peeled away, the same happening on the right.

"Is that what I think it—"

Salinger never got to finish his sentence as an explosion tore through the van ahead of them. Isabelle slammed her brakes on, coming to a stop only feet away from the rear bumper, the fireball roaring into the night sky, flickering off the windows of the surrounding buildings. She shoved the car into reverse and hauled ass back about fifty feet before bringing them to a halt. Grabbing her radio, she stepped out of the car, Salinger doing the same, just as tires screeching behind them had them both spinning.

"Look out!" shouted Salinger as he dove to the side, Isabelle spinning and throwing herself to the ground as a tow truck slammed into the back of her car. She flipped onto her back to see a car sailing off the back of the tow truck and over her own, smashing into the inferno that was the transport vehicle.

Salinger rounded their car, rushing to her side. "Are you okay?"

She nodded and extended a hand. "Help me up." Salinger hauled her to her feet and she handed him the radio. "Call it in."

"You okay, miss?" She looked at the tow truck driver rushing over, beer gut proudly displayed, three day's growth peppered with crumbs of some forgotten meal.

She nodded then looked at what turned out to be a Jaguar joining the inferno. "Shit, that's going to be expensive," she muttered, looking over at the tow truck, a man climbing out of the passenger side, jumping up and down, clapping his hands together.

If that's not a happy dance...

"He doesn't seem upset."

The tow truck driver looked over his shoulder at the man and laughed. "You kiddin' me? He's my best customer. I'm actually on his speed dial." He lowered his voice, placing a hand to one side of his mouth. "Between you and me, I hope he buys another Jag. I've got two kids to put through college." He roared in laughter then turned, heading back to his truck.

Isabelle looked at the raging fire, her heart heavy, there no way anyone was surviving, the two police officers in the front lost.

Two good men. Dead. And for what?

"This case just got more interesting."

She looked at Salinger. "Did it? I think someone just ended our investigation."

"How so?"

"We've got four dead perps, all taken out by the Secret Service, the investigation taken over by the FBI, and now our only two suspects, who we were transporting to hand over to the FBI anyway, are now dead. "You and me, Salinger, we have no case. None. Nada. Rien."

Salinger smiled. "So what you're telling me is we're done for the night?"

Isabelle laughed and looked at her watch. "Give her a call, maybe you can get a nightcap."

Salinger grinned then raised his arm. "Taxi!"

"Wear protection, little one."

Salinger laughed and waved on an arriving taxi.

"I thought you were actually going to leave for a moment."

Salinger shook his head, motioning toward the inferno as the first emergency vehicles arrived, all levity gone. "Our night is just beginning."

Isabelle nodded, their coping with the helplessness of the situation through humor over.

"Let's get to work."

Chinquapin Round Road, Annapolis, Maryland

"What've you got?" asked Red, lying prone on a rooftop across the street from a warehouse they had tracked Acton to. Sherrie White's quick thinking in having him swallow a GPS tracker was proving prescient, he and his team arriving less than half an hour ago. A quick review of the data using codes provided by Sherrie showed Acton had been taken here for about ten minutes then left for his university.

"Acton's moving," replied Sergeant Zack "Wings" Hauser, watching a laptop display showing the man's movements. "It looks like they've left the university and are heading back here. Good call."

Red had decided to check out this location first, his hunch that the side trip to the university was to retrieve the painting that had started this entire fiasco. The New Orleans op was wrapped—everyone was either dead or in the air, the Secret Service taking over from Dawson's team as soon as they were on the ground, which wouldn't be for over an hour.

Dawson had requested his help, the op center stood down by Clancy now that his men were safely in the air. They were an hour away, Dawson several. And with it being the professors, there wasn't a man on the team who wouldn't drop everything to help.

Sergeant Eugene "Jagger" Thomas was to his right, peering through thermal imaging goggles. "I'm showing three people sitting in chairs, two on guard."

"Can you tell who they are?"

"Negative, but from body size, I'm guessing one is Professor Palmer and the other two are the students." Jagger lowered his goggles and looked at Red. "We can take them pretty easy, then we'll just have to deal with whoever is with the Doc."

Red shook his head. "Too risky. They could have some sort of check-in protocol. If we take them out now whoever has the Doc could be tipped off." He pursed his lips, motioning for the goggles. Jagger handed them over and Red took a look for himself. "No, we're going to sit tight and take them all at once."

"We're taking a hell of a chance," said Wings.

"I know, but I don't think we have a choice. We can't risk the Doc."

Jagger rolled to his side, looking at Red and Wings. "If I know the Doc, he'd rather have us save his wife and sacrifice him."

Red nodded, thinking of his own wife. There wasn't anything he wouldn't do for that woman, she the best thing to ever happen to him. She had taken care of him like no other woman could and had given him a fantastic son that was the light of his life. They were why he fought for his country as hard as he did. His family, his friends, his unit. They were everything to him, and it was his duty and his privilege to make the world they all lived in a better place.

Even if it meant not coming home one day.

His wife understood that, though she worried every time he deployed. She wouldn't be human if she didn't. But she never complained. She knew the life, she knew the job, and she had signed up for it the day he was allowed to read her in, it just after he made The Unit. He would never forget how proud she had looked when he told her. So many times he had heard about the wives and fiancées showing fear. But not Shirley.

She beamed.

Her only complaint was that she could never tell anyone what her husband did, instead sometimes suffering jabs from her family and friends about how her husband was just a records clerk when "real soldiers" were off fighting and dying.

It had made her cry in frustration sometimes, yet she never broke.

I'd die for her.

And so would Professor Acton for his wife. He looked at the heat signature of the woman he was pretty sure was Laura Palmer, then handed the goggles back to Jagger. "I have no doubt he would. Fortunately for him I'm in charge and sacrificing him shouldn't be necessary." He looked again at the scene below. It was a large warehouse, modern, with tinted windows for the top half of the walls giving them an excellent view of the heat signatures inside.

And clear shots if they could remove those windows.

He turned to Sergeant Jerry "Jimmy Olsen" Hudson setting up his M24A2 SWS Sniper Weapon System. "Jimmy, you stay here, hold your fire until you hear from me or it becomes clear a hostage is about to be killed."

"Roger that."

Red pointed to Wings and Jagger. "We're going to get some charges on those windows. I want clear lines of sight for Jimmy when the shit hits the fan."

"Too bad BD isn't here," said Wings, looking below.

Red decided to have some fun. "Why, not happy with my orders?"

"Ooohh," grinned Jagger. "Fight! Fight! Fight!"

Wings gave Jagger a look then returned to his goggles. "*Nooo,* I mean we could use four extra guys. We've already got two hostiles with an unknown number on the way. Four more guns could prove useful."

Red had to agree. Eight guns were almost always better than four, though not always. Today would *not* be one of those exceptions, though he had gone into worse situations with fewer. "Unfortunately for us we're all that's available. Besides, we've got the element of surprise and I'd like to think we're a little bit better at this than they are." He turned to Wings. "What's Acton's location?"

"Still looks like they're headed back here. Five minutes out."

Red pushed back from the roof edge then rose. "Time to plant some charges."

Operations Center Four
CIA Headquarters, Langley, Virginia

"Ilya Mashkov is a Russian national, billionaire, one of the oligarchs who for some reason hasn't been touched by Putin."

"Buddies?" asked Morrison, sitting across from Leroux, everyone tired, it now well into the night.

"They seem to meet regularly, always formally though privately. There's been none of the typical macho photo ops though, riding lions, hunting dolphins, scoring eight goals against former NHLers."

"When your wingers carry AK-47s, it's easy to score," muttered Child.

Morrison chuckled. "Interesting. I wonder if it means anything."

Leroux shrugged. "Could. There's nothing Putin likes better than a staged photo op, especially when he can look more macho than the guy he's with. Like when he tried to embarrass the Canadian Prime Minister by walking over and asking to shake his hand in front of other world leaders."

Morrison smiled. "Yeah, I loved that. What did he say? I'll shake your hand but I've only got one thing to say to you: get out of Ukraine?"

"Sounds about right."

Morrison shook his head. "Nice to see the man neutered by a Crazy Canuck." He motioned toward Leroux's tablet. "Continue."

"Yes, sir. Mashkov has holdings all over the world, especially England. Deals in hi-tech, weapons, oil, natural resources, everything. Incredibly diversified." Leroux waved the tablet. "It'll take a team of forensic auditors to figure out just what he's into."

Morrison tapped his chin. "But he's definitely part of The Assembly?"

"I think without a doubt. After that email was received, his business empire exploded. Look." Leroux swiped a chart on his tablet, sending it to one of the large screens, a bar chart with the CIA's estimate of Mashkov's net worth. "His net worth went from two billion to six in a matter of a year, and that's just what we know about. Whoever these people are, they have money. I'm guessing that they buy from each other, so with each new acquisition, their empire grows."

"Anything illegit?"

"Nothing we can find. He's squeaky clean."

"And his contacts? Any indicator of who the others are?"

"Well, if he's number twelve, then I think we can safely assume there's at least eleven others."

Child laughed, spinning in his chair.

Leroux and Morrison both looked at him. "What?" asked Leroux.

"Oh, you're gonna love this, boss! This idiot had his emails all routed through his own personal server."

"Are you kidding me? Who does that?" A smile started to spread on Leroux's face. If Mashkov were stupid enough to have all his email routed through his own server, a massive violation of any type of security protocols, they might have the break they needed. He looked about the room, everyone having stopped what they were doing, all just in as much elated shock as he was.

Morrison cleared his throat. "So just what does that mean for us?"

Leroux turned to his boss. "It means that every email he sent and received exited their Dark Web and went onto the clearnet, the regular Internet."

"So we have copies?"

"Oh yeah, Echelon would have picked them up. Now we just need to crack the encryption and we'll know everybody he ever sent an email to or received an email from."

"Why would anyone do that?"

Leroux shrugged. "My guess is their entire communications network is on their own set of hardware, possibly satellite based, and requires the use of a special piece of hardware. I'm guessing Mr. Mashkov found that inconvenient, so had his own IT guys set up the system to route all of the email through his own server so he could read them on his laptop or iPhone, whatever. By doing that it's secure from normal prying eyes since it's still encrypted—"

"But not ours," finished Morrison.

"Cuz we ain't normal!" laughed Child.

Morrison gave him a look.

Child clammed up, then pointed at the screen. "I'm pulling data now."

"So what you're telling me is—"

Leroux smiled at his boss. "We might be able to find out who the entire Assembly is."

Morrison inhaled audibly, looking at the screens, lines branching out across the globe showing hundreds then thousands of communications.

"We've got you now."

Chinquapin Round Road, Annapolis, Maryland

Large delivery doors rolled up, Acton's captor pulling them through and bringing the SUV to a halt. The ride back from the university had been somber as he pictured Tucker at the end-of-term barbecue less than a month ago. He had been so proud of his first granddaughter, a cute little thing that had behaved remarkably well for having so much attention heaped on her.

Always smiling, always whistling.

He had to admit he hated whistlers—it drove him nuts. Yet for some reason Tucker's whistle was always reassuring—and only heard when he thought he was alone, patrolling the halls.

A whistle that would never be heard again.

He just prayed it wasn't a student that walked in to find the body. It might be something they'd never recover from.

He looked at Laura as he stepped out, she immediately sensing his mood, giving him a "what's wrong?" look. "Tucker's dead. She shot him."

Laura gasped, Mai sobbed and Tommy moaned.

He's going to die soon. Probably a brain hemorrhage or something.

"Here they come," said one of the guards, opening the doors that had just closed a moment before. Another black SUV rolled through, the doors sealing them in once more as two of the woman's henchmen climbed out. They opened the rear doors and Acton's heart sank as he recognized the new arrivals.

We're all going to die.

Steve Wainwright stepped to the ground, helping another woman out whom Acton assumed was the man's wife, his sister Judy following.

Everyone looked terrified, and Steve's eyes widened when he saw Acton and Laura.

Acton turned to the woman. "What are they doing here? You said you'd let us go once you had the painting."

The woman shook her head. "No, Professor, I said we would part ways." Acton's stomach flipped as she raised her weapon and pointed it at Steve. "It's time to clean up the mess you created, Mr. Wainwright."

Steve was terrified, that much was clear to Acton, but he was of a generation that was a hell of a lot tougher than most alive today. He squared his shoulders, drew a long breath and glared at the woman, placing himself between her and his family.

And said nothing.

"This isn't necessary," said Acton, stepping slightly to his left to block any clear shot at Laura and his students. "You have the painting. If anyone asks, we'll just say it turned out to be a fake. End of story, nobody will ever know. You don't have to do this!"

Her expression was cold, not even an inkling evident that he was getting to her. She looked at him. "I have my orders. But don't worry Professor Acton, you'll live until your former student appears to save the day." Confusion gripped Acton and he was about to ask who she meant when he suddenly realized it was Kane she was after. Yes, she was eliminating anyone who had been exposed to their secret about the Titanic, but she was also using it as an opportunity to get her hands on Kane.

But why?

He was about to ask when her weapon fired.

Steve flinched, his wife screamed, and Judy fell back against the side of the SUV, sliding to the floor, blood pumping from a hole in her chest, the shocked look on her face triggering a white rage deep within Acton. He took a step toward the woman but six guns were immediately trained on him.

"You bitch."

It was Laura who said it, Acton's rage contained for a moment by reality. He looked over at a sobbing Steve, his sister cradled in his arms as she bled out, the life draining rapidly from her face as she looked up at her brother.

"I'm so sorry!" he cried, "So sorry! I should've left it alone, I should've never unlocked that door!"

Judy reached up with a shaking hand and pressed it against his cheek. "It's…" She didn't have the strength to finish, her hand falling to her lap, her head lolling to the side, all life gone from her eyes.

Steve turned to the woman, still holding his dead sister. "I'm going to kill you. I'm going to kill everyone who means anything to you. I don't care what it takes, if I have to come back from Hell itself to torment you until your dying days, I'm going to end you."

The woman raised her weapon and pointed it at Steve's wife. "Who else have you told?"

"No one."

She cocked the weapon, it a needless action that impressively made a point.

"Steve!" cried his wife, cowering behind him, his own bravado broken with the single click. He held out a protective arm, tears streaming down his face, a face Acton was quite certain had shed few tears of fear and sorrow in its life.

"Please, I'm begging you. We told no one, I swear. Just Congressman Mahoney and the professors, that's it."

"Didn't you tell Dean Milton?"

Acton felt his stomach tighten at the mention of his best friend's name.

God I hope he's safe somewhere.

"Right, yes, I forgot, he was there."

"Who else?"

The look of shame on Steve's face spoke volumes to his character as his eyes involuntarily darted toward Mai, the tiny girl shaking like a leaf, holding onto an unresponsive Tommy as she squeezed her eyes shut, her head buried in his shoulder.

"Miss Trinh," said the woman, Mai yelping at the sound of her name. "And no one else?"

"N-no. Once we figured out that this might be a big deal, we went home and decided no one else should know, at least not for now."

The woman lowered her weapon. "Good. It appears the infection is almost contained." She raised her weapon and pointed it at Wainwright. "Thank you for your assistance."

"We've got a target down, I repeat, a target down. Looks like one of the new arrivals. I don't have a clear shot on the shooter. There's a metal girder in the way."

Shit!

Red sprinted down the side of the building, Wings and Jagger on his heels. They had been forced to retreat when the second SUV arrived. The cover of night was helpful, though nothing could hide three men standing against a completely smooth wall. They came to a stop at an employee entrance, Red pointing at the handle. Wings tried it and shook his head, quickly rigging it with an explosive charge.

"Can you reposition?" asked Red, activating his comm.

"Negative, if I do I lose my angle on the other targets. I'm reading six hostiles now. Better move quick, I think someone is about to get it. Wait, she's lowering her weapon. Ah shit, taking the shot."

"Fire in the hole," hissed Red, squeezing the detonator. Glass shattered overhead, half a dozen heavy panes obliterated, the shards falling straight down, the charges enough to take out the windows though not send the deadly pieces hurtling toward the very people they were trying to save. At the same time Wings triggered the detonator on the door, blasting the locking mechanism apart, Jagger yanking it open. Red surged forward, Glock raised as Jimmy's first shot rang out from across the street.

Acton spun around, ducking, rushing toward Laura and the kids as glass rained down from above. He heard a shot and looked over his shoulder to see one of the gunmen that had arrived with Steve's family drop, a massive hole in his chest. The others turned, weapons raised, looking for the shooter as another dropped only feet from Acton.

He made a decision.

He dove for the man's gun, grabbing his weapon and scurrying behind the front of the second SUV, taking aim at the woman. She dropped, spinning toward him, one leg extended in front of her as both her weapons came to bear on him, both barrels blasting deadly lead in his direction.

He ducked as Laura screamed, scrambling around to the other side, putting the large tire between him and their captor. He popped up to take a look and spotted three men surging around the office enclosure.

There's more of them!

Several shots rang out, slamming into his cover, sending him back into hiding. He leaned out, the angle not giving the woman a shot, and took aim at the new arrivals.

Then hesitated.

You don't know who they are.

He had to consider they might be friendlies, someone clearly attacking their position from outside. He lowered his weapon, hoping his gut was serving him well today. He rushed down the passenger side of the vehicle, someone delivering suppression fire from the rear bumper toward the outside, silencing the sniper for now. Acton rounded the bumper and put his weapon to the man's head, squeezing the trigger.

He dropped in a heap.

Katz rose from behind the SUV, spotting the three new arrivals coming directly toward her. She raised her weapon and aimed at the fuse panel on the wall twenty feet away, pumping several rounds into it, sparks bursting from the shorted circuits, the entire warehouse suddenly bathed in complete darkness.

And she the only one prepared for it.

She rushed toward the second SUV, its driver's side door still open and dove inside. Standard protocol was to leave the keys in the ignition in the event a speedy exit was necessary and she was pleased to see her men had followed their training. She jammed her foot on the brake and pushed the ignition switch as she reached over and pulled the door shut. A hail of gunfire slammed into the side of the SUV, the bullet resistant window splintering as she shoved the vehicle into gear and hammered on the gas. Gunfire continued to tear into the SUV as she aimed the vehicle toward the far side of the warehouse, keeping her head down so the sniper across the street wouldn't have a shot. The closed doors to the rear loading dock beckoned and she rose, bracing herself for the impact, unsure how strong they might be.

A bullet tore into her dash, scoring the leather and passing through the windshield.

And she knew that was the best shot the sniper had.

Red flipped down his night vision goggles and rushed forward, weapon raised. Someone who had been standing behind the second SUV was suddenly exposed and Red immediately recognized him as Professor Acton.

"Friendly at two o'clock!"

He opened fire on the rapidly accelerating SUV, as did Jagger and Wings, though it appeared to have some sort of upgrades, their bullets not penetrating the door, only the window splintering. He took aim at the tires but it was too late, the vehicle blasting through a set of rear doors and into the night.

"Clear!" shouted Wings, quickly followed by Jagger.

He scanned the area, confirming his teammates' assessment, finally relaxing. "Clear!" He activated his comm. "Any shot on that SUV?"

"Negative, she's gone."

Shit!

Acton hit the ground, lowering his weapon when he heard the shouted "Friendly" advisory, it crystal clear the new arrivals were on his side. Rather than add his own bullets into the mix and possibly become a target, he let the three men try and take out the SUV as he instead looked to make sure all the other hostiles were down for the count.

The SUV slammed into the far doors, the thin metal and glass tearing away as thousands of pounds of motor vehicle forced its way through.

And then it was over.

Emergency lighting took the edge off the darkness as his eyes adjusted, and he cautiously pushed himself to his feet.

Then smiled as he recognized their saviors.

"What are you guys doing here?" he asked, stepping forward, hand extended.

Red shook his hand, as did the others. "A friend said you needed some help." Red motioned toward Steve Wainwright, still holding his dead sister. "I'm sorry we were too late to save her."

"So am I," said Acton, wrapping an arm around Laura as Mai watched Jagger and Wings examine Tommy. He looked toward the rear doors, now hanging off their hinges. "Any chance you'll be able to catch her?"

Red shook his head. "Doubt it. This is off the books so we don't have any assets in the area. There's more going on here than you know, Doc, and it isn't over yet."

Acton frowned, not liking the sound of that. "Care to fill me in?"

"Absolutely. But first we need to get you to safety."

Assembly Covert Communications Facility, Moscow, Russia

Ilya Mashkov was exhausted, he graduating to copious amounts of coffee now, his usual pale tea not enough to keep the juices flowing. He was sure the other members of The Assembly were just as exhausted as he, though their silhouettes revealed nothing.

And nor did his.

He assumed.

He always wondered if he was the only one who couldn't see their faces. Perhaps everyone could see his, or perhaps everyone could see the faces of those who came after them, since they already knew their identities through the vetting process.

Perhaps some day I'll start to see some faces on the screen.

The very thought that those anonymous figures could actually see him forced him to be at his best whenever he arrived at the secure site set up for him. He wished they would set one up at his primary residence in Moscow, but his request had been refused.

Security reasons.

No matter, he was an IT expert and had tapped the hardware himself, bringing a little convenience to his life. He used it to read the emails as they came in so he would have time to prepare responses if necessary, and sometimes skipped his onsite check-in to send replies or new emails, instead batching them then sending them all at once, giving the impression he had actually logged into the hardline.

He was certain everyone was doing the same thing, it simply ludicrous in today's world to expect someone to travel fifteen minutes in each direction when the touch of a button from anywhere in the world would allow him to accomplish the same thing.

But he never faked the meetings.

That he would never dare risk, though he had been debating it over the past day, there so many meetings in the past 48 hours it was beyond ridiculous.

"Number Twelve, our intelligence reports indicate the CIA have been gathering quite a bit of intel on you in the past several hours."

Mashkov felt his throat go dry almost instantly, his tongue stuck to the roof of his mouth. He reached for his coffee, taking a large sip, swishing it around. "That's odd," he said. "Do we know why?"

"No," said Number One, his screen surrounded by a pulsating green box indicating who was speaking, there no mouth to see.

"Are they looking into anyone else?" Mashkov hesitated for a moment, his mind still processing the implications of what had been revealed, he never being privy to a special meeting that discussed one of the members specifically. "I mean, any of you?"

"No."

"Then that's good, right? If it had anything to do with The Assembly they'd be pulling data on more than just one of us. It might be because of my meeting with the Russian President scheduled for next week."

"Perhaps."

Mashkov's alarms were ringing. There was no way they would have called an emergency meeting for routine government inquiries into his background. It must happen a hundred times a day, and if these people hiding in the shadows were as powerful as he knew they were, then their names most likely had been run at some point as well.

So why are they so concerned?

"If you want, I can look into it."

"That won't be necessary. We have someone taking care of it as we speak."

Mashkov's blood ran cold as all the screens went blank.

Approaching Washington, DC

"They'll use me until they're done with me."

Christopher Jones sat facing his wife, the security detail at the rear of the plane, leaving them alone. He had decided he had to tell someone what was going on, and his wife was the only one he could trust completely.

But the fear on her face had him regretting his decision almost immediately. Tears had rolled down her cheeks when he described the sniper aiming at Kaitlin and the promise to kill everyone descendent from his grandfather.

He wondered if it included her.

She was married to him, but she wasn't blood, and this organization seemed to be very precise, very cold, very calculating.

It made sense. The promise to his grandfather was to eliminate his entire bloodline.

He looked at Constance. "I think you and your family are safe."

She looked at him, wide-eyed as she dabbed the corners of her eyes. "*You* are my family. Our children are, our grandchild. How can you say such a thing?"

He leaned over and took her hand in his, squeezing it gently. "You know what I mean. I think they mean the bloodline, so *you* will be safe. It's everyone else we love we need to worry about."

"If they kill you, they better kill me too. There's no way I want to live if everyone I ever cared about is dead."

He smiled slightly, trying to comfort her, not sure of what to say.

I have to get us out of this.

She drew in a deep breath then exhaled, slowly. "Okay, let's think of this logically."

"Logically." He smiled, her analytical side starting to show. It was how she had fought her cancer, it was how she fought all her battles. And this apparently was going to be no different. It was a coping mechanism that was actually useful. "We'll figure out a way through this, together."

"We don't know who these people are."

"No."

"But we know Pete Quaid was one of them."

"An underling is my guess. Not one of their leaders."

"These twelve shadows you saw on the screens."

"Right. But he's dead, remember, so no use to us."

Word had just arrived about the assassination of the only two suspects in custody. There had been six men when the hotel was assaulted with two drivers apparently waiting at the underpass he had been told about. That meant eight men. Four had been killed by the security team sitting behind him, but the other four had obviously escaped.

And silenced the only possible leaks.

NOPD had no success in tracing those involved, and with him no longer in New Orleans, they were most likely out of the state by now too.

They'll never find them.

And it wouldn't matter if they did. They were foot soldiers. They would know even less than Saunders.

Saunders!

He still couldn't believe the man was involved.

I wonder if his grandfather made a promise.

"If you don't do what they ask, they'll kill everyone."

"That's what they said."

"And they want you to become President."

Jones looked at his wife, sensing something. "Yes. Why? What do you mean?"

"What would happen if you didn't?"

"Huh?"

"What would happen if you lost?"

Jones' eyebrows climbed his forehead slightly as he leaned back in his seat, contemplating his wife's words. If he were to lose the election, then he wouldn't be betraying his country since they'd have no way of using him. And if he lost, without revealing their secrets, they'd have no reason to kill him.

It made sense.

He looked at his wife, smiling. "I think you may have just saved all our lives."

Her eyes twinkled. "It's what I do."

He laughed, leaning over and giving her a peck on the cheek. "So how does the runaway front runner lose an election?"

"There's only one way I can think of."

"And that is?"

"We need a good scandal."

Leif Morrison's Office, CIA Headquarters, Langley, Virginia
The next day

"How's Sherrie?"

"She's well, sir, at least as well as can be expected." Leroux stifled a yawn. "Sorry, sir, I was up most of the night with her then had to drive back here."

Morison's eyes narrowed. "She's having trouble sleeping?"

"No, not at all. The painkillers they've got her on are knocking her out pretty good. It's the wheezing. They say it'll go away soon, but I guess I'm just paranoid that she'll stop breathing."

Morrison rose from his desk and took a seat closer to Leroux. He leaned forward, elbows on his knees. "She's going to be fine, Chris. You need to stop worrying." He raised a hand, smiling. "I know, I know, it's easier said than done, but this is the life you've signed up for."

"I know, being the boyfriend of a CIA operative means I need to learn to expect these things."

Morrison shook his head, his smile spreading. "No, that's not what I meant. What I meant was you've signed up to love someone. And that means you're going to spend the rest of your life worrying about that person when they're not well, whether it's cracked ribs from two shots to the chest, or the flu. It doesn't matter what it is, or how routine it is, you're going to worry." He patted Leroux's knee. "It means you love her. And as long as you worry, you know you still do." Morrison rose and returned to his chair behind his desk. "Now, what's the latest?"

Leroux gathered himself for a moment, Morrison always like a father figure to him, though rarely one to give fatherly advice. "Well, actually we've made a lot of progress in the past twenty-four hours. We were able to trace the hack in New Orleans to the same Dark Web jump-off point as several emails routed through Mr. Mashkov's server."

"So that confirms the New Orleans incident was committed by The Assembly."

"Yes, sir, it appears so. Mr. Jones came clean to the Delta operative, telling him everything in an effort to solicit his help."

"I read that in the briefing notes," said Morrison, tapping a file on his desk. "*Very* interesting idea. It could work. When is the leak scheduled?"

"It will be hitting several news desks within the hour. We should be seeing it on the six o'clock news. Mr. Jones has a news conference scheduled at eight p.m. which should mean his speech will be on the eleven o'clock."

Morrison pursed his lips. "It's too bad, he was a good man. An honest man."

"Too honest, it would seem."

"What do you mean?"

"Well, if he had been after the power, he could have agreed to Quaid's terms in the hotel room instead of forcing their hand. And it was his idea to do what he's about to do. He could have done nothing, continued his campaign, and no one would have been the wiser. The New Orleans incident might have actually got him even more votes."

"I see your point. And the Titanic thing?"

"Well, we know it's definitely an Assembly thing as well. But here's the thing. We've been combing through Echelon intercepts of the emails and think we may have identified at least two other Assembly members."

"How?"

"The emails never use names, just numbers, but they don't bother encoding things like locations or meetings. It's almost as if the number system is to protect their identities from each other."

"Makes sense. What did you discover?"

"Well, there's been a lot of emails that reference different conferences or meetings that some of them will be attending. We've begun checking out guest lists for those conferences and looking for overlap where the same person shows up at multiple events, matching the emails."

Morrison smiled, leaning forward. "And you found two that match?"

Leroux nodded, grinning. "Yes, sir. And once we knew who we were looking for, we were able to pull their files. They both inherited massive corporate empires and both do business not only with each other, but Mashkov as well."

Morrison shook his head. "All because some idiot was lazy and wanted to be able to check his email at home."

Leroux rapped his knuckles on the arms of his chair. "Yup. But I think we have an opportunity here."

"What?"

"Well, I had a crazy idea on how we could use our newfound knowledge as leverage."

Morrison's eyes narrowed slightly. "Leverage? For what?"

"To protect the Professors' lives, and the others."

Morrison smiled slightly.

"And yourself."

Leroux blushed slightly.

"And myself."

Moscow, Russia

"Turn that up!"

Ilya Mashkov leaned forward, his butler Dimitri doing as requested, the CNN simulcast over his car's satellite radio suddenly cranked up, leaving Mashkov's heart pounding at the announcer's words.

"In a stunning revelation earlier today, it's been revealed that the widely perceived front runner for the presidency, Christopher Jones, has received extensive campaign financing from questionable Russian sources. Leaked campaign documents show multi-million dollar donations from several individuals and companies linked to Russian President Vladimir Putin. Campaign insiders, speaking on condition of anonymity, confirmed reports that Jones was kidnapped two days ago in New Orleans by possible members of the Russian mob, demanding he tone down his recent rhetoric regarding increased Russian sanctions. That kidnapping resulted in the deaths of at least six individuals including one of Jones' largest financial contributors, Peter Quaid, CEO of Silidev, a large multi-national with significant operations in Russia. A spokesperson for the Jones campaign said he will be holding a press conference later this evening. We will bring that to you live when it happens. In other news—"

Mashkov waved his fingers in front of his throat and Dimitri muted the broadcast, leaving him alone with his thoughts.

It's a disaster.

There was no other way to describe it. And it was bullshit. He had made certain that Jones' backers were all American. Quaid himself was American. Most large businesses in the United States now had some ties with Russia. To claim that this meant the financing came from there was ridiculous.

Then again, the press today never seemed to be interested in the truth, just clickbait that would drive their ratings.

Presidential Hopeful Christopher Jones' Financing all Above Board.

It was a headline that wouldn't grab anyone's attention. Claim the Russian mob was involved and all hell would break lose. He had no doubt the 24-hour news stations were talking about it fulltime, bringing in questionable experts to discuss the implications, Jones already guilty in their eyes as it made for the most sensational newscast. And if it were proven false, it would only get airplay if they could make a story out of Jones being the victim of someone. If they couldn't, it would be a buried story, simply dropped by the press, leaving the majority of those who got their news in sound bites to wonder what had ever happened, ignorant to the man's innocence.

The others aren't going to be happy.

He was already on their radar for some reason.

Perhaps this was why!

It made sense. If someone was looking into the Jones campaign's finances, they would definitely have found Quaid. Quaid did have business dealings with several of his companies here in Russia and abroad. The link would be easy to make. Chances were that anyone connected to Quaid was being looked into.

He breathed a sigh of relief.

It makes perfect sense!

He frowned.

Then why was it the CIA?

The West hated the Russian leadership, that much was obvious. Even he, a loyal Russian, hated the Russian leadership. It was a dictatorship run by a testosterone junkie with a Napoleon complex. Nobody wants to see their leader with his shirt off, whether he thinks he has abs or not.

It's just not presidential.

That hatred for what Russia had unfortunately become meant the propaganda machines on both sides were in full gear, churning out their preferred message to the populace. It was unfortunate that here in Russia the message was quite often so absurd it reminded him of the Soviet Union. And in Mother Russia, where almost the entire press was controlled by the state, its citizens too often believed the rhetoric.

Morons.

The greatest gift they had was access to information, yet too many of them believed their government when that information contradicted the official message.

Lies from the corrupt Russian-hating West!

But that same propaganda machine was working on the other side of the Atlantic as well, and it made sense that the CIA, masters at psychological warfare, would be involved.

Which would be why it was them *that were looking into me.*

He smiled.

Surely my associates will come to the same conclusion.

These things always blew over, and so would this in time, especially with the short attention spans of the populace.

He frowned.

But what about New Orleans? What about Jones?

He might be clear, but his operation with respect to Jones appeared to be a disaster. Even with the stories not true, it could be enough to destroy the Jones campaign, especially with the anti-Russian sentiment sweeping America.

What will Jones say?

He had been listening to the conversation between Quaid and Jones in New Orleans after they had kidnapped the man. Brett Jones' past had been revealed and the threat made, Jones capitulating in the end.

He agreed to cooperate under threat of death to his entire family.

There was no way he was behind the leak. The question now was what Jones would say at his press conference. Would he deny the allegations? He would have to, wouldn't he? After all, they weren't true.

Then Mashkov had a thought, his jaw dropping.

"He wouldn't!"

Walter E. Washington Convention Center, Washington, DC

"Ready?"

Jones looked at Kitty Carmichael in the mirror, her head poking through the door. "Give me a moment."

"Okay."

She disappeared and his wife clucked at him, pushing herself up from the couch and walking over. She gently turned him and adjusted his tie, giving him a pat on the chest when she was done. "There you go."

He looked down at her, smiling. "What would I do without you?"

"I don't know, but I *do* know you'd never be presentable in public."

He laughed then sighed, all happiness draining from him. "After tonight, I don't think it will matter."

"You don't know that."

He took her by the shoulders and leaned in, giving her a gentle peck. "Oh, I think we do."

He sucked in a slow breath, took a final look in the mirror, then held out his hand. "Shall we?"

She smiled, taking his hand and squeezing it. "We'll get through this together."

He nodded, the urge to cry barely held at bay, his lifelong dreams about to be shattered, his entire way of life about to be completely upset, all because of something his grandfather did a century ago.

It's not fair.

They had struggled over the past two days with their decision, though it was the right one, Agent "White" helping them with the covert side of things. It was essential that no one know he himself had been the source of the leak. It had been handled expertly. And with the latest revelation from the CIA that they had identified at least three Assembly members, he had rewritten his planned speech, it now much more final than what he had planned. It was something he had wanted to do from the beginning, but until what he had heard only two hours earlier, he hadn't felt safe enough to do so.

But that had all changed.

Tonight he would go out with a bang, not the planned whimper.

Then leave the public eye.

Permanently.

He opened the door, White and his three partners in the hall.

"Sir."

Jones nodded. "Agent. How about we get this over with?"

"Sounds good to me, sir."

Agent White and his Asian partner, Agent Green, led the way, security heavy with local police and Secret Service providing security. There was no way there was going to be a repeat of what happened in New Orleans.

Nobody would be kidnapped tonight.

Assassinated maybe.

He could live with that, if it meant his family was left untouched. His wife probably wasn't long for this world—it was his children and grandchildren he worried about. They deserved long, happy lives. And if that meant sacrificing his, then so be it.

Somebody announced him and the partisan crowd roared, none aware of the bombshell he was about to drop. He cleared the side curtains and raised his hand in the air, his wife doing the same. He glanced at her, her smile mixed with sadness, something the cameras would catch later as the talking heads picked apart the entire evening.

The stage was filled with his senior staff, none of whom knew what was about to happen. It felt lonely. Normally when back on his home turf his children would be on stage with him, but he had told them to stay home.

He feared what might happen.

As he reached the podium, he let go of Constance's hand and she stepped slightly back to give him the spotlight. He glanced over to see Agent White and his men manning either side of the stage, hundreds of camera flashes blinding him, all the major networks with their own crews recording this historic event.

It will be forgotten within a week.

He gripped the side of the dais, squeezing hard, trying to draw strength from the pain of the wood eating into his palms.

Pain is weakness leaving the body.

His high school football coach had used that line on them. It was about the only useful thing the man had ever said. Or at least the only thing Jones could remember him ever saying.

Why are the painful memories always the ones you remember?

He had so many distinct memories from his early childhood, but they all involved pain. Getting bit by the neighbors terrier, skinning his knees on the neighbor's driveway, stepping on a nail in the neighbor's yard.

Kids should be avoiding their neighbors.

As he looked out at the cheering crowd he thought of today's helicopter parents. They'd never let their kid near the neighbor's dog, let them run for their Big Wheel or go near a yard where a fence was being built.

If kids don't learn about these things, how will they be able to teach their own children?

From those moments onward he was always cautious around strange dogs, tied his shoelaces and watched out when men were working.

All without his mother hovering over him.

SINS OF THE TITANIC

He raised his hands, quieting the crowd.

He raised his hands, quieting the crowd.

He decided to open with the joke his wife had suggested.

"The reports of my death have been greatly exaggerated!"

Laughter filled the room followed by a roar as a smile spread across his face, his wife clapping and laughing just behind him.

"It's been a crazy year, a busy year, and I think we've done a lot of good, don't you?"

More cheers, a chant of his name struck up until he raised his hands again.

"I appreciate that, I appreciate that." He paused, leaning forward over the podium slightly. "Now, you've all heard the news reports from earlier today."

Boos.

"I know, I know, I'm not happy about them either. But unfortunately the evidence presented appears to suggest that the stories are true." Shouts of dismay erupted and he gave them a moment. "I know, I'm as shocked and disappointed as you are. I can assure you that I had no idea, but the evidence seems to indicate that the majority of the funding provided to my campaign through the late Mr. Quaid has ties to Russian companies and possibly Russian criminal and even *political* elements."

Fists were thrown into the air, the anger clear.

"You're right to be angry. I'm angry as well. In fact, I'm livid. You *know* me, you *know* what I stand for. I believe America needs to be strong in the face of its adversaries, and to think that these very adversaries were financing my campaign is an outrage."

He paused, holding his hands up to keep the audience quiet. He looked over at his wife for a moment.

"I almost lost my wife last year."

307

His voice cracked, eliciting awws from the audience. He held out his hand and she took it. He gave it a squeeze and whispered an "I love you" before letting go.

"My wife is my rock; I don't know what I'd do without her." He took in a deep breath. "What happened to me the other night made me realize just how precious life is. Two people I had known for years are dead, directly as a result of my campaign. During the time I was a hostage, I was told to tone down my speeches about Russia and the sanctions I believe should be toughened. I was told that should I become president, I should drop those very sanctions. And if I didn't, they would kill my entire family, including my precious little grandchild."

Rage and horror were written across the faces. He stole a quick glance at his wife, a tissue dabbing at her eyes.

"These events, and these recent revelations about the source of the funding of my campaign have forced me to make some tough decisions. Everything I do I do for my family and for my country. If the Russians believe that me being president is in their best interests, then there is no way I should be president. And for this reason, as of tonight, I am withdrawing from the race."

Roars of protest filled the room, the crowd clearly as disappointed as he was.

If only they knew the whole truth.

"I'd like to thank my wife and family for their support during these difficult times, my staff for their unwavering efforts from when this was just a crazy idea, and to all of you who have been steadfast in your belief in me and a better America. I know you're all disappointed, and believe me I am as well, but I cannot in good conscience allow a foreign, belligerent power, to have any influence in the campaign for the most powerful post in the world. It is time to make America strong again! It's time to take America back!"

The campaign slogan began to be chanted again and he raised his hands, reaching out to his wife, who raised hers as well.

"God bless you all! And God bless America!"

He stepped back from the podium, waving to the chanting crowd, many of the faces stained with tears as the press corps rushed forward, shouting questions at him.

But he blocked them out, turning for the stage exit and quickly disappearing. He turned to Agent White, deciding against going back to his dressing room.

"Get me out of here."

"Yes, sir."

Within moments they were in the limousine, just he and his wife in the back, White and the driver behind the partition.

No one would see him tonight.

He turned and buried his head in his wife's shoulder and sobbed, a life's work destroyed, wiped out by the act of one man, a century ago.

He squeezed his eyes shut, stemming the tears as his wife patted his head, saying nothing, knowing words weren't what he needed now. He sat up, pulled a handkerchief from his pocket and wiped his eyes and cheeks dry.

"Sorry for that."

She smiled at him. "Never apologize for having feelings."

He laughed. "I wonder how many points I'd have dropped in the polls if they saw that display."

"You'd probably pick up a few."

"Always my biggest supporter."

"And your biggest fan."

He sighed, stuffing the handkerchief back in his pocket. "I can't believe it's over."

"You did what you had to do. You did the right thing."

"I know," he said, looking out the window as the buildings whipped by. "But I wonder who they'll go after next."

"Do you really think they'll try again?"

He nodded. "Absolutely." He tore his eyes away from the streets and looked at his wife, fear in his heart. "These people want their president, and they have the money to buy anyone they want."

Ilya Mashkov Residence, Moscow, Russia

Dimitri opened the car door and Mashkov stepped out. It was a cool, brisk morning in Moscow, the sun overhead a mere glow behind a dull gray sky. In the distance storm clouds threatened any afternoon plans.

It looked like he felt.

It was going to be a tumultuous few days, but he would make it through them. There was a reasonable explanation for the CIA investigation into him, and the press conference he had just listened to, though infuriating, couldn't possibly be blamed on him.

Jones had betrayed them.

And he'd die for it.

As would the entire lineage of Brett Jones.

It was sad really. He took no joy in the thought. A lot of innocent people were going to die. They wouldn't be murdered all at once, that would raise too many suspicions. Somebody would die on vacation in Mexico, there'd be a freak natural gas explosion in someone's home, someone would be hit by a bus. There were thousands of ways to die that would appear to be accidents.

Though Christopher Jones would die with a bullet to his head, after the rest were all dead, so he'd have the opportunity to live with what he had done.

Because nobody betrayed The Assembly.

He stepped into his ridiculously ostentatious house and handed his gloves to Dimitri who placed them on a nearby rack. His butler helped him out of his overcoat.

"Can I get you anything, sir."

Mashkov shook his head. "No. I need a little time alone."

"Very well, sir. Until lunch, then?"

Mashkov nodded, dismissing the man with a wave of his hand. Dimitri may work for The Assembly, but he was *his* butler, and he'd be damned if he was going to treat him any differently than any other butler. *He* was a member of The Assembly, not his manservant. *He* was one of the twelve most powerful men in the world and this was *his* home.

He quickly crossed the marble floors into the living room, heading toward the wet bar as he undid his top button.

A throat cleared behind him.

He spun around and smiled, the beautiful agent he had been unable to stop thinking about sitting on his couch, her leather pants and tight top revealing every luscious curve.

He had asked Dimitri to find out who she was in the hopes that he could meet her at some point, but he had never dreamed the man would actually arrange a meeting with the woman.

Perhaps I've underestimated you, my friend.

"To what do I owe the pleasure, Miss—?"

"Katz."

"Katz." He felt his heart race a little faster as she stretched an arm across the back of the couch. "Do you have a first name?"

"Of course."

"And it is?"

"Nadja."

"May I call you Nadja?"

"You may."

It was odd. If she were here at Dimitri's behest, she had to know why. She was a very sexually attractive woman, so she had to be expecting this meeting to be for the purpose of starting some sort of relationship. A business relationship, but of a personal nature. He had them with many women, though none so attractive as her.

Perhaps it's the gun?

Her shoulder holster hung loose, as if she had made herself comfortable while waiting for him.

A good sign.

What he couldn't figure out was why her voice was so monotone.

Perhaps she's here against her will?

He'd have to ask Dimitri what he had said to get her here. He'd hate for it to have been some sort of threat.

Sleep with him or else.

His eyes explored her body, deciding he didn't care why she was here, just that she followed through with what he wanted.

Something stirred below.

But her stare was almost unnerving.

Cold.

That wasn't it.

Indifferent.

That was it. Indifferent. It was as if she had no clue the effect her sexuality had on him, or if she did, couldn't care less.

She obviously isn't attracted to you.

That was of no matter. He had slept with dozens of women, hundreds, that hadn't found him attractive.

Though they had all found his money attractive.

And so would she.

"So, Nadja, can I get you something to drink?"

She shook her head. "No."

Curt. No nonsense.

I bet she likes it rough.

He sat down on the other end of the couch, reaching his hand out across the back, stopping only inches from hers. He breathed in, gently, not wanting to come off as creepy. Her smell was intoxicating. It wasn't a perfume, but something else.

Her shampoo?

Whatever it was she smelt like flowers.

His fingers inched closer.

"To what do I owe the pleasure?"

"I'm here to clean up your mess."

His breath caught in his throat and his heart slammed a little harder.

She wasn't invited here, she was sent here!

He had to get control of the situation, though he had no idea how. He resisted the urge to look for a method of escape. "I assume you're referring to what happened in New Orleans? It was indeed unfortunate, however there's nothing that can trace back to us. And the Titanic incident was certainly not *my* mess. I had no involvement there whatsoever."

"I'm afraid, Mr. Mashkov—"

"Ilya."

"—that you're mistaken."

It appeared his charms were wasted on this woman, which made her even more attractive to him.

You always desire what you can't have.

Fortunately there were few things in this world he couldn't have.

"Nadja, we're all friends here, how can I help? My first duty is always to my colleagues—I would do anything for them."

"Except apparently follow the security protocols laid out for you when you were first admitted into the organization."

Mashkov's chest tightened instantly and he could hear the blood rushing through his ears.

They know about the email server!

He tried to keep the panic off his face. He had to assume they knew everything, and lying wouldn't help. But they couldn't possibly know what was going on in his mind. "I assume you're speaking of the external email routing I set up?"

"I am."

He waved his hand as if it were nothing. "That's nothing. My server is completely secure, it's impossible for anyone to crack the encryption. I merely set it up so I could save time. It allowed me to devote more of my limited time to the organization's business."

"I'm afraid the others don't see it that way."

His heart was pounding rapidly now, sweat trickling down the back of his neck, his fingers recoiling instinctively, a little more distance now between him and the woman who a moment ago was the object of his desire, and now the source of nothing but fear. "I'd be happy to explain my reasoning, and of course comply with any security protocols they feel are necessary."

"Unfortunately it's too late for that."

"Wh-what do you mean?" It was the first crack in his voice, the first break in the façade he had been trying to maintain.

"I mean, Mr. Mashkov, that because of your actions, the CIA was able to locate one of the darknet routers the organization uses. Because of that, they were able to track your unsecured server, and through that, all of the messages you sent through it."

"But they'll never crack the encryption!"

"It's the CIA, Mr. Mashkov. They *will* crack it, it's just a matter of time."

"What are you saying? Are you saying that the CIA will be able to identify who we are?"

315

Katz suddenly stood, stepping back from him. "I've been told to give you a message."

He breathed a sigh of relief.

A message. A message I can handle.

"Y-yes, what is it?"

"The Assembly doesn't tolerate mistakes."

She quickly drew her weapon and pointed it at him.

"Wait!" he cried, raising his hands in front of him, jumping to his feet. "There has to be another way! I'll pay you! Whatever they're paying you, I'll double it. Triple it! Anything you want, I can get for you. Anything!"

She tilted her head slightly to the side. "I want nothing you could possibly offer."

She squeezed the trigger.

The round slammed into his chest, there no real pain at first, just the shock of being hit. He stumbled backward, the bottom of his legs hitting the couch, sending him back into his seat as he grabbed at his chest.

And then the pain came.

Intense.

White hot.

Unlike anything he could have imagined.

He looked down and felt a surge of adrenaline at the sight of his own blood oozing out over his fingers. Katz stood in front of him, her weapon pointed at his head.

"Please, wait," he said, raising a hand. "Do one thing for me, please."

Katz paused, moving the weapon aside. "What?"

"Tell my son I love him."

"Very well."

She put another bullet in his chest as the doors to the room opened, Dimitri stepping inside.

"Is it done?"

Katz nodded.

"Very well. I'll clean up."

You bastard.

Acton & Palmer Residence, St. Paul, Maryland

Acton looked at the patio table as he flipped the hamburgers and smiled. Milton and his wife were laughing with Laura, Tommy, looking much better than he had several days ago, was casually whispering to a giggling Mai.

It was good to see her so happy.

She had been really shaken up by the events of a few days ago, though once Tommy had been released from the hospital, they had been almost inseparable. He had worried about how she would adjust to life in America after having been torn from her home in Vietnam, but it looked like she was going to be just fine. Even if Tommy ended up breaking her heart, as young boys were prone to do, she would do fine.

He caught Laura looking at him, a slight smile on her face. He winked, flipping the next burger. After Laura had been shot they had received the devastating news that they wouldn't be able to have children because of it. It had been a crushing blow to both of them, and sometimes when she thought she was alone, Acton could hear her crying.

And that always got him started.

It was odd that a young Vietnamese woman in her early twenties could somehow fill some of that void, yet she had, Acton starting to think of her as an adopted daughter, Laura even voicing the same thing only last night.

The way Mai clung to Laura when saying goodbye, and now gave Acton a quick hug instead of a handshake showed him that the bond being created was mutual.

The doorbell rang and he handed the lifter to Laura. "I'll get it. Just finish flipping them for me, will you?"

"I think I can handle that."

She rose and took the lifter as he walked by, giving her a little smack on the bum.

"Get a room!" shouted Tommy, laughing.

Acton's eyes flared suggestively at Laura. "Sounds like a good idea." The doorbell rang again. "I'm coming! I'm coming!" He hurried through the patio door and into the kitchen, rushing toward the front door. He pulled it open and nearly shit his pants in shock.

"Hiya, Doc."

Acton shook his head, mouth agape at the sight. Dawson and Red were standing on the doorstep, their arms full of groceries. "What are you two doing here?"

"Heard you were having a barbecue."

Acton's eyes narrowed. "What? I…"

He was flabbergasted, his mind still not comprehending what was going on.

"Umm, these are getting kind of heavy, Doc."

Acton looked at Red, the words not registering for a moment. "Oh, shit, sorry guys! Come in, come in! Your timing couldn't be better. I just started cooking a few minutes ago." He looked at the bags. "Christ, looks like you brought enough to feed an army."

Red shrugged. "We's hungry boys."

Dawson stepped inside, Red following. "We would have been here on time but *somebody* got lost."

"I didn't get lost. You just give horrible directions."

Acton led them deeper into the house toward the backyard, still not believing these two Delta operators were actually here.

Laura's not going to believe this!

"You know, Doc, BD can find his way out of the Arabian peninsula with a toothpick and a candy bar wrapper, but throw some street signs up and he gets all confused."

"I have a tendency to want to go as the crow flies."

"It's true. You don't know how many times he says 'through there!' and points at some office complex. If he were a GPS they'd be banned."

"Look who's—"

Acton's jaw dropped again.

"Hiya, Doc!"

Ten guys were standing in the back yard, beers already in hand, all Delta operators they had come to know over the years.

"What the hell—"

"Sorry, hon, it's my fault. BD called to give us an update and I invited him over."

"Then one thing led to another, and this little surprise was born," said Dawson.

"I hope you don't mind," said Niner, stepping forward and shaking Acton's hand.

"He would be the one thing that led to another," said Dawson, taking a beer offered up by Atlas. "Once Niner hears there's meat involved, he's unstoppable."

"Hey, I've got family back in Korea to feed. If I can save on groceries, then I can send more to them."

Eleven men groaned, Acton laughing, his head still shaking. He put an arm around Laura.

"This is great, guys, absolutely great. A few years ago if you had arrived here, I'd be returning fire"—laughter erupted—"but now, after all we've been through together"—he squeezed Laura against his side—"our home is your home. You're always welcome here."

Beers were raised amid shouts of "Hear! Hear!"

Dawson looked at the small barbecue. "You call that a barbecue?"

Acton looked at it, suddenly feeling a little less masculine. "It does the job."

"Ha!" cried Atlas, slamming his hand on a large oil drum barbecue Acton hadn't noticed until now. "*This* is a barbecue."

"Yeah, for *one* if Atlas is manning it." Niner pointed at the massive man. "He eats half of what he cooks."

"Taste testing, my man, taste testing. I want to make sure you guys get only the best."

Spock guffawed. "If we're to believe *you*, half the meat in the country is bad."

"*I'll* man the grill," said Dawson, stepping over to the large barrel and flipping open the top.

"Grill Master Dawson to the rescue!" laughed Jimmy as a bag of charcoal was brought forward.

That was when Acton noticed half a dozen coolers filled with beer, lawn chairs already being opened.

They go into battles and barbecues fully equipped.

Acton took over from Laura on his puny barbecue, Dawson soaking his charcoal in lighter fluid beside him. He struck a match.

"Fire in the hole!"

Acton ducked to the side as a fireball launched itself half a dozen feet into the air, Bravo Team roaring in approval. Laura handed Acton his beer, taking up station beside him.

"So, anything we need to know about?" asked Acton, dying to know what was going on, Dawson only having told him several days ago that something was in the works and to not worry, they were being watched. He had tried to spot the protective detail, but hadn't caught anyone.

Satellite?

He had no idea, but these guys were all in the neighborhood for some reason. It made him wonder if they had been their guardians over the past couple of days.

"The painting has been taken into custody by the Feds," said Dawson, taking a swig of his beer.

"Yeah, they've got a nice spot for it, right beside the Ark of the Covenant," said Niner, laughing. "Did you see in that opening scene of Kingdom of the Crystal Skulls where you can see the Ark in one of the shattered crates?"

"Are we back on the movie trivia again?" groaned Atlas. "Give it a rest."

"Hey, pop culture is the only culture some of us have."

"I'll pop you some culture." Atlas made a fist. Niner darted behind Acton.

"Save me, Doc."

"You're on your own, kid."

The others roared.

"I'm hurt, Doc, genuinely hurt. After everything I've done for you." Niner sniffled. "I'm going to go over here. Atlas, get me a tissue."

Acton shook his head, grinning. He turned back to Dawson. "So the painting is gone. That will be a bit embarrassing on the academic circuit for a few years but I'll get over it."

"Nothing we can do about that. There's no official record of Captain Wainwright's ship being in the area, but the Navy isn't willing to risk the story getting out so it's been buried."

"And the Wainwrights? They've agreed to keep quiet?"

"Yes. They're terrified of losing any more family so they won't be saying anything, and without the painting, they have no proof."

"But are they safe? Are *we* safe?"

322

"You will be shortly."

"I don't understand. Who was behind all this?"

Dawson shook his head. "The less you know, the better. Let's just say they shouldn't be bothering you anymore."

"How can you be so sure?"

Dawson leaned toward Acton and Laura, lowering his voice slightly. "Because our friends at Langley are sending them a message."

Acton's eyes narrowed. "What kind of message?"

"The kind they won't like."

Assembly Covert Communications Facility, Moscow, Russia

Nadja Katz waited for the last of the members' monitors to activate. She was now facing a grid of eleven silhouettes, the twelfth blank.

Thanks to her.

She hadn't been certain Mashkov was one of the twelve, though she had a strong suspicion. It didn't matter to her, though it did seem to cement her position in the organization. She was their go to person, clearly trusted to carry out the most sensitive of missions, even if she had failed in Maryland. The professors were alive, the infection hadn't been stopped, though there had been no further evidence it was spreading. Her sources told her the painting had been confiscated and the feds were burying it.

Leaving no real evidence of whatever it was these people were hiding.

"Welcome everyone," said Number One, his digitally modified voice always giving her a curious sensation in her spine, almost an instinctual reaction to a distant memory. "There's been a development that you must all be made aware of."

"I assume by Number Twelve's absence he has been taken care of?" asked Number Six.

"Yes. Number Twelve unfortunately died earlier when his private plane lost power."

"Clever."

That had been Katz's idea, Dimitri taking care of the details.

"Number Twelve is no longer our concern," said Number One. "However his legacy is. We have received a message."

"A message?" It was a question echoed by several.

Katz leaned forward, curious herself.

324

"Yes. It was received through an old server used to monitor our security taps of the US Navy's personnel records."

"Who sent the message?"

"The CIA."

There was a pause, nobody saying anything.

Finally Number Six broke the silence. "Was it to us?"

"Yes."

"What did they want?"

Katz was completely absorbed now, it somehow interesting to hear the discomfort in the voices of people so powerful.

A door opened behind her.

She looked to see Dimitri enter the room, closing the door behind him. She nodded, returning her attention to the screens.

"The message was quite clear. Quite specific. I'll read the pertinent details. It says, 'We know who you are. If you harm any of our operatives, specifically Chris Leroux, Sherrie White or Dylan Kane, you will be exposed. If you harm Christopher Jones or his family, you will be exposed. If you harm Professor James Acton or any of those affiliated with him, or Steve Wainwright or any of his family, you will be exposed.'"

"A fairly specific list," said Number Four. "Why is this of any concern to us? We will continue our work. The Assembly is eternal."

"Normally I would agree," said Number One. "However, the email also lists several names."

Again silence. Katz sensed Dimitri behind her, standing against the wall.

"Whose names?"

"Some of yours."

Several people audibly gasped.

"How many?"

"Three including our late associate. All accurate."

"But how? Even in our communications with that idiot we never used names."

"We're not sure yet, but the fact is, they are aware of two more of you so far."

"What are we going to do?" asked Number Six.

"Contain the infection."

"But how?"

A gunshot sounded, a flash on the monitor labelled #2 actually startling Katz. Another gunshot, another flash, the silhouette of #6 gone.

"The infection has been contained. For now."

No one said anything, even Katz slightly stunned.

They're more ruthless than I realized.

Which meant she had to be even more careful when dealing with them.

Dimitri was closer now.

She shifted her feet.

"What do we do now?" asked Number Three.

"Nothing for now. But in time this infection will be contained, and when it is, we will eliminate all involved." There was a pause, no one saying anything. "Meeting adjourned."

Dimitri's jacket rustled behind her. She knew instantly it wasn't going to be a gunshot, he would have stood back and done it. It was going to be something silent.

Not a knife.

The back of the chair was in the way, and reaching around to slice her throat would be awkward.

She shoved her arm high, lowering her chin as she used her already prepared feet to push away from the chair.

She felt the wire of the garrote slice into the leather, but he had failed to get it around her neck.

Which meant he was already dead, he just didn't know it yet.

Her free hand pulled her weapon as she felt the thin wire slice into her arm.

The pain was a mere sensation, not to be ignored, but not to be distracted by. She spun, raising her weapon, firing two rounds into Dimitri's shocked face.

Pulling the wire free, she realized the monitors were still live, all remaining nine silhouettes still watching her. She aimed her weapon at the screens.

"You shouldn't have made an enemy of me."

THE END

ACKNOWLEDGEMENTS

This one took a little longer than usual, stupid life getting in the way of what I love to do. This was fun, the Titanic always an interesting subject to me. Though the motivations of the characters on the Titanic are entirely my own invention, some of the lines delivered on the bridge and when Astor said goodbye to his wife are taken from witness accounts. Heroism was in full display that night. As was dignity.

The SS Californian was not a work of fiction. It existed, saw the Titanic as it floundered, and did nothing. I think it is safe to say their captain honestly did not believe the Titanic was in any danger, though many felt he should have hung for his inaction. The Californian's captain spent much of the rest of his life a pariah, the Californian itself sunk by a U-boat in World War I.

And the other ship? That too *may* have existed, some witness accounts reporting rowing toward what they thought was a ship that seemed to never get closer.

No proof was ever found that she existed.

Hmmm.

Here's a fun fact: the story Leroux tells of his mother calling to tell him his father is in the hospital is true. It happened to me! And yes, my mother has learned her lesson.

Lots of people again to thank. My Dad of course for the research, Jennifer Dunn for some naval terminology, the real Chris Leroux for some French help and tech info, Fred Newton for some poker help, Ian Kennedy for some EOD stuff, Greg "Chief" Michael for some US Navy help, Marc Quesnel for the "mayday fun fact", Brent Richards for some weapons info, and Chris Holder for some tech info. And as usual my wife, daughter, mother and the rest of my family and friends for their continued support.

To those who have not already done so, please visit my website at www.jrobertkennedy.com then sign up for the Insider's Club to be notified of new book releases. Your email address will never be shared or sold and you'll only receive an occasional email from me as I don't have time to spam you!

Thank you once again for reading.

ABOUT THE AUTHOR

USA Today bestselling author J. Robert Kennedy has written over one dozen international bestsellers including the smash hit James Acton Thrillers series, the first installment of which, The Protocol, has been on the bestsellers list since its release, including a three month run at number one. In addition to the other novels from this series including The Templar's Relic, a USA Today and Barnes & Noble #1 overall bestseller, he writes the bestselling Special Agent Dylan Kane Thrillers, Delta Force Unleashed Thrillers and Detective Shakespeare Mysteries. Robert lives with his wife and daughter and writes full-time.

Visit Robert's website at www.jrobertkennedy.com for the latest news and contact information, and to join the Insider's Club to be notified when new books are released.

Available James Acton Thrillers

 ### The Protocol (Book #1)

For two thousand years the Triarii have protected us, influencing history from the crusades to the discovery of America. Descendent from the Roman Empire, they pervade every level of society, and are now in a race with our own government to retrieve an ancient artifact thought to have been lost forever.

 ### Brass Monkey (Book #2)

A nuclear missile, lost during the Cold War, is now in play--the most public spy swap in history, with a gorgeous agent the center of international attention, triggers the end-game of a corrupt Soviet Colonel's twenty-five year plan. Pursued across the globe by the Russian authorities, including a brutal Spetsnaz unit, those involved will stop at nothing to deliver their weapon, and ensure their pay day, regardless of the terrifying consequences.

 ### Broken Dove (Book #3)

With the Triarii in control of the Roman Catholic Church, an organization founded by Saint Peter himself takes action, murdering one of the new Pope's operatives. Detective Chaney, called in by the Pope to investigate, disappears, and, to the horror of the Papal staff sent to inform His Holiness, they find him missing too, the only clue a secret chest, presented to each new pope on the eve of their election, since the beginning of the Church.

 ### The Templar's Relic (Book #4)

The Vault must be sealed, but a construction accident leads to a miraculous discovery--an ancient tomb containing four Templar Knights, long forgotten, on the grounds of the Vatican. Not knowing who they can trust, the Vatican requests Professors James Acton and Laura Palmer examine the find, but what they discover, a precious Islamic relic, lost during the Crusades, triggers a set of events that shake the entire world, pitting the two greatest religions against each other. At risk is nothing less than the Vatican itself, and the rock upon which it was built.

Flags of Sin (Book #5)

Archaeology Professor James Acton simply wants to get away from everything, and relax. A trip to China seems just the answer, and he and his fiancée, Professor Laura Palmer, are soon on a flight to Beijing. But while boarding, they bump into an old friend, Delta Force Command Sergeant Major Burt Dawson, who surreptitiously delivers a message that they must meet the next day, for Dawson knows something they don't. China is about to erupt into chaos.

The Arab Fall (Book #6)

An accidental find by a friend of Professor James Acton may lead to the greatest archaeological discovery since the tomb of King Tutankhamen, perhaps even greater. And when news of it spreads, it reaches the ears of a group hell-bent on the destruction of all idols and icons, their mere existence considered blasphemous to Islam.

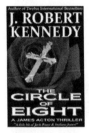

The Circle of Eight (Book #7)

The Bravo Team is targeted by a madman after one of their own intervenes in a rape. Little do they know this internationally well-respected banker is also a senior member of an organization long thought extinct, whose stated goals for a reshaped world are not only terrifying, but with today's globalization, totally achievable.

The Venice Code (Book #8)

A former President's son is kidnapped in a brazen attack on the streets of Potomac by the very ancient organization that murdered his father, convinced he knows the location of an item stolen from them by the late president.

A close friend awakes from a coma with a message for archeology Professor James Acton from the same organization, sending him along with his fiancée Professor Laura Palmer on a quest to find an object only rumored to exist, while trying desperately to keep one step ahead of a foe hell-bent on possessing it.

Pompeii's Ghosts (Book #9)

Two thousand years ago Roman Emperor Vespasian tries to preserve an empire by hiding a massive treasure in the quiet town of Pompeii should someone challenge his throne. Unbeknownst to him nature is about to unleash its wrath upon the Empire during which the best and worst of Rome's citizens will be revealed during a time when duty and honor were more than words, they were ideals worth dying for.

Amazon Burning (Book #10)

Days from any form of modern civilization, archeology Professor James Acton awakes to gunshots. Finding his wife missing, taken by a member of one of the uncontacted tribes, he and his friend INTERPOL Special Agent Hugh Reading try desperately to find her in the dark of the jungle, but quickly realize there is no hope without help. And with help three days away, he knows the longer they wait, the farther away she'll be.

The Riddle (Book #11)

Russia accuses the United States of assassinating their Prime Minister in Hanoi, naming Delta Force member Sergeant Carl "Niner" Sung as the assassin. Professors James Acton and Laura Palmer, witnesses to the murder, know the truth, and as the Russians and Vietnamese attempt to use the situation to their advantage on the international stage, the husband and wife duo attempt to find proof that their friend is innocent.

Blood Relics (Book #12)

A DYING MAN. A DESPERATE SON.
ONLY A MIRACLE CAN SAVE THEM BOTH.
Professor Laura Palmer is shot and kidnapped in front of her husband, archeology Professor James Acton, as they try to prevent the theft of the world's Blood Relics, ancient artifacts thought to contain the blood of Christ, a madman determined to possess them all at any cost.

Sins of the Titanic (Book #13)

THE ASSEMBLY IS ETERNAL. AND THEY'LL STOP AT NOTHING TO KEEP IT THAT WAY. INCLUDING KILLING MEDDLING ARCHEOLOGY PROFESSORS.
When Professor James Acton is contacted about a painting thought to have been lost with the sinking of the Titanic, he is inadvertently drawn into a century old conspiracy an ancient organization known as The Assembly will stop at nothing to keep secret.

Available Special Agent Dylan Kane Thrillers

Rogue Operator (Book #1)

Three top secret research scientists are presumed dead in a boating accident, but the kidnapping of their families the same day raises questions the FBI and local police can't answer, leaving them waiting for a ransom demand that will never come. Central Intelligence Agency Analyst Chris Leroux stumbles upon the story, and finds a phone conversation that was never supposed to happen but is told to leave it to the FBI. But he can't let it go. For he knows something the FBI doesn't. One of the scientists is alive.

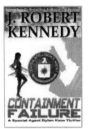

Containment Failure (Book #2)

New Orleans has been quarantined, an unknown virus sweeping the city, killing one hundred percent of those infected. The Centers for Disease Control, desperate to find a cure, is approached by BioDyne Pharma who reveal a former employee has turned a cutting edge medical treatment capable of targeting specific genetic sequences into a weapon, and released it. The stakes have never been higher as Kane battles to save not only his friends and the country he loves, but all of mankind.

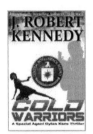

Cold Warriors (Book #3)

While in Chechnya CIA Special Agent Dylan Kane stumbles upon a meeting between a known Chechen drug lord and a retired General once responsible for the entire Soviet nuclear arsenal. Money is exchanged for a data stick and the resulting transmission begins a race across the globe to discover just what was sold, the only clue a reference to a top secret Soviet weapon called Crimson Rush.

Death to America (Book #4)

America is in crisis. Dozens of terrorist attacks have killed or injured thousands, and worse, every single attack appears to have been committed by an American citizen in the name of Islam.

A stolen experimental F-35 Lightning II is discovered by CIA Special Agent Dylan Kane in China, delivered by an American soldier reported dead years ago in exchange for a chilling promise.

And Chris Leroux is forced to watch as his girlfriend, Sherrie White, is tortured on camera, under orders to not interfere, her continued suffering providing intel too valuable to sacrifice.

Available Delta Force Unleashed Thrillers

 **Payback (Book #1)**
The daughter of the Vice President is kidnapped from an Ebola clinic, triggering an all-out effort to retrieve her by America's elite Delta Force just hours after a senior government official from Sierra Leone is assassinated in a horrific terrorist attack while visiting the United States. As she battles impossible odds and struggles to prove her worth to her captors who have promised she will die, she's forced to make unthinkable decisions to not only try to save her own life, but those dying from one of the most vicious diseases known to mankind, all in the hopes an unleashed Delta Force can save her before her captors enact their horrific plan on an unsuspecting United States.

 **Infidels (Book #2)**
When the elite Delta Force's Bravo Team is inserted into Yemen to rescue a kidnapped Saudi prince, they find more than they bargained for—a crate containing the Black Stone, stolen from Mecca the day before. Requesting instructions on how to proceed, they find themselves cut off and disavowed, left to survive with nothing but each other to rely upon.

Available Detective Shakespeare Mysteries

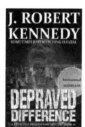 **Depraved Difference (Book #1)**
SOMETIMES JUST WATCHING IS FATAL
When a young woman is brutally assaulted by two men on the subway, her cries for help fall on the deaf ears of onlookers too terrified to get involved, her misery ended with the crushing stomp of a steel-toed boot. A cellphone video of her vicious murder, callously released on the Internet, its popularity a testament to today's depraved society, serves as a trigger, pulled a year later, for a killer.

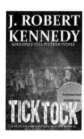 **Tick Tock (Book #2)**
SOMETIMES HELL IS OTHER PEOPLE
Crime Scene tech Frank Brata digs deep and finds the courage to ask his colleague, Sarah, out for coffee after work. Their good time turns into a nightmare when Frank wakes up the next morning covered in blood, with no recollection of what happened, and Sarah's body floating in the tub.

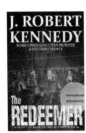

The Redeemer (Book #3)

SOMETIMES LIFE GIVES MURDER A SECOND CHANCE

It was the case that destroyed Detective Justin Shakespeare's career, beginning a downward spiral of self-loathing and self-destruction lasting half a decade. And today things are only going to get worse. The Widow Rapist is free on a technicality, and it is up to Detective Shakespeare and his partner Amber Trace to find the evidence, five years cold, to put him back in prison before he strikes again.

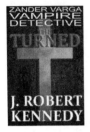

The Turned: Zander Varga, Vampire Detective, Book #1

Zander has relived his wife's death at the hands of vampires every day for almost three hundred years, his perfect memory a curse of becoming one of The Turned—infecting him their final heinous act after her murder.

Nineteen year-old Sydney Winter knows Zander's secret, a secret preserved by the women in her family for four generations. But with her mother in a coma, she's thrust into the front lines, ahead of her time, to fight side-by-side with Zander.

Made in the USA
Coppell, TX
25 January 2022

72295036R10201